Mostly
Sunny

Also by Jamie Pope

The Hope and Love Duo:

HOPE BLOOMS
LOVE BLOOMS

MOSTLY SUNNY

Coming in April 2019:
ONE WARM WINTER

Published by Kensington Books

Mostly
Sunny

Jamie Pope

Kensington Publishing Corp.
http://www.kensingtonbooks.com

DAFINA BOOKS are published by

Kensington Publishing Corp.
119 West 40th Street
New York, NY 10018

All Kensington titles, imprints and distributed lines are available at special quantity discounts for bulk purchases for sales promotions, premiums, fund-raising, and educational or institutional use. Special book excerpts or customized printings can also be created to fit specific needs. For details, write or phone the office of the Kensington Special Sales Manager. Kensington Publishing Corp., 119 West 40th Street, New York, NY 10018. Attn. Special Sales Department. Phone: 1-800-221-2647.

Dafina and the Dafina logo Reg. U.S. Pat. & TM Off.

ISBN-13: 978-1-4967-1825-9
ISBN-10: 1-4967-1825-9
First Mass Market Printing: October 2018

eISBN-13: 978-1-4967-1826-6
eISBN-10: 1-4967-1826-7
Kensington Electronic Edition: October 2018

10 9 8 7 6 5 4 3 2 1

Printed in the United States of America

Chapter 1

It had been so dark in the closet that Sunny couldn't see her hand in front of her face. She didn't know how long she had been in there. Mama had made her get in again.

Stay where you'll be safe, baby.

It was the same thing she had always told her before she made her go in there. But this time Sunny had been in there for a long time. So long that she had lost track of the days. So long she thought her eyes had stopped working and she couldn't see anymore. She could still hear things. The muffled noises coming from the next-door neighbors, the ambulance sirens that went by the apartment every so often. She could hear herself breathing and her heart beating. She could hear her stomach growl because she ran out of the food Mama had left for her. She could smell herself, and feel the stickiness of her skin.

But she couldn't see.

Mama had always thought they were safer in the dark because no one could see them.

She wanted to make sure no one could see Sunny in particular.

And if no one could see her, no one could hurt her again.

She scratched the scab on her shoulder. Mama told her it would never heal as long as she kept picking at it, but she couldn't help picking at it because the more of her skin she picked off, the less of the round scars she would see. And then she wouldn't have to remember what happened to her. The thing that made Mama even sicker. The thing that made Mama move them out of the last apartment and into this place. The thing that made Mama lock her in a closet every time she left the building.

She heard the jingle of keys at the door and voices. Too many voices. Two men and a woman. Even through the wall she recognized the super's voice. The walls were so thin there. She could almost make out what he was saying, but not quite. Her mama told her to always be quiet because they never knew who was listening.

The people must be going in the apartment next door. Whenever she heard the keys she thought it might be Mama coming home, but she hadn't come. Sunny was starting to think she would never come.

But then she heard the door open. And then she heard the heavy footsteps on the floor and then she heard the voices again.

"The lady down the hall says she knows that a little girl lives here. That the woman who rents the apartment never lets her out. She says the little girl used to come to her at night and she was always dirty and hungry."

"And you say that the woman who lives here hasn't been back in three days?"

"No sign of her. Her rent is two months late. We're going to evict her. Can you just make sure she doesn't have a kid stashed here?"

Sunny was listening so hard her head hurt. It had been three days? Mama had never been gone three days. Something was wrong. Something had happened to her. Mama wouldn't leave her this long unless she had to. Unless there was a reason.

Sometimes Mama needed a break. She needed to be free like a hummingbird. If she was caged too long she would start to vibrate and move and get all jumpy like there was somebody behind her trying to scare her. It was hard to live with her when she got like that. She did things like cover all the windows with thick blankets so the light couldn't come in. She made Sunny stop going to school. She made them move again and again.

But the breaks made her calmer. Better to live with.

Sometimes she was gone for a few hours. Sometimes it was a day. Sometimes a little more. But she always came back for her.

Always.

But this time it was more than a day. This time Sunny was worried that her mama had turned into the hummingbird she called herself and flown away.

She wanted to say something. To call out and let them know where she was, but her mouth was so dry and her throat hurt and she was scared. Scared for Mama. Scared that someone had hurt her. Scared that someone was going to hurt Sunny.

The closet door opened and immediately her eyes stung as the light hit them.

"Shit," she heard a man say but her eyes hurt so bad she couldn't see his face. "Call for an ambulance," he ordered.

She was lifted into the arms of a man in a dark blue uniform and he held her like she was a baby, like Mama used to when she was smaller. His hand felt warm on her back. His smell was clean.

Her eyes focused on him for a moment before they started to go blurry again. Her throat was burning so badly.

It had been so long since she had seen anyone but Mama.

Mama had told her not to trust men. She had told her that most of them were bad, but Sunny had to trust this one. He was taking her out of here. She never wanted to be in there again.

Her eyes finally cleared up enough so that she could see him. He had brown skin like hers but his eyes were so sad.

"Hello," she said to him. Her voice cracked. It had been so long since she had used it.

"Hello, little one. My name is Officer Rodgers." He nodded toward the badge on his chest so that she could see. "That's my partner, Officer Martinez." He looked behind him at a woman who looked just as sad as he did. "We're here to see if you're okay. Can you tell me your name?"

"I'm Sunny. It's nice to meet you."

"It's nice to meet you too." He smiled softly at her and glanced back at the lady that was with him and shook his head. "Are you hurt?"

"My shoulder is almost better now. But I'm thirsty. I tried to save the water, but I couldn't."

"We'll get you something to drink, Sunny," Officer Martinez said. "Anything you want."

"Can I have soda?"

"I think so." Officer Rodgers nodded.

"And a hot dog? I hid two dollars in my book. I can pay for it."

Officer Rodgers looked even sadder if it was possible. "You don't have to pay for it. We'll buy it for you."

Sunny shook her head. "Mama said I'm not supposed to take things from people. Please, don't tell her."

"You don't have to worry about that." He took a deep breath. "Where is your mama, Sunny?"

"I don't know. She'll come back. She said she was coming back."

"Oh, sweetheart," Officer Martinez touched her face. "I don't think your mama will be back this time."

"Sunny!"

Sunshine Gibson snapped out of her daze and looked up at her supervisor. "Yes?"

Maxine was standing just in front of her with that concerned motherly expression that she sometimes had. "I called you three times. You were gone for a moment."

Gone.

That was the right word for it. She didn't often think about the day she was found. She was one of those always-look-forward-never-look-back kind of people, but today had been hard. She had gotten an invitation to Officer Rodgers's retirement party. She shouldn't call him officer anymore. He had been promoted to detective years ago. And he was more than just a police officer to her. He was one of the few people in her life who was special to her.

He had kept up with her after the day he took her from that closet. *Kept up* were not the right words to describe what he had done. They weren't strong enough. She still remembered how he had stayed with her while the doctors checked her out in the hospital. How he rubbed his hand over her back while she slept on his shoulder. He had made her feel safe when her world was spinning so far out of control.

He had come with her to her first foster home and every other foster home she had been placed in until she had emancipated herself at seventeen. He was in the stands at her college graduation. He called her at least once a month to see how she was. He had cared about her. He was the steadiest person in her life.

She wouldn't call them close though. She had always kept her distance because she didn't want to impose on his time. He had his own life, his own children to care for. He shouldn't feel obligated to look after her. But still he meant a lot to her and now he was retiring. Moving to Florida with his family. He was starting a new chapter of his life, but it made Sunny feel like it was the end of an era.

She was an adult now. Nearly thirty. She had her own place that no one could take her away from. She had a small group of friends that were more like family, but her first protector was leaving and she couldn't shake the heaviness that settled on her shoulders.

"I'm sorry." She smiled at Maxine, trying to

inject some happiness into her voice. "I was just thinking."

"Are you okay?"

"Yeah. Of course." Sunny started to tidy the stacks of papers on her desk. "What did you need?"

"Ms. Romano called and asked if we could put off her home visit again."

"Why?" Annoyance rose inside her and she tried to push the feeling away but it was too hard.

She was a social worker in the Family and Children Services department for the city of New York. She had worked her butt off in school to get good grades but when it came time to choose a career she chose to go into social work. She had been with so many foster families that her social workers were the other constant in her life, her safe place when the world felt so damn scary.

She wanted to be that person for someone else. She worked mostly with children in foster care. She got to witness the joy of seeing some of them leave the system when they were adopted. But she also saw the other side of it. The children who had to be removed from their parents. The older kids that were no longer cute and nobody wanted.

She had been one of those kids. One of those sad statistics. Kids like her usually ended up in jail or dead. She tried to prevent her kids from being the ones who fell through the cracks.

"She made some excuse about having an appointment."

"Appointment my ass." She stood up and grabbed her purse. "That's the second time she's rescheduled.

I'm making a surprise visit right now. She's hiding something."

"Don't bother." Maxine put her hand on her shoulder. "She's not at home. She took Kev to New Jersey this weekend. And it's after five on a Friday. Go home. Enjoy your weekend. Do something fun."

"I'm a social worker. I can't afford to have any fun," she said, grinning at her boss.

"Don't I know it." Maxine grinned back, but the smile didn't stay too long. The concern never left her eyes. "You need to tell me what's up. And don't lie and tell me nothing. I've been doing this job for thirty years. There's nothing you can tell me that I haven't seen, heard, or experienced before."

"Detective Rodgers is retiring and it's put me in a weird space. It made me think about Soren."

Soren was one of her kids. Or clients, or consumers, whatever the politically correct term was for the people Sunny worked with. She was a little girl with caramel-colored skin who had been abandoned by her mother on the footsteps of their office. She was frail and terrified and wouldn't talk for almost an entire year. But she did start to speak eventually. To Sunny, and Sunny learned that they had a lot more in common than the way they looked.

"We're not supposed to have favorites, but she's yours."

"I will neither confirm nor deny that," Sunny said, trying to prevent the smile from creeping across her face. "I love her so much though."

"Yes. You've done a great job with her. You shouldn't be worried. She's one of the kids I know will turn out fine and I don't say that a lot. You found her a great foster family who is going to adopt her. Cases like these are why we do what we do."

She nodded. "You're right. I'm in a funky mood. I think I just need to get out of this place. I've got spring fever or something."

"Yes. Have a nice dinner. Drink an extra glass of wine."

"I know by nice dinner you mean have something with multiple courses that looks pretty on a plate. But a nice dinner for me is getting dollar slices and a hot dog with those red onions I immediately regret eating."

Maxine shook her head. "I'm surprised you don't have an ulcer. At least tell me you buy decent wine."

"No wine. Milkshakes. I'll spend a whole five dollars for a good one."

"You can come home with me to Westchester. My husband is making chicken marsala. My daughter will be coming home from school this weekend. She loves you. You could stay over and I can cook breakfast in the morning. I would have two girls to mother and would be in heaven."

Sunny was tempted to take Maxine up on her offer. She hadn't been mothered much in her life. Even with her own mother. Sunny was the one who took care of her. But Sunny would feel too . . . too . . . in the way, if she went to Maxine's. Like she wasn't really wanted. Like she was there just because she had no place else to go. It was one of the side effects of spending most of her life in foster care.

"Maybe another time. My best friend is nearing the end of her first pregnancy and I'm going to stop by to see her."

Spending time with her friends sounded like a good idea, but Sunny just didn't feel like being social. Instead, she returned to her tiny hole in the wall apartment, the one that was in a less than desirable neighborhood, with the rent that was too high, and dined on leftovers and chocolate ice cream.

Her mama had moved them to New York when she was four. She tried hard to remember her life before they had come here but her memories only came to her in small snatches and what she could remember was blurry. It was almost as if she was looking back at her life through frosted glass.

She did remember her preschool. It had been inside of a small church in a town that was near the ocean. The people were nice there. She remembered the warmth of the place. She remembered the smell of the sea.

Her mother used to take her to the beach after school. They used to take their shoes off and run through the waves. But then something happened and there was no more school with the kind people, story time, and friends. And there were no more trips to the beach. No more feeling the sand between her toes. There was no more home.

There was sleeping in the car and eating fast

food if there was any food at all. There was constant moving. Constant restlessness.

Her mama had turned them into gypsies. At first it had been fun, but then it got hard. She never made friends, never felt grounded, never felt like she had a place to call home.

No roots.

She had missed school and people and everything that was normal.

"Don't be sad, baby," Mama would coo when she saw Sunny's spirits crash. *"You don't want to be one of them. You are an original. You are phenomenal."*

"Yes, Mama." It was all she could say.

A little twinge of resentment toward her mama would start to grow, but then Mama would let her do something outrageous like color on the walls with permanent marker, and Sunny would forgive her.

Her mama kept popping into her head lately almost every day, and Sunny would hear her voice, maybe it wasn't her mama's voice. She hadn't seen her mama since she was seven, and as time passed she was beginning to forget little things about her like the way she smelled, her smile and, most important, her voice. The woman in her mind always sounded like Claire Huxtable, which wasn't right because Sunny's mama was white, with light blue eyes and long, blond hair that stopped right above her behind. Sunny wasn't white; her skin was caramel, her hair was neither straight nor down her back. She never knew her father but she supposed he was black. Mama only told her that her daddy was a soldier, a beautiful dark man with full lips, straight white teeth, and no hair. She would always ask for more.

"What's his name, Mama? Where is he now? Did he love me?" Mama would never answer her directly. Instead she would simply reply in her Claire Huxtable voice, *"Why do you need to know about your daddy? You've got me and I've got you."*

Sunny now realized why her mother sounded like Claire Huxtable. As a child she watched the sitcoms religiously before her mama got sicker and shut everything off. She clung to them like it was her lifeline. Those women were her fantasy mothers, smart, beautiful, caring, and most important stable. They were married to men who loved them. The families ate dinner together every night and their house had paintings on the walls instead of marker. They had roots. Each child, no matter how foolish they had been, could come home to a mother and father and feel safe. Sunny never felt safe. Sunny longed for that, so much that it hurt sometimes. Still, she missed Mama even after everything she had put her through, even after the constant moves, the paranoia, the extreme mood changes and the abandonment. She missed her, ached for her, and on days like today wondered what ever happened to her. She had never gotten the real story. She only knew that she was gone and that she never came back.

Sunny only had a few pieces of her mama that she kept as mementos, a crystal barrette, a tiny jade statue of Buddha that she let Sunny hold when she was afraid, and two letters that she had sent on her thirteenth and eighteenth birthdays.

To My Sunshine,

I haven't seen you now for five years, my love, I want to, but I can't. I'm not sure where you are or how to find you, but maybe that's for the best. I know you don't understand what happened, but Mama couldn't take care of you the way you needed to be taken care of. You know Mama, Sunshine, she just couldn't stay any longer and I couldn't ask you to leave one more time. You would be so proud of me baby, I'm different now, I'm a grown-up now. I've got my own place without marker on the wall, and a job, a real job, and I've been here for six months. I think about you every day. You must be so pretty by now and so smart, smarter than everybody in your class. Don't be afraid to show them how smart you are. You're thirteen today, soon you will be entering womanhood. There are so many things I wish I could tell you, so much knowledge that I feel a mother should share with her daughter, but there isn't one thing I can say to you that is profound, not one piece of advice I can give you that is magically going to make you turn out all right. I can only tell you not to be me. Try not to make my mistakes. That may not be helpful to you because you don't know me, and maybe that's for the best. I hope you're not angry with me, Sunshine. I did things to you that a mother shouldn't do to her child, and I'll always be sorry for that. I just wanted you to know that I was alive and that I still think about you every day and most important I love you. Mama will always love you, Sunshine.

*Pray for me. baby, and maybe one day I will see
you again.*

Mama

Sunny had read that letter at least six hundred times, until the piece of notebook paper it was scrawled on had become soft and yellow, fragile from its constant use. She had memorized it and probably could recite it word for word, but knowing what it said wasn't enough for Sunny. She needed to see it, look at it, touch it. Study the big soft curves of her mama's handwriting. It made her feel closer to the woman who was so far away from her. Sunny wished she could just push her mama to the back of her mind. She had work to concentrate on, cases that needed attention, foster parents to find, but none of that was important, because her own case kept making its way to the forefront of her mind. She needed to know exactly what happened to her mama.

It was time she searched, but frankly she was terrified to find out what happened to her.

Chapter 2

Julian King peered down at the naked woman in his bed. To describe her in one word would be difficult. Gorgeous came to mind. Not just any kind of beautiful. Many women could be described as beautiful. Models, actresses, women on the street, but this woman was more than that. Her always sleek hair was slightly mussed. But that was it. After an hour of steamy sex most women would look languid, flushed, satisfied. Regina looked regal. Like she could single-handedly perform a hostile takeover of a Fortune 500 company as soon as she got out of his bed. It was one of the reasons he wanted to permanently claim her as his own.

But she was one of the women who didn't want to be claimed. He liked that about her. She was no average woman. She wasn't like the pretty, sweet girls he had grown up with or the nice young ladies he spent time with in college. At this point in his life, Julian didn't want anyone sweet. He had been down that road before. He had been with women who required too much of him. Too much of his time. Too much of his money. Too much of his life.

He didn't want a woman who couldn't hold her own at a cocktail party. He didn't want to be with anyone who couldn't help his career grow. And for his career to grow he needed to impress the senior partners at his firm. He had to project his success and for that he needed the right kind of wife.

Regina Richardson was the kind of wife he needed.

He had it harder than most of the people in his position. He was six-foot-five, a former professional football player. He had been a jock all his life. He was a superstar in college. He went to the Super Bowl his rookie year. He had been on boxes of cereal and in sports drink commercials. He had posed naked for the largest sport magazine in the country and because of his massive fame he had gotten everything he wanted with just a snap of his fingers. But then he got hurt. The third game of his second season was his last. He landed wrong after a tackle and got a neck injury that caused spinal damage. The doctors told him if he played again he faced paralysis.

He spun out of control for a while after. Too much booze. Too many women. Too many close calls. But then his father barged in and grabbed him by the shirt and shook some sense into him.

"You've used your body to get you through your entire life and now it's time for you to use your brain."

He went to law school. His professors underestimated him. His classmates underestimated him.

The media had underestimated him. He graduated top of his class. He passed the bar in three states. He was hired at the most high-profile firm in the city. He thought he wouldn't have to prove himself after that, but he was dead wrong. People still thought he was the dumb jock. His colleagues thought he was only hired because of his former celebrity status. They always underestimated him, thinking every win he got was because someone had let him slide.

But if he could land a wife like Regina, it would show the world he was good enough to be among them.

Regina spoke five languages. She was from one of the oldest families in America. She ran an international cosmetics company. Women lived and died for her approval. She was indisputably a good catch.

His only problems were small.

His family hated her.

He couldn't blame them. His father and sister were nice people. Regina just didn't know how to act around them. She came off cold even when she tried her hardest to be friendly.

He had one other problem when it came to her.

She didn't want to be his wife or anybody's wife. She had been through one failed marriage and didn't want to travel down that path again. That made sense to Julian, especially since they didn't love each other. But Julian didn't believe in love. Love didn't keep his parents together and love certainly didn't keep his mother from walking out on him and his sister. He didn't want love. He wanted something more tangible. What he wanted was a guarantee, and with love there was none.

His sister told him that he shouldn't waste his time with someone who didn't make him feel warm all over. He laughed at her when she said this. Warm was for blankets. Not for society marriages. And that's what he wanted—an old-fashioned marriage where two families merged to gain greater power.

He gazed down at Regina again as he put on his shirt. He was tired of searching, tired of coming home to an empty apartment, tired of having to schedule time alone with this woman. He was ready to settle down, but all Regina seemed to be inclined to do was play games. She wanted to be chased, and for a while Julian was happy to play along. It made her feel desirable. But now Julian had become bored with chasing what should already be his.

"Where exactly do you think you're going?" She spoke to him like he was her subordinate. She may have been eleven years his senior, but she sure as hell wasn't his boss.

Julian didn't answer her, only stood there looking down at her as he fastened his cuff links.

"Did you hear me? Where are you going?" she demanded.

He raised one brow at her, reminding her who she was speaking to.

She changed her tone at once. "Julian, darling, where are you going? I'm getting lonely in this big bed all by myself."

It was then he decided to answer.

"I have to go back to work."

Regina's gray eyes flashed with anger for a second. "Work? Really, Julian, you just left there two hours ago. I thought you could spare a little time for me." Even though Regina was complaining, her voice was still sexy, smooth, like silk, yet husky at the same time.

"I can't. I have to go in. You know I'm trying to make senior partner."

Regina looked up at him as if he were declaring a challenge, and let the sheet that was wrapped around her body slip so that one perfect bare breast was visible. Tempting, but he knew her game and he wasn't about to play. It was always like that with them, always a chase, always a battle of wills. Julian was done with that. He would not chase her, nor would he bend to her will.

"Come back to bed," she purred. "It's cold without you."

"I can get you another blanket and you can stay in my bed as long as you want but I have to go back to work."

She rolled her eyes and got out of bed, naked as the day she was born, and wrapped her perfectly sculpted arms around his neck, pressing her small, naked chest in to his much larger one.

"Please, please, get back in bed. I want you in the worst way." Her voice grew to its most seductive pitch but Julian fully recognized that he was being played.

"I have to go."

She dropped her arms and the sex kitten act

quickly. "Damn it, Julian. I cleared my entire afternoon to be with you. Don't you realize my time is valuable?"

"My time is valuable too. You aren't the only one with a job and responsibilities. You didn't even bother to check with me to see if I was free today."

"Why should I have to?" she spat. "If you want to be with me then act like it."

"The whole world doesn't revolve around you, and neither do I." He kept his voice calm. Julian rarely lost his temper but today her whining was annoying him. "I'm a grown man and I'm tired of playing games. I wanted to be with you because I thought you were mature."

"Are you trying to say I'm old?"

"Not old but there's a reason that I'm dating someone who is closer to fifty than to twenty-five."

She recoiled as if she had been slapped in the face. She hid her age very well, almost treated it as if it were some top-secret government information. Julian knew she was just a mere four years away from celebrating the birthday she dreaded the most.

"You bastard," she whispered.

He shook his head. "Don't treat your age like it's a bad thing. I like that you're mature. I want to be with a woman. You're everything a woman is supposed to be."

"You make me sound horribly old." She pouted and for the first time that day he saw signs of softness lying behind her icy exterior.

"You're not old. You're smart and beautiful, and cultured. I want to be with you."

"If you want to be with me, then stay with me. Get

back in bed. I don't ask for a lot, Julian. It wouldn't be so hard for you to cancel this one client and spend the day with me."

Julian sighed. Regina was the most persistent woman he had ever met, but she was about to find out how stubborn he could be. "I already told you, I can't stay with you today, but I will make you a deal. I will cancel all my plans tomorrow if you agree to be my wife."

"Your wife?" she said, amazed and horrified at the same time. "You want to marry me? You aren't in love with me."

"So? You aren't in love with me either, but we work well together and you can't deny that, no matter how hard you try. What have we got to lose? You can't tell me that you want to come home every night to an empty apartment."

Julian knew that wasn't the life he wanted for himself. Despite all the friends, the parties, and the social influence, he couldn't deny that lately he felt a deep ache in his chest.

"I can't marry you, Julian. Not like this. I just can't."

Julian put on his jacket, and shook his head. "I need to know that this is going somewhere. We've been on and off for years and I simply can't do this anymore. We either have to take the next step or end this." He turned and began to walk out.

"So, that's it," she called. "You have nothing more to say."

"Are you going to marry me?"

She paused for a moment then lifted her chin. "No."

He had a feeling she was going to say no. But he had wanted her to say yes. He didn't love her, but the rejection stung more than he thought it would. He was wealthy. He was young. He was smart. He was going places. But she didn't want to marry him. What the hell would it take? "There's nothing left to say."

"That's bullshit, Julian. You need me but I sure as hell don't need you and I will not come running after you. I refuse to lower myself."

"You feel like marrying me is lowering yourself." He nodded. "Well, I guess that says it all. Enjoy the rest of your life, Regina."

And with that statement he left. There really was nothing more to say.

Sunny went back to work that Monday, still feeling that ache that had arrived the same day as her invitation. The ache was always there, the ache of not knowing who she was and where her roots were and if there was anyone out there who she was connected to, but lately it had grown stronger. She was determined to push it back down because her life had turned out okay. She had an education and a good job that she liked. She spent her days helping kids, which filled her up. She hadn't had it as bad as some other kids. None of her foster parents had beat or starved her. Most of them had been nice enough. She had remembered what it was like to feel loved. It wasn't a bad life. Some people had it worse. She needed to be thankful for what she had.

Her final foster mother, Flossie, had taught her that. Flossie had loved her. At sixteen Flossie had wanted to adopt her, but she died before the process could be finalized. It had been another blow, but Sunny tried to be grateful for the time she did have with her, grateful that she got to be a part of that small stable family as long as she did. She had experienced what it was like to be loved again, the same way her mama had loved her before the voices got too loud in her head.

Sunny picked up the phone during her lunch break and dialed her best friend, Arden, who was nearing her eighth month of pregnancy and home on bedrest. She had met Arden her freshman year of college at Columbia when they were placed in the same dorm. Arden took her home with her upstate every time she went. Holidays, birthdays, and special occasions were spent with her and her family. They had been best friends for over ten years and now her best friend was married and going to become a mother. And Sunny was so happy for her because Arden deserved happiness more than anyone she knew.

"Hello, Sunshine."

"How are you today, princess?"

"I can't see my feet. I don't know what they look like anymore, but I know they are swollen. I still made my husband paint my toe nails last night. He said they look like sausages."

"Did you smack him for that?"

"How could I? How many federal agents do you know rush home from work to paint their pregnant wives' toenails?"

"He rushed home to do that?"

"Yes. He's been amazing since I've been on bedrest. I think he feels guilty because he got me pregnant. He keeps apologizing, like I wasn't the one who told him I wanted a baby."

"You're spoiled as hell."

"I know. I wish I could do something special for him, but I'm not allowed out of bed."

"You love that man. That's all he wants. He's so happy that he's going to be a father, he could bust."

"He is very happy. We were talking about how we are going to decorate the baby's room in the new house last night and he was rubbing my belly and he got a little teary eyed."

"Daniel is a sweet. When I first met him I thought he was a raging asshole, but he's such a good guy."

"Yeah. He is. I want you to find one of those. Did you ever plan a second date with that agent we set you up with? He told Danny that he thought you were really cute."

"I never called him back. He was nice. Just not for me."

"You say that about every guy."

"I don't!"

"You do. I would never tell you that you need a man in your life, but you deserve a good one that is going to put you first and make you happy. How are you ever going to find one if you don't put yourself out there more?"

"I've got a lot of stuff going on right now." It was the truth. She used to tell Arden everything, but she hadn't lately. Arden was newly married and soon to be a homeowner and a mother and she was happy. She had a new life to live. She had her own stuff going on. Arden didn't need to hear about Sunny's issues because in the large scheme of things they seemed less significant to the big new life her friend was embarking on.

"What's the matter?"

"Just work stuff. It's been crazy these past few weeks." As soon as the words came out of her mouth she saw Jeannie Earl walk through the door with a paper in her hand and a panicked look on her face. "I've got to go, Arden. I've got an emergency here."

"Call me later."

"I will." She hung up and stood up to meet Soren's foster mother as she reached her desk. "What happened? Is Soren okay?"

"No." She shook her head. "I'm mean yes. I sent my husband to go get her from school."

"Why? What happened?"

"This." She shoved a manila envelope at Sunny. "It came in the mail. I don't know how she knows where we live. How did she find us?"

"Who?" Sunny asked as she opened the envelope. The first thing she saw was cash, two stacks of neatly wrapped hundred dollar bills. Sunny looked back up at Jeannie, her mind spinning, but no clear thoughts emerging.

"There's a letter," Jeannie whispered. Her eyes filled with tears

Sunny looked back into the envelope and there was a letter on folded notebook paper. She felt sick to her stomach then and almost too afraid to open it, but she did and she looked at the soft curves of the handwriting, her eyes too blurry to see the words clearly at first.

Dear Soren,

It's been more than a year since Mama has seen you. I know you must be angry with me for leaving you the way I did, but I had to. I was getting bad again, and if I let myself slip again I would no longer be the mama you love. I couldn't take it if you didn't love me anymore. I didn't want to make the same mistakes with you as I did with your older sister. I loved her too. I loved her so incredibly much, but I couldn't keep her from getting hurt. I made a promise to myself that I was going to be a better person, and I am. I started all over again, my baby, you don't know how hard that is to do. I feel like I am being reborn, but this time I am smarter. This time I can't fail. I lost your sister forever, and that pains me every minute of every day. I won't lose you, Soren. I will come back for you. I promise you that. Pray for Mama, baby. I will see you soon.

~Mama

"Sit down, Jeannie," Sunny told her as she sank into her own chair.

Jeannie obeyed her, but she reached across Sunny's desk and squeezed her hand. "You look like you've seen a ghost."

Maybe she had, but the letter had taken her back. She had been a little older than Soren when her mother had sent her a very similar letter. She remembered the excitement she felt when she had first received it. Her mother was alive. But then devastation has set in. Her mother had known where she was but she never once tried to see her, tried to get her back.

She shook thoughts of her own life out of her head and focused on Jeannie before her. "I'm just shocked."

"We are too. This came to our house. How did she know how to find us? We're not even listed in the phone book."

How had Sunny's mother found her?

She once again forced her mind off of herself and put her attention back on the terrified woman who sat before her. "She can't take Soren away. She abandoned her, thus terminating her parental rights. Soren was so traumatized she didn't speak for nearly a year. There's no way she's getting her back."

"Look at all the money she's sent. There was a note for me in there too!"

Sunny looked in the envelope again and this time on pink stationery there was a note in that same softly curved handwriting.

Mrs. Earl,

   *Thank you for taking care of my baby. I know
this isn't enough to repay for all you have done for
her, but it's a start. Please use some of it to buy
Soren something special.*

~ *G*

G. She signed a G. As hard as Sunny tried, she
couldn't pry the name of Soren's mother out of
her. But Sunny knew her own mother's name. It
was Grace. She used to sign her name with G sometimes. It must be another coincidence. But it was a
hell of a one.

Sunny looked back up at Jeannie, not sure what
to say. "How much is there?"

"It's two thousand dollars. Soren told me they
were homeless. Where did she get that kind of
money from? Who the hell is she involved with?"

"I don't know." Sunny didn't want to say it to
Jeannie, but it was like the woman was attempting
to pay child support.

"What if she kidnaps her?"

"She wouldn't do that," Sunny said so firmly she
believed herself. "If she wanted to kidnap her she
would have taken her. She wouldn't give you a clue
it was coming."

"What am I supposed to do with this money?
Should I go to the police?"

"I'm not sure what you would tell them. Or if
they could do anything about it. Does Soren know?"

"No. It came today while she was at school.
Should I tell her?"

Sunny shook her head. She remembered how the letter she got from her mother had sent her reeling. "Not yet." She closed her eyes. "Let me think about what we should do. It took a long time for Soren to trust. She used to hide her food because she wasn't sure when she was going to be able to eat again. She used to hide under her bed at night. I don't want her going backward."

"No." Jeannie shook her head. "She hugs me now. Unprompted. She smiles freely. She's not afraid to ask for things. She loves us and we adore her. I cannot lose her. I cannot lose another child."

Jeannie's daughter had died of a rare form of cancer. She would have been Soren's age. The Earls deserved Soren as much as she deserved them. They needed to stay together.

"Put the money away in an account just for Soren. Please, don't panic right now. Soren is very perceptive and we don't want to scare her. Just go home and be with her. Take her on a little trip. Get out of the city. Let me worry about this." She handed back the envelope with the cash, but held onto the folded notebook paper. "Can I keep this for a little while?"

"Of course."

"Can you just let me know where it was mailed from?"

Jeannie looked at the envelope and then at Sunny. "It says Hope, South Carolina."

Sunny's heart beat so hard it was starting to hurt. Jeannie left her and Sunny tried to go back to work as if it were just any other day, but she couldn't concentrate. She felt sick to her stomach.

It's a coincidence. It's a coincidence. This can't be happening.

Maxine noticed that there was something wrong with her. Her entire office noticed there was something wrong with her and there was, but she couldn't give voice to it. Maxine thought she was sick and when she suggested she go home, Sunny left without a fight. For the first time she had been eager to get out of there and return to her tiny apartment.

She rushed home and went straight to her jewelry box, the place where she kept the few things she had from her mother. Her crystal barrette, her jade Buddha statue, and the two letters she had sent Sunny out of the blue, five years apart.

They were still in their original envelopes. Neither of them had return addresses but one was postmarked from Maryland and the second was postmarked from Hope, South Carolina.

Sunny took the letter she received on her eighteenth birthday out of the envelope even though she had read it so many times, she had memorized it.

To My Sunshine,

I can only get up enough strength to write to you every five years or so. But please do not think it's because I don't think about you. I think about you every single day. I think about the woman you've turned into. How beautiful you must be. I wish I could have been there to see you grow, but

*we both know I was too sick to take care of you, to
be your mother. I know you were starting to hate
me. I don't blame you. I couldn't protect you. I
couldn't give you a fraction of what you needed. I
can't tell you what happened to me after I left. I
broke. I went back south. I pulled myself together.
I had a job and an apartment without marker
drawings on the wall. I met a nice man. I was
normal for a while.*

I had another baby, Sunny.

*You have a sister. I know I should have told you
sooner, but I thought it might make you angry with
me. How could I take care of another child when I
couldn't even take care of you? I thought of her
as my second chance, but every time I looked at
her all I could see is your face. All I could feel
was guilt for failing you. I wish I could see you,
Sunny. I wish I could hug you. I know you're in
college now. I know you're doing something that
is going to end up changing the world and I
just want you to know how proud of you I am.
And I want you to know that I'm sorry for what
I did to you and that it's something I'll never
be able to forgive myself for no matter how hard
I try. I pray that you are happy, my Sunshine.
I pray for the day when I can have both of my
girls with me.*

~Mama

Sunny sank to the floor with the letter in her
hand. Both letters were written in beautiful cursive.
Both mailed from Hope, South Carolina. Both

women called themselves Mama. Both women had two daughters they couldn't take care of.

It had to be a coincidence, but what if it wasn't? What if the little girl Sunny had grown so attached to was her sister? The math worked. Soren was eleven. Sunny had been eighteen when she got the letter. It would have been right around the time Mama had given birth.

It had been over ten years since Sunny had heard from her mother. Part of her thought she was dead, but what if she were alive now?

This nagging thought wouldn't go away. She could try to push it down. She could hand this new development in Soren's case off to her supervisor or the police or anyone who knew more than Sunny. It was probably the right thing to do but she couldn't bring herself to do it.

She needed to know. It was time she found her mama.

Chapter 3

Julian had waited outside for his mother to pick him up from school. She was late. He looked down at the digital watch he had just gotten for his birthday. It was almost four. She was never this late. Galen was at the babysitter's. She was smaller than him. She was probably worried. He wasn't worried. Not really. His stomach just felt weird. Mom had been . . . different lately. She stayed in her room a lot. And when she was out with them her mind seemed to be far away, so even when she was with them she seemed gone.

Maybe she was still sleeping. She did that a lot lately. She seemed like she slept more than she stayed awake and Julian didn't understand how anyone could be so tired. He had asked his father about it once, and his father said she might be sick. But she didn't look sick to Julian. She just seemed like she didn't care anymore.

He started walking away from school. Almost all the teachers had gone for the day. A few of them asked him if he was okay. He told them he was, but as he got farther and farther away from the school he wasn't so sure. She *had never been this late. She had always called if she was going to be. She had always sent his father if she couldn't make it.*

They didn't live far from the school. Less than a mile. He was ten now. He went to the store by himself sometimes to buy candy. He could probably walk home alone every day now. He would stop to get Galen from the babysitter first. He wasn't sure why she needed a babysitter when Mom didn't work. Galen went to preschool in the mornings. Mom said she needed some more time to herself. That had caused an argument. His father had pulled her into their bedroom so he and Galen wouldn't hear and maybe she was too focused on the TV to notice, but Julian had heard.

"They're your children too! You need to spend time with them."

"I didn't sign up for this life."

"So what? You think my life has gone according to plan? Nobody forced this on you. You made the choice ten years ago. You are a mother. You need to act like one."

He remembered hearing something smash against the wall and Mom running out. She didn't come back that night. Dad was the one who picked him up from school the next day.

He tried not to think about it as he got to the babysitter's house. It made his stomach hurt more and more.

He knocked on the door and it flew open immediately. Mrs. Standish was standing there looking very angry for a moment, but then she saw it was him.

"Julian, where is your mother? I told her I had a doctor's appointment today. I can't miss it."

"I'm here to get Galen. We're walking home."

Mrs. Standish frowned. "Why? Where is your mother?"

"Dad is going to meet us at the house." He didn't know why he had lied. He didn't know why he couldn't tell her that he didn't know where his mother was. But he couldn't bring himself to. He hadn't been afraid of her being hurt. He was afraid of her hurting them.

"Jules!" Galen came running up to the door with her backpack on, her pink sneakers untied. *"Where's Mommy?"* She looked up at him with big eyes and he knew she was worried too.

"I'm going to walk you home today." He got down on his knees and tied his sister's shoes and then took her tiny hand in his. *"Come on, Galen. We'll see Mommy soon."*

Only they didn't. The next time they saw her was a year later when she had asked his father for a divorce.

He walked into the building that contained his law offices after a lunch meeting with one of his best clients, a reality television star that had somehow turned her limited talents into a multimillion-dollar empire. Maybe he wasn't in the best head space since Regina had turned down his proposal because he could barely feign interest in his client's story today. She had been accused of ripping off an indie designer's work and was now being sued. For over an hour Julian had to listen to her explain how she came up with the design, but in the end even he thought she was guilty. Sometimes it was hard for him to care about the cases he was presented with. His father was a police officer, turned civil rights attorney, turned magistrate. He had made an eighth of what Julian had made, but he had never lost his passion for the work. Julian wondered what had happened to his passion.

He had been with the firm for many years now, and when he used to walk into the swanky lobby of the building he had been awed by it. Historic cases had been won here. Huge settlements had been negotiated and wars either started or prevented here. This place is where the wealthy went when they had trouble. It was one of the top firms in the country. He had felt such immense pride being there. No one thought the ex-football player would land in the top firm in the city.

He proved he could make it there and that should have been enough, but seven years in, he was still proving that he belonged there. It was starting to grate on him.

"Good afternoon, Mr. King," Brenda, his long-time assistant greeted him. She was in her late fifties and was close to retirement. He had never begged. He considered it beneath him, but he had begged her to stay on as his assistant. She had taken better care of him than his own mother.

"Hello, Brenda. I think I must have told you a million times not to call me Mr. King."

"I, for the millionth time have told you that you are my boss and that's what I am supposed to call you."

"If I fire you . . . would you call me by my first name?"

"If I whoop your behind . . . would you stop being so cheeky?"

"Maybe," he grinned. "But you like seeing my cheeks."

"Mr. King!" She blushed deeply. "I'm old enough to be your grandmother."

"You're not too old for me, Brenda." He winked.

"Oh hush. Your one o'clock is waiting in your office."

"Give me the rundown. Who is it? An athlete with a pending assault charge? An heiress with a drug conviction hanging over her head?"

"You'll see," was all that Brenda said.

"I'm not liking the way you're saying that. If it's a dog custody battle, send them away right now. I refuse to use my years of legal experience arguing for a Maltese again."

"No, I think you'll be pleasantly surprised."

"Is it something big like a murder case? I haven't defended someone accused of murder before. It would be a huge change of pace."

"I'll never understand you lawyers. Murder cases excite you?"

"I wouldn't put it like that. But a high-profile case that could drag out for years is great for the firm because it puts us in the spotlight. And anything that I handle that is good for the firm is good for me. It will bring me that much closer to partner."

"I doubt the young lady in your office has been accused of murder. Shoplifting lip gloss from a store, maybe, but probably not murder."

"Famous?"

"Not that I could tell."

He nodded, thinking he was about to walk in

and meet another heiress who couldn't keep her privileged self out of trouble. He was tempted to make up an excuse to send her away because after his last meeting he didn't think he could stomach someone who didn't know what it was like to put in the work.

But when he walked into his office he found someone completely unexpected. There was a pretty girl there. Maybe girl wasn't the right word for her. A lot of women didn't like to be called girls because they thought it diminished them. Brenda had called her a young lady. But that didn't seem like the right term for her either. The woman in his office was lovely. Lovely wasn't a word in Julian's vocabulary either and he was having a hard time today coming up with words. His mind felt like it was stuck in mud. But the woman before him was the kind of pretty he didn't often see in New York City.

There was no hardness to her. No jaded edge. The woman stood before him in a simple sundress, a prim cardigan wrapped around her shoulders and a pair of baby pink ballet flat shoes. She had a mass of thick curls that she had attempted to tame in a low bun.

She didn't belong in his office. Every bone in his body knew he was going to have to turn her away even before she stated her case.

"Hi, I'm Sunshine Gibson, but everybody calls me Sunny."

Her name fit her.

She wasn't one of the cultured young women who had spent their days in finishing school. He

had met his share of New York society women,
young and old, and he knew he hadn't seen her in
any of those places. Yet he did know her from somewhere. Or at least he thought he did.

She reminded him of all the girls he grew up
with in Virginia. The nice ones who had married
right out of college and were presidents of the PTA
by the time he was a first-year attorney.

She shouldn't be there.

"I'm Julian King." He reached out and shook
her hand. He held on for a moment longer than he
should have. He had gotten caught up in how soft
and small her hand felt inside of his and felt something pass between them as they looked at each
other.

He mentally shook his head, realizing he must be
imagining things.

He was just in a weird headspace after ending
things with Regina. The young woman before him
didn't look more than twenty-two. He had been attracted to older women as long as he remembered.
Younger ones were trouble. They weren't as deci-
sive. They always wanted a world of things he
couldn't deliver. He steered clear of anyone who
was under thirty.

He cleared his throat and gestured to the chair
in front of his desk. "Please have a seat and tell me
what it is that I can do for you."

"You don't remember me, do you?" she asked.
He had known she looked familiar but he couldn't
place her.

"You're too young to have gone to high school with me so, no I don't remember you."

"We met briefly at a Christmas party last year."

Julian had been to many Christmas parties, each one of them upscale. Maybe his snap judgment was wrong; maybe she was a society girl.

"Really? Which one?"

"Clive Daniels."

"You know Clive?"

Clive was old money, but as down to earth as someone who grew up with everything could be.

"I know his wife. Her sister is my best friend. She spoke very highly of you. Said you could handle nearly any legal problem."

"I'm glad to hear that." Julian knew one of the reasons he was hired at this firm was because he had connections. He could bring in big clients and earn the firm millions each year. He also knew it made the other lawyers hate him. But he didn't give a damn. He wasn't here to make friends. "Tell me what I can do for you."

Sunny took a deep breath and for the first time in their short meeting he saw something besides sweet innocence in her almond-shaped eyes. For a second she looked almost tortured.

"I'm a social worker . . ."

"You're a social worker?" She wasn't a society girl and she wasn't some mixed-up college kid. She definitely couldn't afford his services. "I wouldn't think you were old enough for that kind of job."

"I'm older than you think. I haven't asked anyone

if they would like fries with that in some time. May I continue?"

There *was* an edge to her. Despite that warm smile and those huge innocent eyes there was something a little fierce there. His respect for her grew.

"Yes." He nodded. "Please do."

"I work for the city, and my job mostly consists of placing children in foster homes."

"A tough job," he commented. He fully understood how difficult her job was and how little the city of New York paid its hardest working employees.

"Yes, thank you. I have one child who is about to come up for adoption, and I'm afraid that the situation might get complicated."

"I'm sorry, but I don't see how I can help." Unless this adoption involved some celebrity or political figure, his firm would not be interested in taking it on.

"Actually, you can help me a lot. That is, if you're willing to waive your fee."

"My fee? The way you say it makes it sound like I shouldn't get paid for my work."

"Of course, you should get paid for your work but what you charge for an hour, I make in a week."

He knew that billing clients over a thousand dollars an hour was a great deal of money, but the way she said it made him feel almost dirty. He didn't set the prices, the firm did, yet he felt the need to defend himself.

"It costs a lot to live in Manhattan." That wasn't

much of a defense, but he couldn't think of anything else to say.

"Yes, and yet there are hundreds of thousands of people here who get by on a lot less. Listen, I'm not here to debate your prices. I'm here because I need your help."

"All right, Ms. Gibson, even if I agreed to waive my fee, I still don't see how I can help you. Most of my work is criminal. Although, if you think you have a lawsuit on your hands I might be able to advise you."

"I need you to be the child's law guardian until the adoption is finalized."

A law guardian was an impartial person who reviewed the child's situation and recommended the best option for the child to the court. It was simple. It basically was sticking yourself right in the middle of somebody else's mess and Julian just wasn't up for that.

"I'm sorry, but I really can't help you with that. Family law is one of the areas I know nothing about. I can recommend a list of lawyers who would be more suitable. My secretary will fax them over to your workplace."

"I don't want anybody else," she said, looking him right in the eye. "You're the best in the city. I want you."

The way she said it, the intensity in her voice, made him pause and stare at her for a moment. There was some toughness there. He didn't expect that from the way she presented herself.

"If you have corporate or trust issues or ever

need to sue somebody, I can help you, but your problem is out of my area of expertise."

"You'll want to take this case. I promise. Just let me explain. It's a lot more complicated than it appears on the surface. The only reason I came to you is because I can't do it by myself anymore."

For a split second, he wanted to say yes. He wanted to help her, but common sense prevailed and he knew he couldn't. She knocked him off balance. He couldn't read her as easily as he would have liked. He couldn't place her into a box like he did with everyone else and that meant he couldn't work with her.

"I'm sorry, Ms. Gibson," he said, standing up. "I really can't, but I will have my assistant fax over the list today." He walked around his desk as she stood. "I hope everything works out." He extended his hand to shake hers again. And there was that feeling again, that something that passed through him when he felt her soft hand in his. He tried to let her go, but she held on and squeezed his hand slightly.

"Thank you for your time, Mr. King."

He watched her walk out, her hips gently switched from side to side, and he had a feeling that he wouldn't be seeing the last of Sunshine Gibson.

Chapter 4

"I didn't think my feet could get this big," Arden said, looking down at them as she and Sunny sat across from each other at the kitchen table. "They've grown two sizes and my mother said they might not go back down. Hers never went back down." She slumped over on to the table as much as her hugely pregnant belly would allow. "My shoes. I have such beautiful shoes."

"Selfishly, I'm happy for your big feet. Your shoes are exactly my size."

"My shoes have four-inch heels and pointy toes. You're much more of a ballet flat girl than a heel girl. I didn't think you liked my shoes."

"You're wrong. I love your shoes, but ballet flats are much more practical for me since I spend the majority of my day walking around New York City doing home visits. But sometimes I want to wear sexy shoes. Sometimes I want to wear a dress that doesn't make me look like a Sunday schoolteacher.

Sometimes I want to not be the person everybody thinks I am."

"What's wrong, Sunny?" Arden reached across the table and took her hand. "There's something up with you lately."

"It's work stuff. I'm afraid that the adoption for one of my kids might fall through."

"I'm sorry, honey, but if you've done everything in your power that you could, you have to let it go. You can't let it get to you."

"I'm not sure I did everything in my power. I went to see Julian King yesterday."

Arden frowned as she rubbed her growing belly. "Why? He usually does big celebrity cases. Plus, there's no way in hell that you can afford him."

"I went to him because we met at your sister's Christmas party and your brother-in-law told me that he was one of the best lawyers in the city and to use him if I ever needed one."

"But my brother-in-law is a millionaire with a food empire. All of his recommendations are top of the line. My husband once asked him where he got a T-shirt and he sent us to a store that was selling them for eight hundred dollars. Julian is the kind of lawyer you go to if you're a famous athlete fighting a charge or if you get caught embezzling from your company. I guess I'm saying he's the man you go to if you have money. He charges your weekly salary in an hour. You don't have any money."

"Okay, Arden. I get it. I'm poor. Do you want to talk about how I don't have any parents next?"

"Sorry." She shrugged. "I just don't understand

why out of all the lawyers in this city you picked the most expensive one just because my rich brother-in-law said he was good."

"I'm not an idiot, Arden. I want him to work for free."

"And he agreed to that?"

Apparently, she was the only one who thought Julian King would waive his fee. "Well, no. He didn't take me seriously at first. He looked at me and immediately thought I was some kid."

"Sunny," Arden said gently. "You do look like a kid. I've been with you when a bartender accused you of having a fake ID."

Sunny rolled her eyes. Maybe she did look young but she stopped being a child twenty years ago. Maybe she never really was a child in the first place. Having a mother who left her locked in a closet had sucked the childhood right out of her.

"I don't care. He had no right to be the smug stuck-up jackass he was."

"So that's why you hate how you look all of a sudden?"

"I don't hate how I look. I just feel stuck sometimes. I've worn my hair like this since I was fourteen. I've had these shoes since college. I feel like everyone around me is evolving and moving on and I'm still here in the same place I was five years ago. And I'm just not so sure I want to be in that place anymore. Does that make any sense?"

"Yes. That makes a lot of sense."

"How do we fix it?"

"I'm not sure, but let's start by looking in my shoe closet."

Being with Arden, playing in her closet, spending a few hours just being silly with her best friend had helped lighten Sunny's mood. But then she went home to her tiny apartment and she was alone with the letters that were sitting in her jewelry box. The ones she felt compelled to read again.

And then Jeannie Earl called her. Another letter had arrived with more cash and a photograph of Soren when she was a baby. And Sunny knew that even if she wanted to give up this search for herself, she couldn't give it up for Soren.

The next morning she couldn't stop thinking about it so she left her apartment and started to walk, finding herself on the upper East Side. She loved this part of the city. She loved the way the old buildings looked. She loved the sidewalk cafés and looking into the windows of the stores she would never be able to afford. She had daydreamed of a life here when she was a little girl. Living in a grand apartment with a huge kitchen and big windows that let in all the light. She had also dreamed of waking up one day and finding her mother back to normal, a mother that would put her back into school, and one who didn't think people were chasing them all the time.

Sunny knew it probably was just a coincidence. That Soren wasn't her sister and her mother wouldn't have reemerged to abandon another kid after twenty years. But she wasn't sure she would be able to let it go unless she knew the truth.

Maybe hiring a high-priced attorney wasn't the right move. She could hire a private detective. But, she couldn't afford that either.

And what information could she give that would help unravel this mystery? She had only known her mother's first name.

Her parents were never married. Sunny was so little when her mother told her about the love she had shared with her father. Girl Sunny thought it sounded terribly romantic. Woman Sunny realized that she had probably been the product of a torrid love affair with a soldier on leave. It probably lasted as long as it took for her father to get his next assignment. But her mother had made it sound so magical. As if they were soulmates who destiny had failed.

What kind of information was that to give to a private detective? Her mother had been mentally ill. As a child she didn't have the right words for it, but now she could see things clearly. Her mother saw people who weren't there. Heard voices that never made a sound. How could Sunny know for sure what was true and what was conjured up by her mother's illness?

She didn't have her original birth certificate. She didn't know who her parents were or where she was born. No one had seemed to miss her or Grace. No one ever came looking for her. Her mother had kept her so hidden from the world she wasn't sure that anyone knew she had existed until that police officer pulled her out of the closet. But Grace had to have had a family once upon a time. She had to have been someone's daughter.

There was a little more information on Soren, which is why she thought she could turn to Julian who worked in a huge law firm and had all the resources one could ever dream of. Soren knew who her father was. He had been in her life briefly before her mother moved her up here. She knew his full name, where he was born, how he lived, and when he died. Sunny had found out everything she could about him. He was from the South and had been married to another woman when Soren was conceived. His name had not been put on any birth certificate and there was no piece of paper that linked him to Soren's mama. She was a mystery too.

Soren refused to speak of her either out of anger or fear. It took Sunny a year to pry that little information from her.

She was walking past a beautiful prewar apartment building on her way to Central Park when she felt a large hand clamp around her wrist. She tensed for a brief moment before she twisted her arm to break the hold and raised her other hand to shove her palm into her assailant's nose.

"Hey!" Julian King stepped away from her. His hands raised in defense. "I wasn't going to hurt you."

She let out a breath as her heartbeat slowed. "What the hell is the matter with you? You can't go grabbing a woman in New York City unless you're prepared to get your ass kicked."

"I called your name twice, but you didn't hear me."

She was surprised to see him, especially since she had just been thinking about the case she needed his help with. New York was a big city. She didn't often bump into many people, especially ones who ran in such different circles. But maybe it was fate that she had decided to come to this section of the city at this time of day.

"I was lost in thought. I'm sorry."

"I'm sorry I scared you." He shook his head. "Damn. I knew you would be trouble the moment I met you. Remind me to never sneak up behind you."

"I can only remind you if this won't be the last time we meet."

His eyes flicked over her as he took her in. He was openly studying her and she wondered what he really thought about what he saw. "I was about to accuse you of stalking me but with that reaction I'm starting to think that your walking past my apartment building is a coincidence."

She looked at the doorman-ed building that was steps away from Central Park. Of course he lived here. Most lawyers seven or eight years into their career couldn't afford to live in a building like this, but Julian King had played professional football. He had been a star. He probably made more money than he could spend in two lifetimes and now he made in a month what she made in a year. "So you live here?" She looked up at him. "You shouldn't have told me that. Now I know where to find you."

He wasn't wearing a suit today unlike the last two times she saw him. He wore a black long-sleeved shirt and gray shorts. He was put together but casual. His sleeves were rolled up to reveal his powerful forearms. Sunny glanced down as his legs to see his thick muscular calves. He looked much more like a football player than an attorney. He was a huge man, one that looked like he picked women up and threw them over his shoulder when he wanted to have his way with them. But then there was his face, which was almost beautiful with his high cheekbones and square jaw. And his mouth. It was pouty and full. He had better lips than most women and for a moment Sunny wondered how they felt brushed across a throat or down the valley of a chest.

She wasn't sure she liked Julian King but she was attracted to him on a primal level. She didn't think much of it. Men who had as much testosterone as he did probably had that effect on a lot of women. But damn, he was nice to look at.

"So now you plan to stalk me? That sounds sinister from someone who looks like they still attend Sunday school," he said.

"A slimy lawyer is calling someone else sinister? He who is without sin . . ."

One side of his mouth curled and he started walking. She fell into step beside him. "If I'm such a slimy lawyer, why did you want me to take your case?"

"I need the best. This family has been through a lot and they deserve it."

"But I've told you that I'm not the right person to help you. I've been working on a lot of divorces lately. I literally tear families apart. I wouldn't know where to begin."

"But you can listen, right? And not brush me off just because I look young."

"No, I brushed you off because you look young and you clearly have no way of paying me."

"You're an ass."

"I was joking, but I'm a lawyer who is trying to make partner, whose firm looks at how much business I bring in, and taking your case wouldn't be good for my career."

"But it might be good for your soul. Wouldn't you feel better if you did something good once in a while?"

"I give plenty to charity."

"But I don't want your money. That's easy to give. I need a little bit of your time. And right now all I'm asking you to do is listen."

"Talk."

"I have a ten-year-old girl who is about to be adopted by a great family. The kind of family every social worker dreams about for her foster kids. Her birth mother left her on the steps of our agency two years ago. We went through the process and searched for both parents but couldn't find them and the child was eligible for adoption. But recently the mother started to contact her." Sunny pulled her phone out of her bag and showed him the picture she had of the two of them together. "This is her."

Julian took the picture from Sunny and studied it. "She's cute, but I still don't see a case."

"There's more. She started contacting the child at her home with her new parents, which should be impossible because once a parent loses rights we seal our records, and there is to be no contact unless both parties agree to it. This mother had completely disappeared. She left this kid half-starved and filthy. Who knows what she exposed her to."

"But this mother found the child."

"Her name is Soren, and yes she had contacted her and her foster mother by letter, and she says she is planning on getting her back."

"She just can't take her child back. Her rights have been terminated. I don't care what she says in her letter, legally it's not possible."

"I know that, but it hasn't been one letter. Another came last night by courier and the mother is sending money. Thousands of dollars at this point."

"It's like she's paying child support. That complicates things. If she goes to court she could use that in her argument. Are you sure everything was done correctly? In a court case she'll use every loophole to her advantage."

"I went over everything myself, but who knows what she has planned and that scares me. This woman has means. She managed to find Soren in a city of millions and now she says she's coming back for her. I don't know what to do. I keep telling the foster parents not to worry, but that's wrong of me because I am worried. Jeannie Earl is a good mother to Soren and she has been through a lot. She deserves to raise a child and Soren deserves this woman's love. She was a mess when her mother left her the last time. What's to say this woman won't slip back into old habits? What's to say she won't leave her again?"

Sunny's chest started to grow impossibly tight as she spoke. She knew what it was like to be left. She knew what it was like to have everything go seemingly well and then have it all ripped from you. She was an adult now. She had set up her life so no one could rock it with one decision. But Soren was a powerless child and the thought of her life being turned upside down again made Sunny want to double over. "I'm afraid." She said the words aloud for the first time.

"Of a custody battle?"

"Soren is going to be stuck in the middle of all this and I'm not sure how she's going to handle it. She didn't speak for months. Two foster families sent her away because they couldn't deal with her issues. You can't imagine how hard it is to be left by your mother. You don't trust anymore. You feel like there is something wrong with you, like you're unlovable. And for a little kid to go through that and survive is amazing."

He nodded once and she saw a mix of sadness and understanding in his eyes. "You do need legal help," he admitted.

"I know the kinds of things these kids go through. Even people who love their kids hurt them. I wouldn't be able to live with myself if she was hurt again because I didn't do everything possible to stop it."

"Enough," Julian said softly, cutting her off. "I don't want to hear any more."

"You should meet Soren. She's smart and beautiful and funny. She's got a chance. I can give her the chance I never got. I don't find matches this perfect. People don't want to take older children, but the Earls did, and they are good people and . . ."

Julian placed his hand on her shoulder and squeezed. He knew he shouldn't have touched her again after her last reaction to him, but he couldn't help himself. He had to stop himself from placing his hand on her cheek. He wanted to comfort her. Yes, she looked younger than she was. Her simple dress, well-worn flats, and messy hair didn't help that, but just by speaking with her he knew she was more woman than girl. She was smart and she cared deeply about this kid she was trying to protect and the family she was trying to place with her. Sunny was scared and if she kept talking he would want to help her. But he couldn't because she was the last thing he needed right now.

"Sunny, I understand, but please stop talking. The last thing I need is a crying girl in Central Park." They were well into the park too. He had stepped outside of his apartment, needing some fresh air on this warm spring afternoon. He had gone into the office early that morning to get some work done on a big case he had coming up. There were lots of young lawyers there, scrambling to get their work done, to make an impression. He brought in the biggest clients. He earned the firm millions and millions of dollars, but Julian was there still trying to prove himself like the rest of them. His colleagues thought of him as a lineman who endorsed sneakers and sports drinks, who only brought clients in because of his days as a pro. But he had gone to a damn good law school just like them and he passed his bar exam with much higher than average scores just like them and he did have his novelty star power to get his foot in the door, but a lot of them had rich mommies and daddies who knew one of the partners. And just like all of them when he screwed up he heard about it. He wasn't immune. He wasn't just a token. Most days he didn't think much about it, but he had been in a funky mood all week. Then he saw Sunny walk past his building and without thinking he reached out and grabbed her wrist, which he probably would never have done if she were anyone else. But he saw her and couldn't let her go by.

He had startled her. He saw the panic and fear leap into her eyes and it was deeper than he expected to see just by catching her off guard. He knew he should have parted ways with her by now, but fifteen minutes later they were standing in the park and he didn't want to let her go yet.

"I don't cry," she said softly. "I stopped a long time ago."

She was probably making a comment about her age, but there was something in her voice that made him think it was more than just that. He looked into her eyes and felt something pass between them again. It was similar to the feeling he got when they first met and he had shaken her hand. He realized that he was still touching her, his thumb gently stroking her shoulder.

What the hell was he doing? He needed to send her away.

"You depress me. Come on. I'll buy you lunch."

They had ended up at the Boathouse in Central Park. Sunny had seen the restaurant dozens of times but she had never eaten there. She had never thought to eat there. Sunny didn't think she would have ended up there when she left her apartment this morning. But here she was with a massively gorgeous man who had just placed his big hot hand on her body and stroked her shoulder with his thumb. He had been trying to comfort her, but she felt more than comfort when he touched her and for a moment she wished that her skin was bare and that there were no barriers between them.

The hostess led them to a small table that overlooked the lake. It was beautiful. One of those gems New York City had to offer that she rarely got to see because through her work, she often was shown the ugliest side of the city.

"You're really buying me lunch, right?" she asked him as they sat down. "You're not going to say that you're buying me lunch and then send me a bill for twelve hundred dollars later?"

"It will only be for five hundred dollars. After

that story, I have to give you a discount. I have a heart after all."

She grinned at him. He grinned back and she was briefly caught up in how sexy his smile was.

"I have one rule today. Don't," he started to say.

"Try to convince you to take my case?"

"No. I'm not doing that, no matter what you do. You can't order a salad. You have to order food. I'm sick of going out and paying for some lettuce you know you don't really want."

"I never order a salad when I'm out. Especially with very rich former football playing lawyers. Do they have nachos here? The ones with the fake cheese are my favorite."

"No nachos."

"Mac and cheese? And I don't mean that fancy kind either. I want the kind that comes out of the box."

"I think you might be a year or two too old for the kids' menu. I'd bet you'd like grown-up food if you tried it."

"What would you recommend?"

"How about I order a selection of things and we share. They serve brunch till four and I worked out hard with my trainer this morning before I went into the office."

"You went into work today?"

"A lot of us do. Eighty-hour work weeks aren't a myth when you're trying to make it to the top."

"So that's how your firm justifies the huge salaries. We pay our lawyers a fortune so we don't feel guilty sending them to an early grave?"

"I'd bet you work nearly as many hours as I do," he countered. "That's what the trainer is for. To keep my mind clear and my body healthy so I can live long enough to enjoy the enormous fortune I'm earning to keep reality television stars out of jail."

She sat back in her chair and studied him. Linemen could be doughy, but Mr. King kept himself in shape. She wondered just how hard that body felt under all those clothes.

A waitress came to their table and Julian ordered enough food for six people.

"It's obvious you find comfort in food. What do the other fancy lawyers do to blow off steam?"

"Some drink. Some turn to drugs. Some screw everything in a ten-foot radius."

"Oh?" She leaned forward and rested her hand on her chin. "Tell me more about that last one."

"I shouldn't."

Her eyes flicked across his body. "Confession is good for the soul."

"How old are you? Really? I can't tell."

"Seventeen and a half."

"Sunny," he warned.

"I'm damn near thirty, Jules. I'm a licensed social worker with a master's degree. How young could I possibly be and why is this such a concern for you?"

"When you work for high-profile people you come across your share of clients who have had scandals with girls and boys who haven't made it to their eighteenth birthdays and get involved with people twice their age. I'm suspicious."

"I'm jaded. One of the girls on my caseload had been a sex worker since the age of . . ."

He put his hand up to stop her from speaking. "You're not allowed to talk about your job. I want to eat carbs and sugar and fat. I'm here to enjoy my day, damn it."

"Okay. Then we talk about your job. Give me the dirt."

"One of the junior partners brings in women he's met online and has sex with them in his office. One time he forgot to lock the door and his assistant walked in on him. She was so shocked by what she saw she screamed. Apparently there was a latex and a dog leash involved."

"Kinky. Did he get fired? I can't imagine that's cool with your bosses."

"No. It was late. We didn't have clients there. My bosses have their own proclivities. They know that everyone needs to blow off steam. And normally that kind of thing wouldn't bother me except that he had a pregnant wife waiting at home."

"Asshole."

"I agree."

"But you work out and eat. How boring. Do you at least smash things with your ham-sized fist when you get angry?"

"No. I'm a former pro athlete who nearly destroyed myself partying after I got injured. I find other ways to channel my rage."

"I guess you don't have a secret sex dungeon either?"

"I tried to put one in. The co-op board wouldn't allow it," he said with a straight face.

She laughed. There was something about him that she liked. But before she could put her finger on it the food had arrived. There were waffles and French toast, eggs Benedict, macaroni and cheese, some sort of chicken dish, and a quiche. There was so much beautiful food before them that she became emotional. It was rare she got to eat like this.

Ever since she had gone into foster care her belly had been full, but before then she remembered the times when she would go more than a day without anything except water. That had left a mark on her. Julian probably thought nothing about the spread before him, but for her food like this was a celebration.

"Is everything okay?" he asked her, appearing truly concerned.

"I could cry. This is beautiful. Thank you."

He frowned at her as if he was unable to process if her gratitude was real. "Eat."

She did. The food was filling and delicious. She felt his eyes on her more than once and when she looked up at him he was openly studying her. "What?"

"Do you eat like this on dates?"

"Like what? Am I being a pig?"

"No. You're eating like you're not trying to impress me."

"Why should I impress you?" She put her fork down. "Judging by the way you're studying me like I'm some kind of new species, I gather you don't date many girls who eat."

"No, I don't date many *women* who like to eat. My ex was one of those meticulous types. Chicken had to be cubed, not sliced, dressing on the side. All organic, no gluten, no sodium."

"No fun. I'd bet she was unnaturally skinny. Not the God-given thinness some people are born with. I bet she exercises away all her breasts, and thighs and hips. That she flips if food is made with butter and not steamed. I'd bet she's trying to keep up with some impossible beauty standard created by the media. Which I don't get because men are hard-wired to desire women who are . . . more bountiful."

"I think there could be something to that theory."

"Then why do you do it? Judging by the way you spoke of your ex she didn't make you very happy. Maybe you should look for a different type of woman in a place you'd never think to look."

"But what if I'm looking for a particular type of woman? A man like me needs someone who isn't ordinary."

Sunny rolled her eyes. "What's that mean? Who is just ordinary? I'm certainly not."

"You certainly aren't, Sunshine," he said dryly.

"Thanks, Jules." She smiled.

"That wasn't a compliment."

"Who cares? I'm choosing to think of it that way."

"You're cute." He grabbed one of her errant ringlets and pulled on it.

She swatted at his hand. "Hey!"

"My little sister had this kind of hair when we were kids. I loved to annoy her by pulling it." He grabbed another strand and pulled that one too. There was a little mischievousness in his eyes.

"Are you biracial?" she asked him.

"I am, but I never call myself that. What about you?"

"My mama was about as blond and blue eyed as they come."

"We have something in common."

"Matching identity crises?"

He laughed loudly. Sunny loved the sound of it, its deep timbre, the way it vibrated through her chest. She wanted more of it.

"Julian?"

Sunny heard a clipped but husky voice call. She looked up to see a blond ice goddess wearing Chanel sunglasses on her forehead and a slate gray dress that matched the color of the woman's eyes.

"Regina."

Immediately Sunny noticed the change in his demeanor. The laughter was gone, the smile melted away. There was a tightness about him.

No longer was he Jules, the funny guy she enjoyed. He was Julian King, high-priced attorney. He was the same man she had met in his office.

"Is this your baby sister? Hello, Galen. It's so nice to see you again."

"This isn't Galen. You've met my sister before. This is Sunshine Gibson."

"Sunshine," Regina said, placing a false smile on her face. "What a cute name for such a cute *girl*. I didn't know Julian was mentoring. Tell me, sweetheart, which law schools are you applying to?"

This was not one of Julian's acquaintances. There

was too much familiarity in her voice, there was possession in her eyes. This woman already knew the ways Julian's body felt pressed against hers. She had probably had the pleasure of his lips on her neck.

Sunny wasn't sure why, but this woman really annoyed her.

"Julian isn't mentoring me," was all she said, giving no explanation of their relationship.

"I'm not."

Apparently, he wasn't explaining things either, which was interesting.

"Sunny, this is Regina Richardson. She is president of Fierce Fire Makeup. Regina, Sunny is a social worker for the city."

Regina fixed her gaze on Sunny as if she was trying to figure out her purpose for being there with him. "You're a *social worker*?" she asked as if she had never heard of the job. "How . . . nice for you. How did you meet? I didn't think Julian crossed paths with many *social workers*."

She said it as if social worker was a code word for social disease.

"I'm going to have his child," Sunny said, feeling a little annoyed. "Tell her, baby. We are going to be married by the end of summer." She reached for his hand and slid her fingers through his. She had done it for effect, but she felt a warm buzzing along her nerves.

Regina looked completely bewildered. "Julian, you just asked me—"

He cut her off and scowled at Sunny. "Sunny was

joking. She's a friend of an acquaintance. We are discussing business."

"So she's your client?"

"Why does it matter to you? You made it perfectly clear what you wanted."

"Nothing was clear." She shook her head. "You gave me an ultimatum and then walked away."

There was pain in her voice. Regina seemed unfeeling but it was clear to Sunny that she was hurting. Julian was tense. She couldn't read him, but she didn't see sadness or longing in his eyes. He seemed a little angry.

It was an uncomfortable moment. One that Sunny wished she wasn't there to witness.

"This is neither the time nor place to discuss this," he said to Regina, and Sunny felt a little pressure on her hand.

His fingers were still locked with hers on his lap, hidden from view but she wasn't sure if he realized that his hand was there.

"Oh, I don't mind," Sunny spoke up, wanting the tension to break. "I love hearing other people's drama. I'm nosy by nature. It's why I became a social worker."

One corner of Julian's mouth curled. "That may be but I'll spare you."

"You're right. You know how to reach me." Regina replaced her sunglasses and walked away.

"I take it you two used to be a couple."

"Yes. Until recently."

"I didn't expect her to be your ex. She's quite a bit older than you."

Julian shook his head. "She would be very offended by your remark."

"Why? I didn't say she looks bad. She looks fantastic. She's just older."

"Are you suggesting she's too old for me?"

"I applaud women who date younger men. If I'm single in fifteen years, I'm going to find a muscular sex god in his twenties to be at my beck and call. I just question that she's right for you."

"I like my women mature. They know what they want from life. They're more emotionally and financially secure. I don't have to worry about getting trapped."

"Ah." Sunny nodded. "You are gorgeous, successful, and rich. You're avoiding gold diggers who can keep you on the hook for child support for the next twenty-one years."

"I'm not going to lie. That is partly why I choose to date the women I do. My brother-in-law and I first became friends when I defended him in a child support lawsuit. A woman produced a five-year-old child, claiming it was his and asking for millions of dollars in back child support. The kid wasn't his. But it could have been. I only played pro for a little while, but I have seen women throw themselves at athletes just to elevate their lives."

"And now you're cynical."

"I'm realistic. I see the ugly side of people every day. I avoid those type of entanglements where I can."

"If Regina had all the things you were looking for in a woman then why aren't you together? From what I gathered, you're the one who ended it."

"She doesn't want to marry me." He just stated it, as if it were a simple fact. "I must not have everything she requires in a partner."

"How did you propose? Was it romantic? Did you whisk her away and ply her with flowers and expensive wine and tell her that you can't bear to go through the rest of your life without her?"

"No. I was on my lunch break. We have been together off and on for a few years. I told her that it was time we take the next step and get married. She turned me down."

"Of course, she turned you down. I would have turned you down too. You don't love her. Or at least you're not showing her you love her. She wants you to be in love with her. Most humans need to feel that. That's why she won't marry you."

He shook his head. "That's not why we were together. Neither one of us were looking for love. I was very upfront about that. And I've done enough divorces to know that love doesn't make marriages work. Mutual respect and common interests make marriages work."

Sunny shook her head. She had seen the worst side of people but she knew that love worked. She had seen it heal. She had seen it get people through terrible times. Everyone wanted to be loved. It was as simple as that. "She loves you, you jackass."

He shook his head. "No, she doesn't."

"That woman loves you and if you can't see that then you don't know what love is."

His eyes narrowed. "How would you know what love is? You confuse love with romance. Romance doesn't last. After all your cuteness is gone and the flowers dry up, what are you going to be left with? Someone whose flaws you finally see clearly and probably can't stand. That's why you don't choose a partner based on emotion. You choose one you can live with. One that complements your lifestyle. Regina and I would work well together."

Logically that made sense and he delivered his argument as perfectly as any lawyer could. But Sunny wasn't buying it. He had to want more than that. Everyone wanted more than that.

"Well, counselor, if it was that simple then why didn't she want to marry you?"

Chapter 5

Julian looked up at his computer when he heard a knock on his office door. It was David Connor, another junior partner at the firm, who was competing with him for the senior partner position.

They didn't like each other. They never had. Julian had been hired later and rose through the ranks faster than David. He thought Julian was a hack and a token hire. Julian thought he was a brown-nose kiss ass who got there through his father's connections.

"What's up?"

"I have a client who would like tickets for the season opener in September. I need you to get them for him."

"I haven't played in almost ten years. What makes you think I could get those tickets? Especially the kind of tickets you're expecting."

"Cut the bullshit. You represent half your former team as well as two coaches. You could get any tickets at any time. It's one of the few reasons they keep you around."

Dave never bothered to hide his disdain for Julian. They hated each other, but they were often forced to work together on very high-profile cases.

"They keep me around because I bring in the most billable hours and I have the highest percent of success rates when I go to court. Can you say the same thing?"

"I'm right on your ass in both areas. We both know you do so well in court because people are surprised that a pro athlete who has been hit in the head so many times can string two logical sentences together. They're so shocked they give you the win just for effort."

"I got into law school, was top of my class, and passed the bar after getting hit in the head. Imagine how much more better I would be than you if I hadn't played football. I also never have to worry about the other side trying to physically attack me. How's your face feeling? I heard your head snapped back when Mr. Roswell punched you after the settlement was read."

"Face is fine. But in order for him to want to punch me, you know I must have gotten his ex a ton of money in that divorce? Billionaire divorce cases give me a rush. I guess you don't get too many of those. You seem to be busy defending your football playing buddies on assault charges or the trashy celebrities when they go off the deep end."

It was true. He defended people he knew were guilty for the stupidest offenses. Sometimes the work felt hollow. Sometimes he wanted to smack the hell out of his clients. But he couldn't do or say a damn thing because those people's bad behavior propelled him to the top of his firm. "I'm at the top of my game and I'll never run out of clients."

"But new money runs out fast. Old money never dies."

"But your old money wants something that my new money can provide. Why the hell should I help you?"

"I'll go over your head if you don't. Wouldn't you rather seem like a team player than a selfish prick to the partners?"

"Why? You never seem to mind coming across that way."

Dave's nostrils flared. "Are you going to help me or not?"

"No promises. I'll see what I can do," he told Dave just before he left.

He could get the tickets. He could get any tickets but it annoyed the hell out of him that that's what half the firm, including some of the partners, only thought he was good for.

He looked back at his computer, shaking off his annoyance that started to creep up more and more as the months went on. But this time he wasn't able to shake it off as quickly. He was having a hard time concentrating. It was after official business hours had ended. The offices had gotten quieter, most of the assistants and other personnel had been gone for a couple of hours.

He thought about going home himself. He usually

didn't leave for another hour, but it was hard for him to concentrate. But then he was faced with going home to his big empty apartment. At first he thought it was because he missed Regina. But that wasn't true. They had dinner or drinks a couple times a week. They never slept over at each other's apartments. He didn't actually find himself missing her company. He missed the idea of her. He was a man in his prime. He liked women. He enjoyed good sex. He needed to start dating again. But frankly the idea exhausted him. He would have to go out to meet a woman who was in a similar place as Regina. He wanted someone who was mature and independent. He wanted someone who was perfectly happy not needing much from him.

"Hello, Mr. King."

He looked up at the mention of his name to see a woman leaning against his door jamb. For a moment he didn't recognize her. Her hair was short. Her dress hugged her curvy body and showed smooth, touchable-looking legs.

But that skin was that same beautiful rich caramel color and those eyes were still huge and dark brown and innocent.

Sunny was standing before him, no longer looking like the girl he had mistaken her for the first time she came to his office.

She was a woman and she was sexy.

"What the hell happened to you?"

"I was expecting, 'hello, Sunny. How are you today? You're looking well.' You work in this fancy

office but apparently you don't have any manners."
She walked farther into his office and he couldn't
help but to notice the swish of her hips as she did so.

"I'm sorry. I just wasn't expecting you to look
so . . . so . . ." Mouth-watering. Incredible. Edible.
"Different."

"I got a haircut. One of my former clients just
graduated from cosmetology school and she cut
my hair for free. She's taking a master class and
wanted to try some techniques out." She touched
her hair self-consciously. Her ringlets were gone,
but the cut she had was sophisticated and sassy.
"Do you hate it?"

"I don't hate it," he said quietly. "What about the
clothes?" She was wearing heels. Not the sky-high
kind that his ex wore. But just high enough. Just
sexy enough to make her legs look phenomenal.

"This?" She looked down at herself like she had
no clue that she looked like a bombshell in a red
wrap dress. She wore a denim jacket over it but that
didn't take away from the sexiness of it. "My best
friend is pregnant and is getting rid of some things
she doesn't think she'll be wearing anytime soon.
She never liked this color on her."

He swallowed as she walked closer and sat on the
edge of his desk. He had realized last week that he
was attracted to her, but he didn't think it was physical at first. He was attracted to her energy. He
wanted to say that she reminded him of his sister,
but that wasn't it. He enjoyed speaking to her. He
enjoyed eating with her. She was someone he might

have as a friend under different circumstances. But he had found himself touching her a lot during those couple of hours, not meaning to. A touch of the hand here, a squeeze of a shoulder. Their knees had been touching while they ate. He was feeling something more toward her that would be hard to ignore for long.

And when they parted ways that afternoon after seeing Regina he thought his ex would have been the one on his mind, but it was Sunny he thought about. He knew that he couldn't see her again. But he guessed he wasn't the one who could decide that.

"What's the matter?" She touched his face with the backs of her fingers in an almost motherly way. "You look ill."

"I'm fine." He removed her hand from his face but didn't immediately let it go like he should. Her hands were so much smaller than his. They were soft. Her nails were bare. Not perfectly manicured like Regina's always were. "I've been thinking about your case."

"You have?"

"I can't take it."

"I truly need help. I wouldn't have come to you unless I did."

"I know and that's why I'm going to personally introduce you to a classmate of mine. Her name is Maria Cordova. She's brilliant and her specialty is family law. I can't promise that she can give you a lot of time, but she will meet with you free of charge and offer advice."

"I don't have the energy to break in another lawyer when I'm so close to breaking you."

"I'll go with you to meet her. And you're not close to breaking me. So get that out of your head right now."

"Aren't I? You care and that means I somehow got to you. I need more than just a quick consultation. I need real help."

"Why me?" he asked seriously.

"You probably don't remember this but at Clive's party someone had bumped into one of the waitresses and knocked a tray of food all over her and on the floor. Unlike everyone else, you put your drink down. You asked her if she was okay and you helped her clean it up, even though she was mortified and tried to send you away. But she was grateful because you could have just ignored her like everyone else. But you got on your knees in your fancy suit and you helped that girl and right then and there I knew that you were kind. I was shocked when I found out you were a lawyer because you people aren't known for your kindness, but I knew if I ever needed legal help I would go to you."

"It had nothing to do with my professional football playing career?"

"I actually didn't know about that until after the fact. And who cares? You passed the bar exam. You work here. That's what matters."

Since he became a lawyer he had been wanting that kind of validation. Someone who thought he was good enough to work with, simply on his merits and not because of his celebrity status.

He didn't expect it to come from her.

"No one has ever accused me of being kind before."

"Maybe you should practice being kind more often by helping me."

"No. But I will go with you to meet Maria and if she can't help you I'll find another classmate who can."

"This Maria person is good?"

He started to feel the stirrings of hope in his chest. He needed to get Sunny out of his hair. He was in a weird place right now. His life wasn't going according to plan and he needed to get his head together. But she was clouding his judgment. She was calling him kind when he wanted to be known as sharp and brutal. Regina's abrupt coldness kept him on his toes. Sunny just disoriented him.

"She's brilliant."

"I'll make you a deal." She leaned closer and spoke into his ear. "If you lock your door and show me how your colleagues blow off some steam, I'll go to her. Just give me tonight. I promise I won't bother you again."

He pulled away from her and looked into her eyes to see a mischievous twinkle there. "Are you suggesting we have sex?"

"Yup. Right here on this desk." She glanced behind her. "Or on your couch. Even in your chair. You won't even have to take all your clothes off, but that would be a pity because I would like to see what's under that suit."

"God damn it, Sunny." He grew painfully hard right then and there. He had never had sex in his office. He wasn't like some of his colleagues. He had more self-control, but there was that primal side of him that was dangerously close to taking her up on her offer.

He had seen a glimpse of this side of her in the park that day. This naughty, fun kind of sexy that most women he knew lacked. It would be so easy to close his door. It would be so easy for him to pull up her dress, grab her behind, and pull her down on top of him. He was just thinking about missing good sex. She was offering him this opportunity no-strings-attached.

But when an offer sounded too good to be true it was. There was something mischievous about her.

"Stop trying to fuck with my head."

"I'm not." She kept her face neutral.

"You're such a bad liar."

"Oh, come on!" She paced away from him and plopped herself down on his leather sofa. "There's a reason we met at that party. There's a reason I bumped into you in front of your apartment that day. You need to help me."

"Come on. Don't tell me you believe in fate. It's bullshit."

"I have to believe in something. Don't you? Don't we all?"

"You sound so . . ." Innocent. Naïve. Sweet. "Ridiculous."

"Give me three good reasons why you won't help me and I'll go. You must think there is something to this case if you went through the trouble of contacting your friend."

"You have no money. I have no expertise and most important I don't want to be saddled with you any longer than possible."

"Not good enough." She folded her legs beneath her, her dress riding up to expose her thighs. "I'm just going to have to stay here until you change your mind."

He almost didn't hear what she said because he was so distracted by her legs. He wanted to run his hand over them just to feel the softness. He usually had so much self-control, so much discipline. It was how he made it to the NFL as a first round draft pick. It was how he did so well in law school. It was how he landed this job and rose through the ranks in this firm.

He shook his head and forced his eyes to her face. "So you're just going to park yourself on my couch until I change my mind?"

"Yup."

"Grow up. You're exactly the reason I only date older women."

"You date older women because you're afraid of commitment."

"I wanted to get married. If that's not the definition of commitment I don't know what is."

"You picked a woman you couldn't possibly fall

in love with to be your wife. You don't want to risk your heart so you choose not to love."

"What the hell would you know about anything? And I'm not discussing this with you. Sit there. I don't care. I have work to do."

He sat back down at his desk and tried to concentrate on his work but he couldn't. He didn't want to look up at her, but his eyes kept going to her. She made a couple of phone calls to foster parents. She spoke to kids, asking them about their day and wishing them good night. He wondered if she was doing this for effect. So that he could see how good of a social worker she was and feel guilty. It was unnecessary. He already knew how much she cared because she had gone through the trouble of coming to him.

They had been in the silent stand off for about twenty minutes when she pulled a package of cookies out of her handbag and started munching on them.

"If you're hungry you can leave and get some food."

"I'm fine but thanks for asking." She gave him a little smile. "When you're not sure when your next meal is coming you make sure to always carry snacks."

"This is New York City. You can't go a block without finding something to eat."

"But when you don't have any money it doesn't matter if there's a restaurant every two feet. You still can go hungry." She ate another cookie.

"I know social workers don't make a lot of money but you can afford to eat."

She nodded. "Yes. Now. Before I lived with the families, I didn't."

"Families?" He couldn't help but to ask; his interest was now piqued.

"I lived with a lot of families. Each one taught me something."

All of a sudden it clicked. "You were a foster kid, weren't you?"

"I guess I still am in some ways."

"How long were you in the system?"

"Eleven-twelve years. I had myself emancipated after my last foster mother died when I was seventeen. I had been admitted to college on a full scholarship. I didn't need anyone anymore."

"I don't think you ever stop needing anyone," he said, feeling something for her that he wasn't sure he liked.

He had a hard time believing that no one had wanted to adopt her. She was so damn cute now. She must have been a beautiful kid.

"Is that pity I hear in your voice, counselor? Don't feel bad for me. I turned out okay."

"What happened to your family?"

She shrugged. "My mother suffered from mental illness. She used to leave me locked in a closet when she went out at night because she was scared that someone would hurt me. The last time she didn't come back. The cops found me three days later. I never knew my father. I'm pretty sure my mother's family didn't know I existed or if they did, they wanted nothing to do with me or her."

"Why do you think that is? What could she have done?"

"I think she was from a wealthy family in the South. She used to say things about debutante balls and white dresses and how much her father loved the Lord. But my mother was sick and probably wild and she was a beautiful blond woman with blue eyes who brought home a baby who looked nothing like that. I could be wrong. They could have been wonderful people, but I'm guessing that they weren't. They had to have known she was sick. How the hell could they have just let her go?"

Her story hit closer to home than he expected. His mother was white. His father was black. They had met in college in South Carolina at a party. A one-night fling turned into a pregnancy and that pregnancy turned into a marriage that probably neither one of them wanted. He remembered his father trying. He remembered him attempting to be happy. His side of the family had been very involved. They had loved Julian and his sister, but his mother's side was different. They were colder. There was always a little judgment there. A little disappointment maybe. It didn't matter that his father was in law school. That he was a defense attorney by the time Galen was born.

Even as a kid Julian could see that they would never be satisfied, that his mother would always be miserable when she was with them. She had walked out too. Just like Sunny's mother. Except he had always known where she was. She had gotten married to someone else. Someone in finance. Someone more like her family had expected. She had another son. One that looked more like her. One that her family seemed to adore.

"Is that why you wanted to become a social worker? Because you spent so long in foster care?"

"Why do I feel like I'm being cross examined right now?" She gave him a quick smile.

"You won't leave my office. I think I'm entitled to my questions."

"What if I don't want to answer them?"

"Please," he asked softly.

"For most of my life the only consistent people I had was my social worker and the police officer who found me in the closet. If it weren't for them I would have been lost. I knew I could be an anchor for someone else."

"And that's why Soren's adoption is so important to you."

"She has the shot at a life that I've always dreamed of as a kid. Not many people are willing to take a kid with such heavy emotional baggage, but these parents not only are willing, they love her. She needs to be loved by them. We all need that kind of love."

"Shit," he said to himself. He looked down at his feet, feeling lucky for what he did have.

"I want to stop talking about this."

He looked up at her. She had shut her eyes. Her body was tense. He knew she was vulnerable in that moment, but she was like steel. She would be damned if she showed him that.

He was a near stranger and she had just revealed so much about herself to him, including that she had been left locked in a closet. What the hell kind of life was that? She looked so innocent with her large, soft-brown eyes. But those eyes had seen a lot and now that they were closed he couldn't see how much hurt must be in them.

"Okay. Let's talk about when the hell you are going to get out of my office instead."

"Are you going to help me?"

"I can't." It was dangerous. He was telling her to get out but part of him didn't want her to go. He could look at her all night. She was not what he wanted. She was not what he needed in his life right now.

She stood up and started walking toward him. Her hips swaying seductively as she did. She wasn't trying to be sexy. She just was. "Can't is different than won't. Tell me why?"

"Because I don't like you."

"I'll grow on you and you're working for the kid. Not for me."

He stood and grabbed her hand. It was the second time their hands ended up locked together. "Let me walk you out. I'll call the car service to take you home." He started to lead her outside. He made it about fifteen feet from his office before she stopped.

"Did you honestly think I was going to leave that easily? I haven't broken you yet."

She gave him that mischievous grin that he was beginning to like and started to pull away, but he wouldn't let her and scooped her into his arms in one motion.

She let out a little scream, but it wasn't out of fear. It sounded like one of delight. He liked that sound. He liked that he was the one to bring it out of her.

"Put me down!"

"No." He walked toward the elevator. The middle of the floor where the paralegals and assistants worked was empty. Most of the associates were gone at this point. There was no one there to see him act so out of character.

There was no one there to see how much he was enjoying himself. He liked the feel of her in his arms, her weight, her softness, that look in her eyes. She squirmed a bit but he held her firmly against him.

"You shouldn't be using your size against me," she complained.

"You shouldn't have used your sexuality against me," he retorted.

"I did no such thing, but even if I did, it clearly didn't work because you are forcibly removing me from your office."

"You should have never come."

"I know, but I couldn't stop myself. I kept thinking about you and this case since I last saw you. It's not going to stop and would you mind at least tugging down my dress? I'm feeling too much breeze on my behind."

He glanced down at her. Sure enough, her thighs were exposed, her dress was bunched up. He could see just a hint of her underwear. It was no black lacy thong like Regina would wear. They were yellow and had daisies printed on them.

That made his groin tighten again. He didn't know why. Full briefs with flowers on them were probably the least sexiest underwear on the planet, but on this woman, they weren't. On this woman they were alluring. Of course a girl named Sunny would have something so cheerful on her bottom.

He placed her on her feet near the elevator, but he didn't give her enough space to get away. He leaned his body against her and slowly pulled on the hem of her dress. Maybe that's not all he did. Maybe his hands traveled up to her hips and slightly around to her behind and smoothed her dress down.

"That's my ass you're touching, counselor." She looked right into his eyes, her chest pressed against his, her lips looking inviting and thoroughly kissable.

"Do you object?"

"If I did, you certainly would have known about it before now."

He took a deep breath, trying to calm himself. He couldn't kiss her, but he couldn't physically pull his body away from hers, either. "I'm calling a car service to take you home. Please go and never come back here."

"I'm not promising that, and I don't need you to call anyone to get me home. I've been getting home myself long before you came around."

"I'm sure that's true, but it's getting late and dark and I don't want to worry about you all night, so let me call the service to take you home."

"See?" She grinned at him. "You do like me."

"I do not." But he did. He didn't like the way she made him feel, but he liked her. He couldn't help it.

"Is everything okay out here?"

Julian froze at the sound of his boss's voice. Davis Cleese was a founding partner in the firm, a man who Julian admired immensely and the one who had a very large say in who the next full partner was going to be.

"Hello, Mr. Cleese." He backed away from Sunny. "Yes. Everything is fine. I was just walking Sunny out."

"I thought I heard a woman's scream."

"That was me." The mischievous twinkle returned to her eye. "I bumped into something really big and hard."

Cleese was the most puritanical of the partners. He lived and practiced by a strict moral code and was more interested in the quality of work they did than the billable hours they racked up. It was in direct opposition of what the other partner, Eric Bruno, believed. "This is Sunny Gibson. She is a social worker for the city. She was seeking some legal advice on behalf of her client."

"Oh?" Mr. Cleese gave him a knowing look. "Are you sure that's all that's going on?"

He knew this partner disapproved of anything that might be deemed sordid happening in the workplace. Usually Julian was aboveboard with his every action. But he had forgotten himself. He had forgotten everything sensible when it came to Sunny.

"Yes, sir. I promise. I was just about to call the car service to take her home."

"Tell me about this case." He crossed his arms and turned his attention to Sunny. "It would obviously have to be pro bono. My sister was a social worker. I know how little they make and I know how much we charge."

"I have a child who is about to be adopted. She was abandoned at our agency. She was underfed and mute and traumatized. But I found a great family for her and the child is finally starting to heal, but a woman claiming to be her biological mom has started contacting the adoptive family. She is sending large sums of cash as support. She has means and we're afraid that she will pull some sort of stunt to prevent the adoption from going through, or worse, try to kidnap the child."

"That sounds incredibly serious. I can only imagine what the adoptive parents are going through."

"I'm sure they are terrified. But as I've explained to Sunny, I don't specialize in family law. None of us here do. I was recommending another lawyer for her."

"I don't trust anyone with this," she said to Cleese. "I came here for the best."

Cleese was quiet for a moment. "Julian is right. We don't specialize in family law, but that's an area we should start branching out into. With the way some of these divorces end up, sooner or later we'll find ourselves embroiled in a nasty custody case. This would be a good way for you to learn the ropes and guide the others if anything like this comes up again."

"You're right, sir. I would just hate to take away time from my current clients. I just got a call from

Charles O'Grady this morning. He punched an off duty cop outside of a bar. He's already been in trouble. His case is going to need my attention."

"You're referring to that big Viking-looking football player?"

"Yes, sir."

"You'll be his lawyer, but only in the honorary fashion. The new associates can handle it. It's a simple criminal case. My junior partners should be handling more serious matters. The challenge will make you better. The pro bono work will cancel out some of the trepidation I feel taking on such wealthy clientele."

"I didn't mean to eavesdrop, sir." David Connor stepped out of the shadows. "I was on my way to file this when I overheard your conversation. If Julian can't take this case on, I would be happy to offer my services. I jump at the chance to do as much work for the community as I can."

Slimy son of a bitch. "Your services will not be necessary. I can take the case on."

"Good," his boss said. "Use whatever resources you need, Mr. King, and keep me updated."

"Thank you for your support, Mr. Cleese." Sunny gave him her most gorgeous smile. "I'm so glad to have met you tonight." He wondered if Cleese had any idea that she knew how charming she was. Regina was practiced and polished; with Sunny it seemed natural and sweet. But he knew she was more cunning than she looked.

"It was nice meeting you as well." He took his leave of them and Connor followed.

"So you're really going to help me?"

"You know I don't have a choice."

"You do. You could say no. You could tell your boss you're helping me and then ignore me."

"If I said I was going to help you, I will help you. I'm many things, but I'm not a liar."

"I'm an orphan with trust issues," she said with a smile that didn't reach her eyes. Her statement had come out as a joke but he knew it wasn't.

How many people had let her down before?

"You have to be on your best behavior with me. I am your attorney. We will be professional."

"You got it, sexy." She saluted him.

He frowned at her, knowing that despite his wishes, his life just got incredibly complicated. "I'm going to take you home." He pulled his keys out of his pants pocket and pressed the button for the elevator.

"I told you I could get home alone."

"And I told you that I'm not going to let you do that while you're with me. So please just save your breath. This is happening."

"What about your stuff? Don't you lawyers carry briefcases?"

"I'll probably come back tonight to finish up some things, but I have my keys, cell phone, and wallet. I don't need anything else. I have everything saved to the cloud."

The elevator doors opened and he grabbed her

by her hand and tugged her inside. He was feeling decidedly disgruntled toward her at the moment. He didn't say anything to her on the ride down or during the short walk to the garage that held his car.

He led her to a BMW SUV. He had always wanted a classic BMW but he was too big for such a sleek car and had to go with a larger model. Not fitting in was becoming a theme in his life.

"Get in."

This time she obeyed without comment. He watched her eyes widen slightly as she did.

"What?" he asked her as they put on their seat belts.

"This car is gorgeous." He watched her run her hands over the dashboard. The move wasn't meant to be sexual, but for him it was. It was a slow stroke of her hands. He could imagine how they would feel on his body. If he were a different type of man he probably would have been having sex with her on his desk right now. But he was who he was and now he was imagining what it would be like to be with her.

This attraction was annoying him. He had the urge to get the hell away from her as fast as he could, but his body liked her near. "It's just a car."

"It's not just a car. It's a symbol of your success. I never imagined riding in one, much less owning such a beautiful thing. I could live in here."

"I know New York apartments can be small, but yours must be bigger than this."

She shrugged. "I lived in a car before. Mama said it was like camping. It was fun for a little while."

God damn it. Why did she have to say things like that? Things that floored him. Things he had no clue how to respond to. "Where do you live?"

"I'm surprised you didn't have my background checked after I bumped into you in front of your apartment."

"I did," he admitted and plugged some information into his GPS. "I remember your address. I just didn't want you to know that I knew it." He pulled out of his space and began the journey to her house.

"I would have thought less of you if you hadn't checked me out. I could have been crazy or something."

"You are crazy. And now I'm stuck with you for the foreseeable future."

She sighed heavily. "I want you to help me. I need to find out who this woman is, but I will go to the other lawyer if you don't want to help me."

"After all that, you're going to simply concede?"

"I'm not conceding. You may think I'm a pain in the ass who doesn't care about your wishes, but I do and I'll feel guilty if you are doing this just so your partnership won't be in jeopardy. Plus, I sure as hell don't need you snapping at me all the time for the next few weeks."

"Too damn bad. I took this case and you aren't allowed to tell me I can't complain about it."

They drove in silence for a while and the bright, clean streets of the Manhattan he worked in faded away. The city had undergone a huge cleanup in the past twenty years or so, but there were some places that had barely been touched. Including Sunny's block. There was some sort of mental health clinic/addiction treatment center there, but not the privately funded ones he sent his wealthy clients to. This one was lacking the spalike atmosphere and staff who were there to serve. There was also a little dive bar on the corner.

It was getting late and people were outside hanging around. There were people coming in and out of the bar. He didn't like this place for her. He wouldn't want his sister, or cousin, or even someone he didn't like very much to stay here.

"You can let me out here," she said as she reached for the door. "Thanks for bringing me home. I'll be in touch."

He grabbed her arm, keeping her inside the car. "You live here?"

"Yeah." She frowned in confusion. "You knew that."

"This is not safe for you."

She smiled and shook her head. "You sound like my friend's husband. He wants me to get a carry permit."

"Is he a cop?"

"A fed. But it's fine and it's in my price range."

"It's fine until somebody hurts you."

"I can defend myself. I learned how at an early age. Trust me, these people aren't going to bother me."

"These people are drug addicts and alcoholics."

"Addiction is an illness. You can't stereotype people based on their appearance or pasts. You of all people should know that."

He did, but he still didn't want to let her out of the car here. What the hell could he do? Take her home with him? That wasn't an option. Not a good one anyway. "I'm walking you up."

"Don't bother. I've been walking myself up for the past three years. I'm fine."

"But I won't be fine unless you let me do this." He was serious. She was too beautiful. Too innocent-looking even if her innocence had long gone away.

"How can you make the feminist in me want to punch you, but the soft part of me want to hug you?" She leaned over and kissed his cheek. "I've learned a long time ago that you can't prevent things from happening and you can't live in fear or else you'll be miserable. You'll end up paralyzed."

It was a wise thing for her to say, but someone so young shouldn't have to be so wise. He could only imagine what she had to go through to get that knowledge. "I'm coming inside. You should offer me water for driving you home. I'm very thirsty."

"Okay, Jules. I'll invite you in for some water. Park around the corner. There's a lot where your car will be safe."

"Didn't you just tell me you were safe here? If my car isn't, then how can I believe you will be?"

"We don't get cars like this driving through here very often. This car is worth way more than me. I'm sure they could get a ton of money for the parts."

"Nothing is more valuable than you." He realized how it sounded and shook his head. "I mean your life. Human life has the greatest value."

"You sound like a motivational poster."

"I was a football player. You don't know how many motivational pep talks I've been subjected to."

"Go park your car."

He did and walked her up to her third-floor studio. It was clean but rundown. He could tell she had done her best to make it homey. There were framed pictures on the wall. Of her and her friends. Of the children she must have helped. Of the cards and letters and drawings she had been given.

"I'm sure your bathroom is bigger than this."

"Only slightly," he said, not really joking. This was vastly different from his apartment that overlooked the park.

"It's not much, but it's all mine," she spoke softly. "And if you hate it, you can keep it to your damn self."

"I don't hate it at all." He glanced at her window to see that there was a sturdy lock on it. He was glad it was there and angry that she needed to have one there.

"Do you want water? I wish I had something fancier to offer, but I don't spend a lot of time here."

"Because you're scared to be alone here?"

She was quiet for a long moment. "I work late. I fill up my time."

"I'm not thirsty, but thank you. We need to set up a formal meeting soon to discuss everything in detail."

"Yes." She nodded. There was an awkward moment of silence between them. But then she stepped forward and wrapped her arms around him and pushed her curvy body into his and she set her lips on his cheek for the second time that night.

He wanted to groan, but it wasn't out of annoyance. He was rarely hugged. He couldn't remember the last time he had been. It was probably six or seven months ago at Thanksgiving.

Regina didn't hug. They had sex. They sometimes napped together in the same bed afterward, but there wasn't this kind of closeness between them. This kind of closeness made him uncomfortable. He found himself wanting it with a longing he didn't know he possessed.

"Damn it, Sunny. You have to stop kissing me. I'm your attorney now."

She didn't let go. He didn't move away. "Thank you."

She finally let go and he gave her one long last look before he left her alone in her apartment.

Chapter 6

There was no food again.

Sunny held on to her stomach willing it to be quiet, but it was angry from not having anything good or filling for the past two days. Mama was extra jumpy lately. All the windows were covered with thick blankets. She had put newspapers on the wall. She had stopped going to the store.

She didn't trust them, she told Sunny. Sunny had asked her who they were but Mama would never tell her. She was tired of asking now. Tired of everything.

She lay near the window on her makeshift bed where a little bit of the light was peeking through. The electricity had been cut off a few days ago. There was no more TV, nothing to keep her mind occupied. There had been books. Mama had taught her how to read a long time ago, but she had read them all and she couldn't see even if she had wanted to read them again.

"Sunshine?" Her mama looked up at her with her now-wild blue eyes. She was too hyper lately. Mama had never hurt her before but sometimes she scared Sunny. "Are you hungry? You must be hungry."

"No, Mama. I'm fine."

"I'll make you something."

She watched Mama get up from her spot on the floor. She had been writing something. She was always writing things, on every piece of paper she could find, in old notebooks that Sunny was never sure where they came from.

She had tried to read her writing sometime, but it never made sense. Sometimes it was random words. Sometimes it was pages and pages of numbers.

"No, Mama. I don't want to eat."

"Nonsense." Mama walked over to the refrigerator, which was just as warm on the inside as the rest of the apartment. There were eggs in there and leftovers that had long ago gone bad. The smell that came out of there made Sunny's stomach squeeze.

Mama lit their gas stove. She cracked the eggs into a bowl and just like they were fresh she began to scramble them. But Sunny could smell the rotten odor from her bed. She could see they didn't look right as Mama beat them with her fork. She pressed her nose into the blanket to block the scent.

She heard the eggs sizzle in the pan. She heard her mama humming like this was normal. Nothing was normal about them. Sunny had just been with Mama for as long as she remembered but she knew that other people had families, that they got to leave the house, that they went to school.

She had seen these people on TV. They didn't have blankets on the windows and writing on the walls.

Mama had put the eggs on the plate and presented them to Sunny, smiling like they didn't stink like garbage. *"Here, baby. Eat."*

"No, thank you."

"You have to."

"Those eggs are not good, Mama. They smell bad."

"But they aren't bad!" Her eyes went wide and wilder if that were possible. "I got them from the man I know. The store will try to poison us."

"I'm not eating!" She always tried to be good. She had always tried to obey, but this time she couldn't.

"I'll show you." Her mother took a forkful and put them in her mouth and then she gagged. The plate smashed to the floor and everything that had been in Mama's stomach had come out.

Sunny got up and went to the bottles of water Mama kept stockpiled in the corner. She wet a towel with one bottle and gave another to her mother.

Her stomach was no longer hungry, but it wouldn't be for long. She knew what she had to do even though she knew it might make Mama mad. Tonight when Mama was out she was going to go for help.

Sunny walked into Julian's office two days later. He had summoned her. She was surprised the call had come so soon. She was going to contact him about meeting to discuss things about the case in detail, but she wanted to give him a few days. She was feeling slightly guilty about how he had accepted. His boss hadn't given him a choice. She wanted him to want to work on the case. She had wanted him to want to work with her. It was unreasonable on her part. Maybe selfish.

There was something about him she was drawn

to, but she didn't think she could go through with this case, possibly uncovering the truth about her identity, if he really didn't want her around. She had spent so much of her life unwanted. Once she had carved out a life of her own she knew she would never have to be in the position to be around people who tolerated her just because they had to.

Julian was behind his desk. His face all business. He looked serious so often that she wanted to tease him. To get under his skin. To coax a smile out of him.

She had teased him the last time she was in this office. She didn't know what had gotten into her when she suggested he lock the door and show her how other attorneys blew off steam. She knew that despite his unconventional looks he was as strait-laced as they came, or at least he was trying to make himself be that way.

She had known that he was going to say no to her proposition, but a little part of her wondered how she would have handled it if he would have said yes. She was attracted to him. There was no doubt about that. She believed that women could be just like men and be able to enjoy sex without emotional attachment or expectations. But would she have been able to go through with it? Long after he had left her place the other night, she could still smell his scent on her skin. She could still feel the ghost of his hands on her hips. She could still remember the way she felt in his arms. Secure. As a foster kid, she never had any say in her life.

She was just shuffled from place to place. But with him she felt safe.

"I can't be Soren's law guardian," he said by way of greeting.

"I had asked you that night if you were going to take the case. You could have said no then. You could have said no anytime between then and now. I didn't have to come all the way down here just so you could tell me to my face. A phone call would have sufficed."

"Relax." He scowled at her. "I didn't say I wasn't taking the case. I said I can't be the law guardian. Guardians are impartial. They hear both sides of a case and then recommend what they think is best for the child. I'm not impartial. I read Soren's file. What you told me was just the tip of the iceberg. I don't think she should ever go back to her mother. The woman doesn't deserve her back."

"You sound angry," she said surprised.

"I'm a lawyer. It's my job to be angry on my clients' behalf."

"Even when you know they are guilty?"

"I don't think my clients are guilty."

"Is being that good of a liar a part of the bar exam? We all saw the tape of that baseball player bash in that guy's windshield. I'm surprised you didn't look at the judge and say, throw his dumb ass in jail."

"My client was exhausted and under extreme duress at the time. He could not be responsible for his actions."

"Extreme duress. Yes, his wife's new lover held a

gun to his head and forced him to destroy his property."

"Marriage vows should be sacred. People who are betrayed like that act out of character."

"You sound like you speak from experience." Had somebody broken his heart? She had wondered why someone like Julian would end up with someone like Regina.

It had nothing to do with age. She had liked that he found older women attractive. It gave her hope, but there was no warmth coming from the woman. No softness. Sunny had lived with many people and placed many kids in homes. She had good judgment when it came to people and she wondered how Julian could think he wanted to spend the rest of his life with a woman who didn't make his heart race.

"I just think vows are sacred and mothers shouldn't abandon their children."

He got up from his desk and motioned to his couch. She sat down and he came to sit beside her, a manila folder in his hand.

"We're going to need to find out everything we can about Soren's biological mother, and I mean everything. Criminal record, drug abuse, mental illness, her last known address. If she ever got a parking ticket we need to know about it. She'll have a fight on her hands."

"I'm not sure that's the best thing. Dragging up that kind of history can do more harm than good."

"And ripping that kid from the family who loves and takes care of her would be better?"

"I didn't say that. But—"

"But what? You come to an attorney like me for a reason. I'm not a family court attorney. I go for blood. I win. That's what you want. I'm not buying the bullshit about helping the waitress at a party. If you wanted a kind person you would have gone somewhere else. But you wanted results so you came to me."

He was right. He was the best. She just didn't want to think about what being the best entailed. Plus there was her, she didn't tell him about. What if Soren's mother was her mother? What if she found out things about her mother that no child should know? What if she found out her mother left her locked in the closet simply because she didn't want her anymore?

What if she ended up more broken by this at the end?

"This woman found where the Earls live. She's sending large amounts of money that we can't trace. Who's to say she won't snatch the child? Who's to say she doesn't have more resources than most of the country and can maneuver the legal system to her advantage? Who's to say she won't smear the Earls and drag out every sordid thing that they have ever done?"

"Smear the Earls?" She was horrified at the prospect. These people didn't ask her to get Julian involved. She had taken that on herself for selfish reasons. She couldn't risk doing that to them, especially if it were all just a coincidence.

"It's what I would do if I were on the other side. I have to be one step ahead of opposing counsel.

And you know if this woman is sending child support, it's only a matter of time before she makes an appearance."

"I've thoroughly checked them out myself. They are just regular hardworking people who took in a child that no one else, not even her mama, wanted. She can't smear them. If she really loves her child then she wouldn't try to hurt the people who loved her."

"Do you know Soren's birth mother personally?"

"No," she said quickly. But she could have known her in another life. "It's just hard for me to believe that anyone who really loved a child would rip that child away from the people who are best for her for personal, selfish reasons."

"Everyone always thinks their reasons are just. I defend people every day who think that way."

She nodded. He was right. But the more he spoke, the more she doubted herself and this journey she was about to go on.

"Why do you seem so unsure?" he asked her. "You were the one who hounded me to take this case and now I feel like you are about to back out."

"As much as Soren's mother put her through, she still loves her. It's clear from the letters she wrote her. I think more than anything that this woman wants a connection with the child she gave birth to."

"If she loved her, she wouldn't have left her," he snapped. "Real mothers don't leave."

Sunny sat there stunned but the intensity of his words, the anger in his gaze. Something had hit home for him. "I don't know what kind of life you had, but my mother left me locked in a closet. She was sick. She couldn't be a mother to me, but she loved me. I felt loved, even when I didn't feel safe. I refuse to believe that I was unlovable just because she never came back."

"I'm sorry." He set his hand on hers. "I didn't mean to imply that you were unlovable."

But for a long time she felt that way. She had been shuffled from family to family. No one had ever wanted her forever and the one person who did, died before she could make it so. She shook off the feeling. She had thought she'd put the death of her final foster mother behind her. It had been over ten years. She had lived with Maggie for only a year. But the retirement of the officer who saved her, and the letters from Soren's mother brought all of it back up. She wasn't as healed as she thought she had been.

"I think you should read the letters, Jules. That's why I'm afraid that this adoption won't go through. You would only go through these lengths for someone you loved."

"If her mother came back into the picture and presented herself as a stable person able to care for Soren, would you think the best place would be back with her?"

"No." She shook her head slowly. The thought had crossed her mind. "You never know if they'll slip again and maybe she won't. We don't like to bet against people. But there was another child, another daughter. Older than Soren. Something happened to her. I can't tell from the letters but it seems like she left that child too."

"I need to see them. Can you get them to me by tomorrow?"

She nodded once, wondering if she was strong enough to complete this process.

Julian felt restless yet exhausted at the same time. He had left work a little earlier than usual and went to the gym. He didn't often miss football. He liked using his mind even if others tried to diminish his intelligence, but he missed the punishing workouts he used to do to get ready for the season. They helped clear his mind. He also missed the team work, being a part of something, having a common goal. That was missing in his law firm.

He sat down on his couch and flicked on the television, but nothing caught his attention. The day still hadn't left his thoughts. He had overwhelmed Sunny. He took all his cases seriously and he wanted to believe that this one was like any of his others, but maybe he was lying to himself.

This case made him think of his mother, far more often than he wanted to. She called him every six weeks or so, her obligatory check in. Pretending that she cared about him, about the children she didn't want to live with.

She had a new life, a new husband in Maryland. He wondered why she bothered to check in with her adult children when they both had done more than fine without her. Still he picked up the phone when she called, maybe just to rub it in her face that both he and Galen had grown up perfectly fine without her.

He remembered that day in court vividly when the divorce was being finalized.

"I want nothing from him," she told the judge with no emotion on her face.

Not the house or the cars. No alimony. She had wanted to erase her husband from her past.

"And have you reached an agreement on custody?"

"He can have them. I can't raise them. I don't want custody."

She didn't even ask for visitation. Julian wasn't supposed to be there that day. But he begged his father to go and he sat in the back of the courtroom in the corner. He didn't know why he wanted to be there. To see her, maybe. For her to see him and realize that she did want to be with her children. She had left a long time before she even bothered to file for divorce. Years. Part of Julian thought his father always expected her to come back. Even though she had asked for a divorce, neither one of them had filed.

But she had initiated things when she wanted to get married to someone else. He had been fourteen at the time and he didn't believe it was possible for love to die all in one moment, but it had that day. He was done with her that day. She had given them up. She had abandoned them again.

It wasn't anything like Soren or Sunny went through. Their mothers probably had much different issues than his own, but he believed that if his mother truly loved him she would have stayed. She would have tried harder to make a connection with them, her bigoted family be damned.

He reached for his cell phone and dialed Sunny's number. She picked up on the second ring.

"Why hello, Jules." Her voice sounded sleepy and kind of sweet. He could imagine her lying in bed in that tiny, hopeful but worn apartment of hers. He could imagine the drunks on the street coming in and out of the bar, the addicts that frequented the clinic just a few doors down.

He knew the statistics of crime that were related to alcohol. He had looked up the incidents that had happened in her neighborhood recently. He didn't like picturing her there. She had no family. No mother to worry about her, no father to disapprove of her place, no big brother to call when someone was bothering her. She was alone and he couldn't stop thinking about that fact. He didn't know why he cared, but he didn't want her to be alone. He wanted her to have somebody.

"I just wanted to make sure you got home."

"You made me leave well before dark. I've lived here for years. I've managed to make it home long before I met you."

And she would probably continue to make it home well after they parted company, but still he felt compelled to call. "I insist on having my clients alive for the duration of my cases."

"My building looks better in the daylight. I promise." He could hear the smile in her voice. "Would you miss me if I were gone?"

"I'd miss you like I'd miss a migraine."

"That's cold."

"Yup. Icy."

She laughed and he suddenly found himself thinking that he would rather be having this conversation with her in person than over the phone. To have her curled up next to him. It wasn't a sexual thought. He didn't long to take her to bed, just to be in the same room with her, and that shook him.

Sexual need he could understand, but this he couldn't. They had just met. They had nothing in common, except maybe they did. They weren't discussing culture and politics, but they did have some very fundamental things in common.

He wished he could say he was projecting his feelings for Regina on to her, but he didn't miss her like he should. He didn't miss her at all.

"I wanted to apologize."

"To me? Hold on. Let me look out of the window."

"Why?"

"I need to make sure the sky isn't falling."

"You're a smartass." He found himself smiling.

"It's better than being a dumbass."

"Are you going to let me apologize?"

"I don't see why you would feel the need to."

"I overwhelmed you today."

"Ah, that. Yes. You did." She paused for a moment. "I don't admit that lightly. I'm not sure what I was expecting, but maybe I didn't think this through all the way."

"Do you want to quit?" He realized he was holding his breath as he waited for her answer.

"No. I don't think I'll ever be satisfied until I know who Soren's mother is."

"Why is this child so important to you?" He had seen the pain in her eyes today. He could see the fear. "You must have other kids whose lives are just as complicated."

"She's been with me the longest. I was there the day her mother left her. I was there when her first foster family sent her back because she refused to speak. I was there when she said her first words after not speaking to anyone for nearly a year. I was the person she told everything to. I see myself in her. I know exactly how it feels to be left that way. Most of the kids we remove, but Soren and I were both just left alone. I want her to have her happy ending. I want her not to have to worry about being abandoned again."

"I need to meet her and her parents. I need to get as much information from her as possible."

"I know. It won't be easy though. It's very hard for her to talk about her biological mother. She's angry at her but devastated by her loss. And yet she doesn't want to go back to her, because she knows that she won't feel as safe with her. It's terrible knowing you aren't safe with your mother."

"You're depressing the hell out of me."

"Just because my name is Sunshine doesn't mean I bring it."

"Apparently not. Seen any good shows lately?"

"Only if you count the two rats fighting over a hot dog in the subway the other day."

"I think I would have liked to see that."

"I recorded it. I'll show you the next time I see you."

"You'll set up the meeting with the Earls?"

"I will."

"Good." He wanted to stay on the phone with her. He wanted to take it into his bedroom and fall asleep with her on the line but that was a ridiculous idea, it was a ridiculous longing. He shouldn't have called her tonight. He shouldn't have invited her to eat lunch with him in the park that day. He shouldn't have taken this case. But he had and now he was stuck with her and these uncomfortable feelings he wanted to push away. "Sleep well, Sunshine."

"I'll see you soon, Jules."

Sunny had made the call to the Earls that morning. It was a surprisingly quick conversation. She told Jeannie Earl that she had a friend who was a lawyer who was willing to help them in their fight to keep Soren. Jeannie had agreed immediately. When Sunny tried to warn her that they might have to dig into their personal lives in case this battle went to court, Jeannie didn't bat an eyelash.

"I'm a mother who lost a child once. I don't care what needs to be done. I can't go through that again."

And that was it. They had agreed to meeting

Julian and allowing him to question Soren about her past. There seemed to be no doubt in their minds, but Sunny was still scared. She didn't know what she wanted out of this. Did she really want to know what happened to her mother?

Was she really crazy for going down this road based on some letters sent from the same location as her mother had last been seen, and sent from a woman who had left two daughters behind?

But even if she took herself out of it, put her selfishness away, she wanted to do this for Soren, to give her the family she had always wanted for herself.

"Sunny?" She looked up to see Detective Rodgers walking toward her desk.

"Hi!" She stood up, happy to see him, but feeling shy at the same time. "What are you doing here?"

"I came to see why you haven't responded to my retirement party invitation."

She never thought he would call her out on it. She thought he'd have his party surrounded by his family and friends and not give another thought to her. "I'm not sure I can make it."

"Bullshit." He sat down at the chair in front of her desk. "If you truly were busy, or you really didn't want to attend, you would have called me and told me. But you're waffling. Something is holding you back."

"Damn, you *are* a good detective."

"I try." He grinned at her and folded his arms across his chest. "What's the matter, kid?"

"I don't want to feel like an outsider there," she admitted.

"What are you talking about? There will be a hundred people attending. Some of them are people I have arrested. I've always said that cops and criminals have the most fun parties."

"I didn't think you'd notice that I wasn't there."

"How would I not notice? I've known you longer than my wife. You've been in my life longer than my kids. I think about you, Sunny. I'm proud of you. I love you, kid."

"What?" She shook her head.

"You heard me. You were so tiny when we found you and you had the biggest, saddest eyes and I couldn't just leave you with child protective services and never know what became of you. And at every turn you surprised me. You could have turned out so differently. You didn't have an easy life. I've seen it before. The world expects a kid like you to be dead or in jail now, but you've got a master's degree. You're helping save kids every day. You're like a daughter to me."

She had wanted to be his daughter. She had wondered every time they had moved her to another home, why he didn't take her.

"I thought about taking you," he continued, reading her mind. "I even asked your social worker about the process, but I wasn't sure you wanted me to."

"You wanted me?" She couldn't believe what he was saying.

"Yes, you were thirteen at the time and you had

just been moved to another home and then you got that letter from your mother. You went all quiet on me. I would call to see how you were and you would barely talk. It was months before we connected. I didn't think you wanted me a part of your life anymore."

"Don't you know that thirteen-year-olds are the most unreasonable people in the world?"

"I didn't fully understand that until I had some thirteen-year-olds of my own."

"I didn't want to bother you."

"I've learned that about you. You don't want to impose. When you called me to invite me to your college graduation you told me that I didn't have to go if I didn't want to about a dozen times. And then you tried to refuse to allow us to take you out to dinner. You were going to eat alone on the night of your graduation!"

She shrugged. She didn't know what to say. He was right. She didn't want to bother him. She had always felt like an obligation. When you're a foster kid, people take care of you because they have to not because they want to.

"I'm glad you came."

"You're going to come to my party. And you're going to sit at the table with my family. And you're going to have a good time."

"Yes, sir. I'll even bring a gift."

"You had better. And when I move to Florida, you'll come to visit me. I have a house on the beach and a little boat." He stood up. "I want you to find love, Sunny. I want you to let yourself be loved without fear of rejection. I want you to be happy. I want you to make your own family. I want to stop worrying about you so much."

She nodded, feeling emotional and overwhelmed again. It was hard for her. It was why she never had a real relationship with a man. It was why she made this job and the children she worked for her life. "I'll try."

"That's all I could ask for." He walked around to her side of her desk and leaned over to kiss her cheek. "I'll see you soon."

"You will."

He left and Sunny sat at her desk for a while unable to concentrate on her work. She picked up her cell phone not really aware of who she was calling until she heard his voice on the other side of the phone. "Sunny."

"Julian."

"What's wrong?" he asked her.

"Nothing. I just wanted to let you know that I spoke with the Earls. They are in support of everything and said I could give you their contact information. They are very thankful for your help."

"What's wrong?" he asked her again.

"Nothing," she said, but this time she choked on the word.

"There's a little coffee shop not too far from where you work that makes the best cake on the planet. Are you in the mood for a snack?"

She had been ready to tell him no, and she didn't know why she hadn't. "I'm always in the mood for a snack."

A half hour later she had met him at the coffee shop. He was sitting at a table in the back, but he stood up as soon as he saw her. His suit jacket was off. His sleeves were rolled up, revealing those powerful forearms of his that she really enjoyed looking at. There was a hint of a tattoo peeking out. She had seen it the day they walked in the park. She liked it on him. It told her that he was more than the buttoned-up lawyer that he liked to pretend to be. "I ordered. A lot of things. I realized that I hadn't eaten since six this morning."

There was a small feast there, but she didn't have time to look at it. She didn't know if she moved toward him or if he grabbed her, but they were hugging. Her head was resting on his chest. His arms were wrapped around her. She felt secure again. Like nothing from the outside could touch her.

She pulled away first. She could get used to that. She could start to like it too much. She could start to need this. "I would like to see how hard you work out in order to eat all this food and keep your body that hard."

"Sometimes I work out twice a day." He pulled out a chair for her and motioned for her to sit. Again he didn't take a seat across from her like most people would, but he sat next to her at the four-top.

"I'd rather be fat," she said with a shudder.

He grinned. "Remember it's how I blow off steam."

"Sex, Julian. You need to have sex. You must be

missing that ex of yours. She might look cold but I'd bet the last thing she was is frigid."

"I make it a point not to talk about my sex life with clients."

"But I'm not your client right now. I want to be your friend."

He nodded. "Fine." He leaned forward, almost placing his lips on her ear. "That's one of the reasons I exclusively date older women. They know what to do in bed and what they want. It makes everything so much more satisfying when a woman knows what she wants."

"But don't all women want a man who can so thoroughly wear them out that they can't walk the next morning? I'm looking at the size of you. I'd bet you have worn out legions of women."

Something flashed in his eyes. He leaned away from her, lessening some of the heat in the air around them, but it was still there. "Behave yourself. Eat. I ordered you a grilled cheese sandwich. It arrived a few seconds before you got here."

"This is fancy grilled cheese." She picked it up and bit into it and then moaned. "What's in this?"

"Brie, bacon, and apricot." He took the other half and started eating. "It's comfort food at its finest."

"You think I need comforting?"

"I could hear it in your voice when I answered the phone. Something is up. I want you to tell me."

This was something she might normally tell Arden, but her friend was so preoccupied with the pending arrival and her move that Sunny didn't want to bother her. "The police officer who found me in the closet came to see me today."

"You're still in touch?"

"Yes. He's kept up with me for over twenty years and now he's retiring and moving to Florida. Besides my social workers, he's been the one steady thing in my life and now he's leaving."

"This man saw where you lived and let you live there?"

"I'm a grown woman, Julian. He can't stop me. And of course he's never been there. He would have had a fit if he had seen it."

"So you do admit how shitty your neighborhood is?"

"You're off topic, counselor."

"You're right. So you're sad about him moving?"

"Yes, but there's more to it than that. I had always kept him at a distance. He saved my life. I had been there for three days. My food had run out. And then he and his partner appeared and he bought me hot dogs and soda and he stayed with me when I was in the hospital and he held my hand all the way up until I had gone into emergency foster care. I was so grateful to him for being my friend to hold on to when I was so damn terrified I couldn't breathe. I didn't want him to feel obligated to me. I didn't want to feel like a burden. The older I got the more I pushed him away. But he never went too far and then he tells me today that he had wanted to adopt me when I was thirteen, but he didn't think I had wanted anything to do with him, so he didn't go through with the process."

"Why did he think that?"

"Because I had just gotten a letter from my mother and it sent me spinning. She was alive and had a job and was doing well and I had just been moved to another foster home. I wanted to be left alone. I wanted to disappear. I felt entirely unlovable."

"And today you found out that somebody had loved you all along."

"Yes." She shut her eyes briefly. She didn't cry. She couldn't remember the last time she had, but the emotion was there, burning in her throat. "I ruined my chance at a family."

Julian took her hand between his massive ones and leaned over to softly kiss her cheek. "You were thirteen and hurting. You can't blame yourself."

"He invited me to his retirement party. I thought he was inviting me to be kind. I didn't want to go. I didn't want to feel alone in a room full of people who were all connected to him."

"You're connected with him too."

"Yes. He told me so. He won't let me stay away. I should feel happy about this, but I just feel so damn sad now."

"You don't want to go to the party?"

"No, but I'm going to go because I owe him that and it was selfish of me to consider not going."

"I can go with you."

She looked up at him, surprised by his offer. "You can?"

"If you don't want to go alone."

"I don't."

"Then it's settled. I'll be your guest."

Chapter 7

Julian hadn't seen Sunny for a week after he left work to meet her at the coffee shop. It had been out of character for him to leave work for anyone. Even with Regina he asked her to schedule their lunchtime dates in advance. But Sunny didn't even ask him to leave. All she had said was his name and he had heard the weight of the world in it.

Something inside him was pushing him to go to her. He had walked out of his office even before she had agreed to meet him. He had felt her presence as soon as she entered the coffee shop, and his entire body started to buzz.

Compared to him she was so small. Her wide eyes and soft rounded features made her appear innocent, almost fragile, but she wasn't. To live that kind of life, to be shuffled around from place to place, to have no one to claim her had to be hard, but she kept her head up. She kept moving forward. He didn't feel sorry for her like some people might; he admired her.

He offered to go to the party with her, that she hadn't invited him to. He had taken nearly two hours of his day to be with her. That was so out of character for him. His body wanted her, but his mind knew he couldn't cross that boundary. He still had to work with her. He had to get to the bottom of this brewing custody battle.

He had to keep his distance from her when he could help it. So he hadn't seen her for a week. But he had texted her at night, and called her once when words on a screen weren't enough.

And now he was going to see her again. In his office this time where he planned on treating her more like a client and less like the friend she thought she was.

She was bringing Soren to meet him. He had spoken to the Earls on the phone more than once over the week. They seemed like kind, hardworking people. They couldn't lavish Soren with gifts, or give her a top-notch private school education. They just wanted to love her. It was so simple.

There were so many people in the world who couldn't conceive or lost the children they had been good parents to, and then there were people who had no problem creating children but treated them like shit, threw them away when they never asked to be brought to earth in the first place.

He wondered how that was fair. How God could punish good people and reward bad. His father had once told him it wasn't that simple when Julian had expressed those feelings to him. But his father

had a strong faith. Julian hadn't been on good terms
with his faith since he was a child.

"Mr. King," his assistant said through his speaker,
"your appointment is here."

"Please, send them in."

He stood up as his door opened and in walked
Sunny, wearing a simple dress that was some shade
of purple he couldn't identify. Her hair was in its
natural state, not a straightened sleek bob, but she
had a head full of springy jet-black ringlets. He
liked her hair like this the best. Short, sexy, a little
wild. It was how he thought of her.

And then there was the little girl with her. He
had to pull his eyes off Sunny to concentrate on
her. They looked shockingly alike. Same caramel-
colored skin, same textured curls. Soren's eyes
were wide and soulful, but they were green instead
of brown.

"You two could be sisters," Julian said more to
himself than to them.

"You think so?" Sunny seemed shaken by his ob-
servation.

"You look so much alike."

"Sunny is beautiful," Soren said, her voice just
above a whisper.

"She is," Julian said without thinking. "And so
are you."

"I would like to have you as a sister," she said,
looking up at her social worker.

"I feel the same way about you." Sunny hugged
the child close to her. "You're the sweetest thing.

Please, meet my friend, Mr. King. He's going to help us learn about your mama."

Soren shook her head, her eyes getting wider. "I don't want to go back. I don't want to go back to her."

"I know." Julian stepped forward and set his hand on the frightened child's shoulder. "We just want to find out all we can about her so that the adoption can go through."

"I don't want to talk about her."

"Okay." He knew he couldn't force her. He knew she had spent nearly a year not speaking. He didn't want to make her uncomfortable. He didn't want her to do anything she wasn't ready for. "You ever have one of those crazy milkshakes? You know the ones with whole pieces of birthday cake on top of them? Or s'mores or whatever crazy thing they had in the kitchen that day."

"My moth—" Soren stopped herself. "Mrs. Earl said they probably cost twenty dollars and even though they looked cool she said she couldn't see herself spending twenty dollars on something that wasn't going to make her more beautiful. Mr. Earl said that she was already the most beautiful woman in the world and she didn't need anything."

"They sound like they love each other," Julian said.

Soren nodded. "I want to stay with them."

"I know. I want to buy you one of those milk-shakes."

Soren's mouth dropped open. "Too much money."

"I've saved up for this day. I was just waiting for the right lady to take with me."

They went out for milkshakes and Julian made it a point not to talk about Soren's mother. He asked about school, about her friends, about her plans for the summer. He spoke of her future with the Earls. If a child was that terrified to go back to their mother, then he would have to do everything in his power to keep her with them.

By the time they had finished, Soren was as relaxed and as giggly as any ten-year-old and Mr. Earl had come to get her.

"Hi, Papa!" she greeted him. Mr. Earl paused and looked at her.

"You've decided?"

She nodded her head. "Is papa okay? I can call you dad, or daddy but I like the way papa sounds."

"Papa is okay." He bent down and kissed her forehead and Julian could have sworn there were tears in the man's eyes when they left.

Julian was alone again with Sunny in his office. "You were very good with her. I'm impressed. I thought she would be afraid of you."

"I'm a giant."

"Yes, you are. But a friendly one apparently."

"The party is tonight, correct?"

"Yes. It starts at eight at his favorite restaurant. They've rented out the entire back room."

"My firm's cocktail party is this evening."

"Oh." Her face fell. "I understand. I'll be fine alone."

"I wasn't canceling. My firm's gathering starts

at six. It's just a thing we do for our clients in the spring. I was going to ask you if you wouldn't mind coming with me first."

"Are you sure you want me to come? I probably won't fit in."

Maybe not. The venue was at one of the city's most prestigious hotels. Most of the old money clients would be there as well as potential clients the firm hoped to snag. "If I didn't want you to come, I wouldn't have asked you. You'll fit in just fine."

"I'll go with you. I bought a dress to change into for the party but I'm not sure it will be fancy enough for your work function. Maybe if I had a pair of heels? I can stop by Arden's place and get some."

He looked down at her feet. "What size do you wear?"

"Nine."

"I've got heels for you in my apartment and some jewelry as well."

"You like to dress up on the weekends, Mr. King?" She grinned at him.

"Yes, but not in what you're thinking." He grinned back. "I'd bet you'd like to see my weekend wear."

"More than you'll ever know."

The exchange was flirty. He had told himself he wasn't going to cross that line again, but he couldn't help it when she was around and now he was going to spend the entire night with her.

He was cursing himself already. He took her to his apartment, which had direct views of Central

Park. She walked in and went straight to the window. "This is gorgeous." She sounded awed. "I mean, I knew people lived like this but I didn't really know until just now."

It was such a stark contrast from her place, with the doorman, concierge, and round the clock security. He could protect himself if he needed to and yet he was much safer than she was at night. They both worked hard. It didn't seem fair.

"Come on. Let me show you what I have for you." He took her by her hand and led her to his bedroom.

"Damn, this bed is huge."

"I'm huge." He went over to his wall safe that was tucked away behind a painting and pulled out boxes of jewelry for her to choose from.

"The wall safe is very rich of you, but I guess my more pressing question is, why do you have so much unworn women's jewelry in here?"

"One of my clients has a store in the diamond district. I cleared up some issues he was having and he gets me really good deals."

"I love a bargain as much as anyone else but you haven't answered my question." She sat on the bed opening the boxes.

"I pre-buy gifts for the women I date. I'm not good with birthdays and anniversaries so I keep stuff on hand in case I run into an issue."

"How long have you been doing this?"

"A while. . . . I hear judgment in your voice."

"You're damn right you hear judgment in my voice. It's not very thoughtful."

"The women I have dated never minded. I always had a gift for them, even when there was no occasion. And I don't recall asking for your opinion." He picked up a set of gold bangles and slid them onto her wrist. "Wear these. You can get ready in the guest bedroom. My sister stayed with me for a while and never took all of her stuff. You're welcome to whatever she has left behind in that closet."

"Thank you."

She left the room then and he went into his closet, stripped off his clothes, and looked for something to wear that night.

He had liked wearing suits when he first started his career in law, but as time went on, he felt more and more constricted in them. His favorite part of the day was when he was able to go home and take them off. But now he was going to have to get dressed again and go be social with a bunch of people he didn't want to see tonight. He'd had a good day with Sunny and Soren. He had forgotten about the mountain of paperwork that waited for him. He had forgotten about the back biting and conniving of his peers. But he was going to come face to face with it again as soon as they walked into that five-star hotel tonight.

And this time he wasn't going to be armed with Regina, who was always perfectly poised and fit in at these events. He was going with Sunny who had an edgy sweetness to her, who had never drank from a thousand dollar bottle of wine, who had never been to Europe or a gallery opening or skiing with a politician. She wasn't going to fit in, and for a moment he thought about blowing off the work function so he didn't have to bring her.

But he wanted her there with him. Not to make him look good, but because he just wanted her comforting presence more than her poise.

"Julian?" He heard her call his name.

"Yeah?"

"I need your help."

"I'm in the closet."

Sunny walked in and her eyes went wide. He was beginning to love that expression. Every time she experienced something new she got that look of wonderment. It was rare to see that. It made him want to show her the world.

"This closet is bigger than my whole damn apartment. It's making me bitter."

"I worked hard to get these things," he said.

"Are you saying if I continue to work hard that I one day can have all this?" The sarcasm was clear in her voice.

"What do you need help with?" It was then he noticed that she was holding her dress up on her body by the straps.

"I can't zip this alone."

He wasn't expecting it to be so sexy. The dress was the color of red wine. It was simple, no sparkle, no adornments, but it clung to her hips and then she turned around in front of him and he saw how it formed to her curvy backside. His groin

tightened painfully and he willed himself not to get
an erection.

It was going to be impossible.

Her back was bare beneath the dress. He skimmed
his fingers over the place her bra should have been.

"I can't wear a bra with this dress," she said, reading his mind. "It shows through the fabric, plus it's
so tight on top I can get away with it."

He intended to zip up her dress and send her on
her way. But his mind and his body weren't working
together tonight. "You've got a tattoo." He wasn't expecting that from her. "Let go of your straps." He
could see just the edge of it peeking out. It was on
the edge of her back, almost on her side. He pulled
the dress away to see wildflowers, delicate and pretty.

He stroked his fingers over the black ink and
watched her tremble a bit. He needed to stop
touching her. "Is it okay that I'm touching you?"

"Yes," she said, but it barely came out as a
whisper.

The straps of her dress fell down her arms and
her breasts were revealed. He looked over her
shoulder at them. They were large, firm and high
with beautiful brown nipples that he knew he was
going to touch before the evening was over.

He kissed the back of her neck. It was going to
be hard to stay in control with her tonight. He
couldn't go all the way with her. They couldn't have
sex. It would be going too far. It would be crossing
a line they couldn't uncross. But he had already
seen her body. He had already touched her. What

was the point in stopping now? He wouldn't be able to make it through the evening if he did.

"Julian." She moved her bottom across his erection. "I'm topless and you're just in your underwear."

"I realize this." He kissed down the side of her neck.

She swallowed hard. "I think it's time to admit that there is something between us."

"I admitted that to myself the first time I met you."

"Damn it, Julian."

"I just want to touch you tonight, Sunny. We can't go any further than that."

"What if I want to? What if I want you so much I can barely think about anything else?"

Her admission almost undid him. All he had to do was spin her around and kiss her. All he had to do was pick her up and take her to his bed and slide deep inside her. "I can make you feel good." He couldn't deprive himself of this. He knew if he did it would build and build and then he would explode and not be able to control himself at all.

She wasn't someone he could just have a sexual release with and then forget. She would stay with him long after it was over.

He pulled her dress down all the way until it slid over her hips and pooled to the floor at her feet. She just was in heels and a pair of simple black underwear. They weren't meant to be sexy, and the fact they weren't, made them impossibly sexier on her.

"I want to touch you, Julian."

"No. It's my turn." He pulled her tightly against him, loving the way her smooth back felt against his chest. He ran his hands down her sides and to her waist before stroking up her belly. She let out little throaty moans. She trembled. He had never been so turned on in his life.

His heart was pounding as his hands went to her breasts. He cupped them at first, feeling the weight, enjoying the soft heaviness in his hands.

She placed her hand over one of his and moved it down her body and into the band of her underwear. She didn't have to say a word. She parted her legs to give him greater access.

He swore. It was the most arousing thing he had ever seen.

She was incredibly wet and he could just imagine himself sliding inside of her. Her tight warmth clenched around him. But he knew he couldn't go there with her tonight, so he just began to stroke her.

She moved against his hand, causing her deliciously round bottom to move against his erection.

She must have realized the effect she was having on him because she started to grind her backside into him, moving her hips up and down as he stroked her.

Her cries grew louder. His breathing became more and more labored and then she broke, her entire body shaking as she cried his name. He came as soon as the last syllable left her lips. He had never done that before. Part of him felt like he was a teenager again. Too afraid to go all the way with a pretty girl.

She turned in his arms, pressing her breasts against him and wrapping her arms tightly around him. They stayed like that for a few moments, recovering, enjoying each other's warmth. And then she kissed his chest with her sweet lips and then the base of his neck.

She tilted her face up, her lips seeking his. He wanted to kiss her so bad. But he couldn't. His sense was starting to return. She had come to him to have her dress zipped up and he had stripped her nearly naked and touched her all over her body.

He couldn't help himself when he was with her, and if he kissed her, he wouldn't be able to stop. He wouldn't be able to stop touching her. They wouldn't make it out of the house tonight. They had to leave tonight.

He took her by the shoulders and gently set her away from him. The disappointment in her eyes was evident and caused something inside of him to squeeze painfully.

"I need to take a quick shower. I'll meet you in the living room in ten minutes."

Julian barely spoke to her since they left his closet. In complete silence, he had driven them to the hotel where the cocktail party was being held.

Something major had happened between them, something that she had wanted. But now that it happened she was wondering if it were all a huge mistake.

She had wanted more from him than he had wanted from her. He wouldn't kiss her. Oh, he had kissed her shoulders, his lips had brushed across her neck in a way that made her tremble with need, but she wanted to feel his mouth on hers. She wanted one of those long, deep kisses that took her breath away.

But he set her away from him and looked at her with a little pity in his eyes. She wasn't as experienced as him. She must have been too eager, revealed too much of her desire for him in that closet. She felt incredibly ridiculous and vulnerable at the moment. But she wouldn't take what happened between them back. She had never thought hands could feel so good on her body or that lips on her skin could make her forget her name. She had felt completely safe with him. That was a rare feeling for her and maybe she was wrong for feeling it, but if she felt it with him she could experience that feeling with another man someday.

A valet took Julian's keys when they arrived and Julian took her hand and led her inside the building. She wondered why he did it. Especially when they were entering a work function. Surely, he wouldn't want anyone to think they were together.

He paused right before they entered the room where the party was being held.

"I feel like I should apologize for what happened

earlier," he said into her ear. "But I'm not sorry that it happened. I wouldn't take it back. I wasn't expecting that tonight. I wasn't expecting you to be you."

"I don't know what to say to that."

"There's nothing to say. We have to work together. We have to solve this case for Soren. I need to keep sharp for it and when you're around everything gets . . . softer."

"Not everything gets softer when I'm around you," she said to him.

He let out a deep chuckle and Sunny's heart flipped in her chest. She could become addicted to that sound. He was right to put space between them. She needed to find out if she and Soren shared a mother. She didn't need to get involved in anything else that could end up hurting her.

"Behave yourself," he said, still grinning. "We've got people we need to pretend to like."

They entered the room where the cocktail party was being held. It was elegant to say the least with waiters in crisp white shirts and black vests passing around hors d'oeuvres and glasses of champagne.

There was a four-piece string quartet in the corner. People were speaking in hushed voices with polite smiles on their faces. Everyone in the room probably made in a week what she made in a month. She had only been around this much wealth one time before. It was the night she had met Julian. But Arden's brother-in-law's party had a much different feel. It was held in a trendy part of Brooklyn in an old factory that had been converted into spacious condos. She didn't feel so out of place there.

She looked up at Julian and saw his smile was gone. He was a little stiffer, more business-like.

"Whose butts are we kissing tonight?" she whispered to him.

"No one. Just have a nice time."

"Tell me who is important. I don't want to say anything to offend anyone."

"Don't bring up sex, religion, or politics and we should be fine."

"I only talk about those things with people I like to argue with."

He surveyed the room. "You see that man by the bar in the gray suit?"

"The one with the very large ring on his finger?"

"Yes, that's a fraternity ring. He was the president and is on the board of directors. He is also one of my firm's founding partners. He has more connections than all the lawyers at the firm combined. Most of them political."

Sunny wasn't one to make snap judgments, but there was something about the man that made her want to avoid him. "He looks slimy."

"Well, maybe he's not as ethical as the other founding partner, but he's a legend and he's not someone you'd want to have as an enemy."

Sunny frowned. "Only villains have enemies. You sound like we're in some superhero movie."

"He's a flashy old school lawyer who got famous for representing everyone from mobsters to huge corporations. In those circles it is easy to make enemies."

"And then there's your other boss, Cleese, who made you take my case because he thinks your firm needs to give back more."

"They need each other to survive and thrive. Bruno would have been locked up years ago if Cleese didn't constantly remind him of his morality and Cleese would probably be practicing in some tiny firm somewhere with just enough clients to make ends meet without Bruno's take-no-prisoners drive."

"And then there's you. Where do you fall on the spectrum? Are you more like Bruno or Cleese?"

He was thoughtful for a moment. "When I first decided to become an attorney, I wanted to be just like Cleese, but then I got to law school and was faced with a bunch of people who thought I was there just because I played ball. I had to prove myself there and when I got hired I had to keep proving that I belonged here and that means bringing in more clients and winning more cases. It means defending people who I know are guilty just because it brings my firm money. I'm probably more like Bruno than I would like to admit."

"You defend pop stars and drunken football players with bad tempers. It's not the same as defending mass murderers and corrupt politicians."

"But the question I have been asking myself is, given the opportunity, would I?"

"Would you?"

"I don't know the answer to that question." He

grabbed two glasses of champagne from a passing waiter. "Drink this."

"You think the alcohol will make me more witty?"

"No. People rarely eat at these things but they do drink. You'll fit in more."

"I hope you realize that there will be ridiculous amounts of food at the next party. You have to eat."

"Don't worry. I will. We don't have to stay here long. Just let me make sure my bosses know I'm here."

"I think he's spotted you." Sunny saw Bruno look their way. Her eyes had connected with him and she looked away. He hadn't just glanced at her; Julian's boss had stared at her from across the room.

"King!" Bruno's voice boomed across the room as he moved toward them. He smiled broadly, showing off all his teeth. He looked like a shark, handsome and slick, his walk a cocky strut.

"I'm going to introduce you to him," Julian said to her, but his voice was resigned. He didn't seem eager to do so and Sunny knew instantly that Julian didn't admire his boss as much as some might.

"There's our pretty boy lineman. How are you, King? I've been working out of the other office lately. Haven't gotten a chance to talk shop with you."

"My cases are going well, sir. I just added that fashion designer who ran into that storefront with her car to the firm."

"That was all over the news." His eyes widened slightly. "Should get the firm some nice coverage, but I don't give a shit about your caseload. If I wanted to talk about the law I would talk to the hundred other underlings I have. I hired you so I could have someone to talk football with. What did you think of the draft picks this year? Who do you think will make an impact?"

"New England got the best unagented picks, but if you're in the office this week we can have a detailed discussion about that. I would like you to meet my friend, Sunny. Sunny, this is one of the founding partners, Eric Bruno."

"Sunny, huh?" He looked at her again, his eyes sweeping over her body. "Is that your real name, sweetheart, or some kind of stage name?"

"My real name is Sunshine and it's nice to meet you." She extended her hand and Bruno shook hers. His grip was a little too hard, making her feel almost trapped.

"Sunshine . . . I guess people really do name their kids that. What business are you in? I'm guessing you're a dancer. Too classy-looking to be the club kind though. Which videos have you been in? I'm friends with a few directors in the business. I could probably get you in a few more."

"Excuse me?" Sunny frowned, confused.

"Sunny is a social worker, sir," Julian said with a little edge to his voice. "She works for the city and our firm is handling a pro bono case for her."

"Are we now? Who cleared that? Wait a minute. Let me guess. It was my partner. If we don't spend at least three hundred billable hours a year helping the needy, he becomes self-righteously pissy and unbearable to work with."

"He was very kind to agree to help us," Sunny said, trying to keep her voice neutral.

"His father was a civil servant or some bullshit like that. He's got a soft spot. So, I guess you're no dummy then, sweetheart. I was going to compliment King here on turning a video girl into someone respectable enough to come to this party and then I was going to ask him to help me turn some of my dancer companions into faux respectable ladies."

"Sunny went to Columbia. She has a master's degree. She didn't need any help from me."

"So you like this one?" There was a knowing smile on Mr. Bruno's lips. Sunny wanted to smack it right off his face. They were speaking about her like she wasn't there.

"I don't just like her. I respect her."

"Ah, so different from our last conquest. Regina must be screaming on the inside. She'll hate that you traded classic elegance for a newer, faster model."

"I'm not an object, Mr. Bruno," Sunny said with all the grace she could muster. "Julian didn't trade Regina for me. We are just friends. He is working on my case. I respect him as much as he respects me."

"Eric," Mr. Cleese had walked over. "You aren't harassing our staff and our clients, are you?"

"Shut up, Cleese. I'm just having a chat with my man, King. He'll always be my favorite at the firm because he helped me win fifty grand his rookie year. I've had money on him since college. He's been well worth the investment."

"Surely, you don't think we hired one of the top

attorneys in our firm just because you earned some ill gotten money off a game he hasn't played in ten years."

"Yeah." He winked. "It's the reason I hired him. Plus if some shit goes down he'll double as security."

Cleese shook his head in disgust and Sunny immediately liked him ten times more than she did the first time she met him. "How are you, Ms. Gibson? It's very nice to see you again."

"I'm doing well, Mr. Cleese. Thank you for asking. And thank you again for your firm's help. The family is beyond grateful."

"It's our pleasure. Come on, Bruno. There are some clients over there that have been asking about you."

"Why are you dragging me away? I was just getting to know Sunny." His eyes dragged over her body and Sunny felt exposed even though she was fully dressed. She forced herself to stand taller. She wouldn't give him the satisfaction of making her shrink away.

"Because your name is on this firm. This get together was your idea and you owe it to your clients to mingle. Now go mingle."

"Fine. King, we'll talk more later. Sunny, I hope to be seeing you again soon."

Sunny said nothing. Julian just nodded and watched as his boss walked away.

"Fifteen more minutes," he told her. "I just have to say hello to a few people and then we're out of here."

Chapter 8

Julian had gotten separated from Sunny during the party. He had stepped away from her, only meaning to be gone for a few moments to have a private conversation with one of his clients. He had left her with a group of acquaintances, hoping that she wasn't too uncomfortable with them. He was worried about how she would hold up. With Regina he didn't have this worry. They could come to a party together and separate for the entire evening without a single thought to how the other was faring. He had wanted that in a woman. He was telling himself that he still wanted that.

But he wasn't sure how true it was. He wasn't worried that Sunny would embarrass him. He worried that someone would say something that would make her feel out of place, like she didn't belong. He had already gone through enough of that in this setting for the both of them.

The conversation had taken longer than he expected and when he returned he saw that she was gone and he was afraid that she had left, but a bigger part of him was afraid that Bruno had gotten her alone. He didn't like the way the senior partner had stared at her. Every dirty thought in his mind was evident in his eyes. Bruno was a man who was used to getting whatever he wanted. Most of the time he wanted women. Young, beautiful ones that he could parade around the city. Ones who were impressed by his wealth and status.

Julian scanned the room for Sunny. He was feeling uncharacteristically uneasy. He was feeling angry, but he couldn't put his finger on why. He wasn't with Sunny. He couldn't claim Sunny. He wanted her, but it was just some attraction he had not learned to control. But when he saw Bruno looking at her like that, he wanted to wrap his fingers around the older man's throat and squeeze the breath out of him. The only clear thought in his head when he saw the other man's eyes travel up her body was *she's mine*.

But she wasn't his and he didn't want her to be his. He wanted to stay away from her. But the attraction was too strong and every time he tried to make the break, something pulled him back in.

He finally spotted her across the room. She was indeed with his boss, but not the boss he had been worried about. She was speaking to Cleese. The man was smiling at her, the conversation they were having apparently entertaining to them both.

He could never make a connection with the man. He was fairly sure if it had been solely up to Cleese, Julian never would have been hired at their firm.

Bruno had loved the idea of hiring a former pro athlete and he never let him forget it. It didn't seem to matter how many years had passed, or how many cases he had won. He was stuck in the same role.

Julian started to make his way toward them, but he felt a hand on his wrist. He looked down to see Regina there. She was looking regal and beautiful. But there was no fire there, no warmth. His body didn't react to her touch. There was none of that adrenaline rush he got when he was with Sunny. There was no pull between them.

There never had been a pull there, yet he had wanted to marry her.

"Hello."

"I thought you said you weren't dating her."

He didn't need to ask who. It was clear that she had seen Sunny, but how could he explain away her presence? He couldn't. He didn't have to bring her here tonight. But he did. He had wanted her with him. It was as simple as that.

"We're friends. I like her. I see her."

"You knew I would be here tonight. You don't have to throw her in my face."

"Excuse me? I didn't know you would be here tonight. I had to ask to have dinner with you two weeks in advance. How the hell do you expect me to know your schedule?"

"We talked about this night months ago. You invited me to come. I cleared my schedule for it."

"But then we broke up. And all the things we did as a couple ended."

"I didn't honestly think the last time I was with you was the last time I was going to be with you."

"I told you what I needed. You couldn't give it to me, so I moved on."

"I couldn't give you what you needed? What about what I needed? It goes both ways."

"How was I supposed to know what you needed? You never told me. You never talked to me about anything."

"You never asked."

He wasn't sure why she was here. She never called him after the day he asked her to marry him. There had been nothing, just the clear message that he wasn't good enough to be her husband. But now she was in front of him acting like he had done her wrong. "What are you looking to accomplish tonight? I can't have this conversation if there isn't a point."

"There is a point. I want to know how you could throw me away after being with me for nearly five years."

"I didn't throw you away. And how much time in those five years did we spend together? We were off and on most of the time. We don't sleep at each other's houses. We talk about politics and art and the news, but when did we ever talk about us? About anything that really matters?"

"What if all that changed?"

He frowned at her. "I don't understand."

"What if I agreed to marry you?"

"Why would you want to marry me? You don't love me."

"How could you possibly know that?"

"Don't answer me with questions."

"You know I'm not like other women. I can give you things she can't."

"This is just about Sunny. You see me with someone else and now you suddenly want to marry me?"

"I always wanted to, but I wanted you to treat it like it was something special and not like a business deal."

"Our entire relationship was a series of negotiations. There was nothing deeper. You want to be chased. You want to be worshipped. I can't give you that. And now if you'll excuse me, I've someone waiting for me across the room."

He left her, feeling angrier that he had been before. This wasn't a good night for him. This hadn't been a good few weeks for him. Sunny must have felt him barreling toward her. She looked at him and then turned back to Mr. Cleese, giving him a quick hug before she rushed toward Julian.

"What's wrong?"

"Nothing." He shook his head. "Did I just see you hug my boss?"

"Yes. I really like him. I'm going to see him again."

"He's married."

She nodded. "I know. It's been twenty-one years."

"Then what are you going to see him about?"

"I'm not sure that's any of your business. What's the matter with you? You're angry."

"I'm not sure that's any of your business."

"Fine, I'm meeting with him to talk about a lawsuit."

"A lawsuit? Who the hell are you suing?"

"You. For being a cranky jackass. You've got to chill with the mood swings."

No one could put him in his place like Sunny could.

"Regina is here. We had a conversation. I'm not very happy about it."

"Oh?"

"Let's go. I don't want to talk about it here."

He led her out of the building and back to his car where they sat for a moment. "What did she say?" Sunny asked, after they had been silent for so long.

"She wants to get back together. She wants to marry me."

"She loves you."

"But she can't say it. She didn't say it. She implied it, but that's not good enough."

"That's important to you. You want her to say it. You need that from her."

"If it's true, she would say it. It shouldn't be hard."

"Do you love her?"

"No." He shook his head. "I want to have loved her, because it would make these last five years seem like not such a waste. My mother didn't love my father. I know he loved her though. I watched him love her and not get loved back and it's hard to see someone so damn decent not get what he deserved. I swore I would never be in that kind of relationship. If neither of us were in love, it could work, but one of us can't have stronger feelings than the other."

He felt her hand on his. "Seeing your ex threw you for a loop tonight. You don't have to go to the party with me. Go home. Relax. I'll take a cab there."

She turned to reach for the door handle and he grabbed her wrist. "You're not getting rid of me so easily. I promise I won't be a morose son of a bitch at the party."

"I'm not worried about your behavior. I'm worried about you. This is bothering you."

It was. These were thoughts that would have never crossed his mind, but she came around and she made him think and feel more than he had in years. "I'm just hungry."

"Okay. Then we'll eat at the party. But if you feel like going just let me know."

He was going to stick it out the entire night. Not just because he had promised her he would, but the thought of going back to his apartment alone didn't feel right after he had been with her all day. It would feel empty and tonight he wanted to be filled up.

The venue for this party was much different than the one they had left. It was in a family owned restaurant. There was no waitstaff in impeccably pressed uniforms. No quiet, elegant music playing in the background. Some Motown classic was on, but it was barely heard over the voices and the laughter that filled the room. It felt warm. The last party didn't. Julian couldn't understand how Sunny wouldn't feel comfortable here. But she didn't. He felt, more than saw her tense up as they walked in. He was right behind her, watching her as she squared her shoulders and forced her head upright. He felt a sharp pang of something inside him that caused him to stop her before they got farther into the restaurant. He pulled her body into his, meaning to offer comfort, but liking the way her curvy backside felt against his front and he hugged her.

He realized his mistake immediately. Thoughts of what had taken place in the closet flooded his mind. The way her curvy little body tucked into his. The way she moaned his name. The way she made his heart race. He wasn't sure who he really was anymore when he was with her and that was crazy. They had met a month ago. How could his world be so thoroughly rocked? How was he supposed to keep things professional with her?

"Don't be sweet to me," she whispered.

"Okay. I won't. You're the ugliest person in the room."

She pulled away and smiled at him. "Thank you. That's better."

"Sunny! You made it." A man wearing a huge grin and a party hat came over to her. His arms were spread. Julian knew immediately that this was the man they were here to honor.

"Detective Rodgers." She hugged him back. "Congratulations. I'm so happy for you."

"Please stop calling me detective. Call me Tom. I've told you that eight million times."

"It's a sign of respect. I'll always call you that."

"You're a silly kid." He glanced up at Julian. "You wouldn't happen to be . . ." He shook his head. "No. It can't be."

He still got recognized by diehard football fans. His future had been incredibly bright to have it all dashed away when he took a hit too hard.

"This is my friend, Julian King. Julian, this is Thomas Rodgers. He's the reason I'm still here."

"It is you!" He grabbed Julian's hand and shook it hard. "How did you know, Sunny? I loved this kid. I followed his career all through college. We went to the same school. I own his rookie jersey and now he's standing here. It nice to meet you, man."

"It's an honor to meet you. Sunny has great things to say about you. You went to Clemson?"

"Of course. Football was my life. Sunny, this is the best present you could have given me."

"He's not a present for you. Julian is my . . ." She stumbled on the word. "Friend. We're friends," she said, even though they were more than that.

Detective Rodgers wasn't buying that they were just friends either and anyone who saw them walk in wouldn't buy that either. He smiled at both of them and hugged her again. "I'm happy for you, honey. Now go eat. Have a couple of drinks. Enjoy yourselves tonight."

Julian did enjoy himself that night. There were a

lot of excited cops eager to talk football to a former pro. Most of them wanted to know what it was like to play in a Super Bowl and hear the roar of the crowd. There were times he hated being known just for his time on the field, but tonight he didn't mind the dozens of questions. It made him miss it.

He made his way over to the table where Sunny was now sitting alone. She had been seated with Rodgers's wife and some of the other wives and girlfriends.

"Hey, stud." She smiled at him. "Your fan club done peppering you with questions?"

"For now." He sat next to her, wanting to reach for her and pull her into his arms again. She looked sleepy and adorable and he craved her closeness.

She leaned over and kissed his cheek. "You made Detective Rodgers's night. Thank you for being so kind to everyone."

"He's a great guy. There's nothing to thank me for."

"Do you get tired of answering football questions? It must be annoying sometimes."

"Sometimes. Especially when I'm at work. I want to be recognized for my skills as an attorney."

"Everyone here was impressed by you. Football and then law school. It's an accomplishment, Julian. A huge one. I hope you know that. I hope you are proud."

Damn it, she was sweet. He reached over and touched her cheek, just needing to feel her skin. She wasn't making this easy on him.

"Why did your boss think I was a music video girl?"

"Your body," he said without hesitation. "Those

little sundresses you wear hide how curvy you are. You're sexy. You might not see it, but you're sexy and every man with a pulse knows it." He paused for a moment. "I didn't like the way he was looking at you. I know I can't tell you what to do, but I would like you to stay away from him."

"What would you say if I told you I was madly attracted to him and wanted to be with him?"

"What could I say?"

"There are a few things that come to mind."

"Sunny . . ."

"Take me home, Mr. King." She stood up. They had been together all day, and if he was honest with himself he would admit that he didn't want the day to end yet. He didn't want to take her home. But he knew he was going to and then he was going to force himself to back away from her for a little while.

Sunny needed some space from Julian if even for a moment. She was enjoying him far too much tonight. The more time she spent with him, the more she saw how kind and decent he was. He had been so good with every person who came up to him tonight, asking about his former career and his endorsement deals. It must have been painful to have such a promising career snatched away from you and then be constantly reminded of it.

She walked over to Detective Rodgers who was standing near the entrance, saying good-bye to his friend. She didn't think she was going to have a good time tonight, but she did. She still felt like an outsider, but she had felt that way her entire life. There was a warmth in the room that was unmistakable. She wanted to live in that warmth. She wanted to create that kind of warmth of her own with a family that she made.

"Sunny." The detective smiled at her as she approached. "Did you have a good time?"

"Yes. You have wonderful friends and family."

He hugged her. "You're included in that. We're not moving until the end of July. Come over for dinner before we go. Bianca had to take her mother home but she told me not to let you leave without asking you."

"I would be happy to come."

"Bring Julian. He's a great guy. I like him for you."

"He's not my boyfriend, you know. We're just friends."

"The way he looks at you tells me a different story."

"You just want me to be happy and settled so you don't have to worry so much."

"Yes. You're right. I worry about you."

"Stop worrying." She pulled away from him. "I'm going to be fine."

"You probably will be, but I don't want you to be fine. I want you to be happy."

She wanted to assure him that she was happy. But she couldn't make herself say the words. How could she really be happy when so much of herself was a mystery? "I'll call you later this week."

He nodded. "Make sure you do."

She looked back at Julian who was standing a little ways away to give her privacy. "I'm ready."

He stepped forward, shook the detective's hand, and congratulated him before they left. It had been an odd night. He had seen his ex. He had been affected by it. There must be some feelings left there. He said he didn't love her, but he had wanted to marry her.

Sunny wondered if it was just a matter of time before they ended up back together.

She was quiet on the ride home. She didn't know if she was just tired or if she was too wrapped up in the day.

"You don't have to park," she told him as he pulled into the lot around the corner from her building. "You can just let me out in front of the building."

"We both know that that isn't going to happen."

She was too tired to argue and allowed him to walk her into her building. He followed her up the stairs. She felt his eyes on her backside as she moved. She tried not to feel self-conscious. He had seen more of her body than any other man had. He had touched her. There was no reason for her to feel shy, but she was.

She turned around to face him as soon as they reached her door. "Thank you for coming with me tonight. I appreciate it."

"You're welcome. Thank you for coming with me tonight. I know you didn't have as much fun with me as I did with you."

"You're okay for a dumb jock." She extended her hand for him to shake, but he stared at it for a moment before he pushed it away. A grin crossed his face and he grabbed her, lifting her off her feet and spinning her around. She let out a little squeal and when he set her down, she stumbled backward. She expected to feel the solidness of her door behind her. But the door pushed opened and she nearly fell into her apartment.

Julian caught her and steadied her, but her heart was racing. She looked up at him, afraid to look behind her. His face said everything she needed to know. The smile had faded away. Suddenly all business.

"You're coming home with me. You cannot stay here."

He pulled out his cell phone and soon she heard him request the police to her address. It was then she turned around. She stood there for a long moment, just taking it in. Everything was disrupted. Her mattress was overturned. Her dresser drawers pulled out, her clothes thrown everywhere.

Her eyes went to the place where she kept her jewelry box. She knew there were no gold or diamonds in there. Just some costume stuff. But her most valuable things were in there. The physical mementos that she had of her mother. The letters she had written. The crystal barrette she used to wear in her long, blond hair and the jade Buddha she had bought from a flea market just before she moved them to New York City.

The box was knocked onto the floor, now empty.

Her letters were still there, folded up, yellow and worn with age but now they were dirtied by a footprint. And next to them was the barrette, but it wasn't intact, it was hopelessly broken, crushed by some thief's foot in the quest for something valuable. She went on her knees before it and started to pick up the tiny pieces. She couldn't let this go. She used to hold it in her hand while she slept those first few nights when she was in the emergency foster care. She used to hold it so tightly that the stones left imprints on the palm of her hand. Sometimes when she stroked it, she felt like she could see her mama clearly. She could remember the shade of her eyes and the softness of her touch and her scent that was comforting even when things around them were insane.

"Sunny!"

She felt Julian grab her and lift her from the floor, but she fought him. She wasn't going anywhere until she picked up all the pieces.

"We'll find you another one. The police are on their way. I need you to pack your clothes."

"We won't find another one. This was my mama's. She gave it to me before she left. I need it."

She had never said that aloud before, but she did need it. Mama was her family. Her only family and she needed this to feel connected to the woman even though she had left her locked in the closet.

"Give me the pieces," he said softly. "I'll hold them for you. I'll keep them safe."

She believed him and when he held out his

large hand, she placed everything she had picked up in it.

"What else do you need, Sunny?"

"Her letters." She picked up the sheets of notebook paper and held them to her chest.

She hurt. That was the only feeling she could identify at the moment. It was the strongest feeling. She had been violated. No one had touched her body this time, but they destroyed her home, her safe place, the space she had created and paid for herself. The one no one could send her away from when they were done with her. The place that was all hers.

"What else can I do for you?"

"Help me put everything back." She stood up, still clutching the letters. "It's not so bad. I can make it nice again."

"Sunny, no. We have to leave it until the police come."

"What are they going to do? I need to clean up to see where my Buddha is. It was hers. She thought it was cute. She said it made her feel calm. She used to rub his belly. I need to find it."

She heard the desperation in her voice, along with the sirens of a police car.

"We'll find it." Julian grabbed her as she tried to push her mattress over. "I picked up some of the clothes that were on the floor and put them in your bag. Now we have to let the police do their job. You have to tell them what's missing."

She could see that her small flat screen TV was

gone and her two-year-old laptop. Probably not worth more than fifty bucks on the street. They destroyed her home for nothing. She would have happily have given those away in order to keep the things that were precious to her intact.

She spoke to the police. She couldn't remember what she had said. She didn't remember the ride back to Julian's place. She didn't remember the elevator ride upstairs. The cloud had lifted when she was sitting on the edge of the bed in his guest room.

Julian came in with a T-shirt in his hand. "You can wear this. I didn't grab anything for you to sleep in."

She took it from him and set it on her lap, smoothing her hands over the soft cotton. She couldn't look at him. She saw the concerned expression in his eyes. She was too close to tears, but she didn't cry. She had stopped a long time ago when she learned that tears never fixed a damn thing.

"Thank you."

He knelt before her and cupped her face in his hands, forcing her to look at him. "Tell me what I can do to make you feel better."

"I'm fine," she lied. "You've done everything you could for me."

He stroked his thumb across her cheek and she had to fight the urge to lean into it. "I feel like it's not enough. We can go back and get the rest of your clothes and things tomorrow."

"No." She shook her head. "I'm going back. I won't need any more of my things."

"You cannot go back there. The guy shouldered through the door to get in. The lock is smashed. It's not safe there for you."

"I'll get stronger locks. I have to go back. It's my home."

"You can make a new home, but you can't stay there. I can't let you go back."

"You don't get to decide what I do," she snapped. "I make the choice. I'm in charge of my own life."

She had been shuffled around from foster home to foster home. She had never had stability. She never knew when she was going to be moved again. She wasn't going to move again unless it was her choice.

"You've had a long day." He rose and kissed her forehead. "We'll talk about this in the morning."

"There's nothing to talk about. I'm going back. I have no other place to go."

Julian shook his head and walked out and she knew then that he wasn't going to let this go.

The next morning Sunny woke up in Julian's guest room. She had slept deeply and was so comfortable that she didn't want to get out of bed. She didn't have to. It was Saturday. She could probably get away with burying her head beneath the pillows and sleeping the day away. But it didn't matter how long she had slept. Last night had happened. Her place was still a mess. Her most important things had been destroyed; her personal effects rummaged through in the search for drugs or cash.

She opened her eyes and stared at her surroundings. His second bedroom was probably bigger than her entire apartment. It was bright and airy with huge windows overlooking Manhattan. She never thought she'd have set foot in an apartment like this, much less have slept in one.

She forced herself to put her feet on the floor and get out of bed. Julian must have been up already. She could smell the scent of coffee wafting through the bedroom door and when she opened it, she stepped out to see him shirtless and sweaty in his kitchen.

The dull throb between her legs returned. This was getting to be too much. Every time she was near him it happened. She had never been this attracted to anyone.

"Good morning," she said, trying to keep her voice neutral.

"Good morning." He came out from behind the counter and took a step toward her. She couldn't take her eyes off his chest. She knew how it would feel against her, and yet she wanted to experience it again, but this time she wanted to run her lips over it. "How did you sleep last night?"

"Very well. Thank you."

"I was worried about you."

"You shouldn't have been. I'm fine. I promise."

He shook his head. She knew he didn't believe her. But it didn't matter. She had no other choice but to be fine. "I made coffee. After I showered I was going to make eggs, but we can go out for breakfast if you want."

"We don't have to go out. I can start cooking breakfast after you get out of the shower."

"You don't have to do anything. You're my guest. You should just relax."

"I can cook, Jules. I'm not going to have a breakdown if I scramble a few eggs."

"I like mine over easy," he said with a grin.

"I can manage that." She went into his kitchen, walking around the other side of the island so she wouldn't brush against him. He was all sweaty and she could smell his scent, but it wasn't a bad smell at all.

He smelled like a man should smell and it was making her want to get even closer to him.

"Do you have a computer and a phone I can use?" she asked him as she opened his refrigerator, so she wouldn't have to look at him anymore. "My cell phone is dead and I didn't think to bring my charger with me."

"In my den. You can use anything that I own."

"Thank you. I have a few calls to make. I hope someone can come over to do my locks today."

"Sunny." He came up behind her, placing his hands on her shoulders. Her heart beat faster. She wanted to push herself closer to him just so she could feel his solid form against her. But she held herself away. "You don't have to go back just because you think you have no other place to go. You know you can stay here."

"We both know that I can't."

He was quiet for a long moment. "I don't want you to go back there."

"I have to go back. I can't move right now. I can't afford anything else in the city."

"You know I can help you with that. I can find you a place. I can pay for it."

"No." She turned around to face him. "No! Are you insane? You think I would let you pay my way? I've got a degree from an Ivy League school. I don't need anyone to support me. I can take care of myself."

"I know, but I wouldn't be doing this for you. I would be doing it for me. I couldn't sleep last night because I kept thinking about what could have happened if you were in there when they had broken in. If we hadn't gone to that party, you would have been."

She shut her eyes, blocking that thought out. "I can take care of myself."

She had sworn the last time someone had hurt her that she would never allow herself to feel helpless again. She had learned how to defend herself years ago. "You say that, but I don't want to hear that they found your body on the news."

"Shut up!" She pushed him away from her. "Don't you think I feel violated enough? Don't you think I feel scared? But I can't let the fear rule me, or I would never stop being scared."

He grabbed her waist and pushed her backward

until her back hit the refrigerator door. "Push me away." He grabbed her wrists and pinned them above her head. "Make me move away from you." He pushed his muscular body all the way against hers. Her nipples went tight. She squirmed against him, which only made things worse. He was so damn strong. All the self-defense moves she had learned had flown right out of her head. But more than that she didn't want him to move away from her. "Stop me from doing this." He bent his head, his lips were dangerously close to her but he didn't close the distance.

The grip on her wrist loosened and his hands came down to touch her body. He slid his hands beneath the T-shirt he gave her to sleep in last night. At first his hands hovered around her hips and then they traveled up to her waist and stomach. His touch made her skin even hotter and her knees nearly buckled.

"Ouch! God damn it." He pulled away from her and grabbed his arm. "You pinched me."

"You dared me to move you. I think I did."

"You did." He took another step forward and grabbed her again, this time lifting her off her feet. He took her to his couch and lay her there, placing his long hard body on top of hers. "How long could you fight me off? How could you stop me if I really wanted to hurt you?"

He was trying to prove a point, prove how unsafe it was for her to live in her place alone, but what he was doing wasn't proving his point. She touched the side of his face with the backs of her fingers. "But it's you, Jules. It's hard to imagine that you could hurt me when you make me feel so damn good."

His nostrils flared and anger shot to his eyes and he yanked himself away from her.

"This is not over," he promised her as he stalked off to his bedroom.

She wasn't sure if he was talking about this conversation or the heated interaction that had just taken place between them, but she didn't want it to be over either.

Chapter 9

Julian took Sunny back to her apartment. He helped her clean up and watched her carefully as she held her head up and try to right things. But things weren't right, no matter how tidy she tried to make them. He saw her last night. He watched her try to pick up the smashed pieces of the cheap barrette that was worthless to anyone else. It was the only tie she had to her past, to her life before foster care, to her mother that abandoned her. At first he didn't understand why she had been so attached to it. The woman neglected her, probably abused her, but those little pieces of her were more important than anything else. She didn't seem to care about the stolen laptop or the television that was long gone. She didn't seem worried about the fact that she could have been hurt if she had been home just an hour earlier. She had cared about saving that connection, having that physical sign of a memory still there.

He realized that she must love her very deeply.

He had nothing from his mother. He didn't even keep a picture of her in his house. There was nothing of hers that he wanted to save. She had left him, just like Sunny's mother had left her. But the only difference was that Julian could speak to her anytime he wanted. He could go and see her. He could even hear her say that she loved him, which he didn't believe, but it was still there and it was much more than Sunny had.

She had been so strong throughout this. He had expected her to break down at one point, to cry, but she didn't. He could have handled her tears; it would have been preferable than the deep sadness he saw in her eyes. It made him ache. It made him want to hold on to her and not let her out of his sight.

She didn't want that. She didn't want his help at all. He felt this wall go up around her. Her smiles didn't come as easily. She didn't tease him throughout the day as she normally would. They barely talked, but he didn't leave her side.

He had gone behind her back once he found out who she had called to install her new locks and paid for stronger ones and an alarm system. He had the technician who installed them tell her that it was all a part of the sale they were running. Sunny had looked at Julian when she heard this, but she didn't call him on it and he was glad she didn't argue about it.

He had gone out and bought them pizza, and when he returned to her apartment he had his overnight bag in his hand. He had his laptop in there as well as his iPad. He was expecting her to question him, but she seemed too tired and distracted to pay much attention to what he was carrying.

He wondered if she had thought anymore about that interaction they had this morning. He had almost lost control again. He had almost kissed her and he knew if he would have done that, he wouldn't have been able to stop. He was a man who prided himself on being in control of his emotions at all times, yet she always made him slip. She had walked out of his bedroom in just his T-shirt, her curvy, bare legs sticking out of the bottom. It was so big on her that it draped off one of her shoulders. He had seen women in nothing at all or the most expensive lingerie, but she was sexier than all of them in that drab olive–colored T-shirt.

They had to work together. He kept reminding himself of that fact. They had to finish what they started, but he could no longer just pretend to be professional because he cared about her too much. He wanted to keep her safe. He wanted her in his sight at all times.

After they had finished dinner he handed her his iPad. "I've got all the streaming apps on here. I like to watch something before I go to bed. It helps me unwind. Or we could watch something together on my laptop."

She frowned at him. "What else is in your bag?"

"Pajamas. My toothbrush. Some clothes for to-morrow."

"Are you going somewhere after you leave here?"

"I'm not leaving here." And to prove his point he pulled off his T-shirt and jeans and changed into his sleep pants in front of her.

"I know it's been a long day, but I don't remember inviting you to stay over."

"You didn't have to invite me to stay over. If you think I'm leaving you here alone tonight after some asshole broke in and destroyed the place, you are out of your damn mind."

"Julian, I'm fine here. What are the chances he'll come back? Besides I've got better locks now. I'll be fine."

"I won't be fine. I'll be up all night worrying about you. It will be better for both of us if I stayed here."

"How long are you planning to stay?"

"Until you agree not to stay here anymore."

"You're being ridiculous."

"For caring about you? I don't give a shit." He got into her bed. It was much smaller than his own. Her entire apartment could fit inside his bedroom, but he wasn't leaving her. He didn't care how uncomfortable it was.

Only he wasn't uncomfortable. Her little place was cozy and, as of right now, he had been with her for over twenty-four hours and at no point had he wanted to be away from her. In the past few weeks he had spent more time with her than he had with the woman he was supposed to marry.

"So you're just going to get in my bed, like you own the place?"

He nodded. "Does that bother you?"

"Hell yeah, it bothers me."

"Well, I guess you know how to prevent this from happening."

"I don't mind sharing a bed. I had to share one with my foster sister for a year. She was a wild sleeper. I used to wake up with her toes in my nostrils."

She walked over to her nightstand and pulled out a nightie. He thought she was going to excuse herself to the bathroom, but she didn't. She stripped off her dress in front of him. She wore plain cotton underwear and a nude-colored bra. He didn't look away. He couldn't look away. "How old were you when that happened?"

"Twelve." She unhooked her bra, revealing her breasts to him for a moment, before she slipped on her nightgown. He put his knee up to hide the monster erection that had formed in his pants. It used to take a lot more than a glimpse of bare breasts to make him hard, but not with her.

"Do you keep in contact with any of your foster siblings?" he asked, trying to keep his attention on the conversation and not how much he wanted her.

"I tried to, but we were all moved around so much that it became too hard." She went around the apartment, tidying up things, plugging in both their cell phones to charge on the nightstands.

He wondered if this is what it would be like to be married, to be married to her. Would it be this comfortable, this cozy? Would there be this kind of warm anticipation every night? He wanted marriage so that he could share his life with someone.

But he had asked a woman he knew wouldn't give him this feeling.

Sunny climbed into bed beside him.

"You can't send me away now. If you want to get away from me, you would have to leave."

"That's what this is about. You're hoping to drive me from my apartment."

"Yes. And do not try to seduce me again. I'm not putting up with it this time."

"Seduce you? You've already seen me naked. My changing in front of you should have no effect."

"The day I stop responding to a woman's nude body is the day I'm ready to pass away. Besides, I was talking about that stunt you pulled in the closet."

"I wanted you to zip my dress! You started that."

"You have a tattoo and no bra on. How did you think I was going to respond?"

"By zipping up my dress."

"You should have smacked me when I started touching you."

"I just wanted to feel good, Julian. With everything that is going on, the opportunity to feel something that made me feel incredible came along and I grabbed it. It was nice to have everything else fade away except you and me and what we were doing."

She said things like that to him. Things that made him want to give her that feeling every single day.

He could take her away from this. He could change her life. It wouldn't be hard for him at all and it was on the tip of his tongue to tell her so. But that was ridiculous. He had told himself just the other day that he had needed to stay away from her. She didn't line up with the goals he had set for himself when he started out at his firm. He had wanted a cultured, independent wife who had her own life that didn't center around him.

But after meeting Sunny, he wasn't sure if that life would make him happy in the long run. He no longer knew what would.

"Come closer." He pulled her to him wrapping his arms around her, liking the way she felt tucked into him. He touched her now wild curls with one hand and stroked down her arm with the other. As his hand traveled up he felt a difference in her skin toward her shoulder. It wasn't creamy soft there. Her skin was raised, not just a regular scar, but one that seemed more intricate.

He lifted his head and studied the scar. He had seen a hint of the scar before through her clothes, but he had never taken the time to look closely. There were three small circles there. They were burns. They must have been very serious to have scarred like that.

"What happened to you?"

"Nothing." She shut her eyes and leaned against him.

"Don't tell me nothing." He persisted. It bothered him to see that she had been hurt.

"I was burned when I was a child."

She didn't say she had gotten burned. *I was burned.* Someone had done that to her.

"Sunny . . ."

"I was five. It was forever ago. I know it's early, but I'm exhausted. Can we just go to sleep?"

He needed to know more but what right did he have to ask? Still he felt the need to kiss her there. "Who hurt you? Was it your mother?"

She looked up at him with her huge eyes. There was pain there. He wanted to kill whoever had done that to her. She opened her mouth to speak but his phone rang.

She rolled away from him and he knew her guard had snapped back into place.

"Your phone."

"Ignore it."

"I would, but I've heard your phone ring before and that ring is different from the normal one. Who is it?"

"My mother."

"Pick it up."

"I do not want to speak with her right now."

"Well, then tell her you can't talk but pick up the phone when your mother calls you. I sometimes forget how my mother's voice sounds. Sometimes I think I would give anything to hear it one more time."

He looked at her for a moment. "You're good at the guilt."

"It comes in handy sometimes."

He answered his phone right before it went to voicemail.

"Hello, Mother."

"Hello, Julian. I called you at home a couple of times this week. I figured I would try you here."

"I'm not at home right now. I'm staying with a friend."

"Oh? Is everything okay with your apartment?"

He glanced at Sunny. "Everything is fine at my apartment. Was there something in particular you wanted?"

"No. I just wanted to talk to you and catch up with you. How are you?"

"I'm fine. Busy. And yourself?"

"Everything is good here. We're going to Europe at the end of the summer. Your brother is thinking about studying abroad."

He objected to the term brother. He had met the kid once when he had come to one of his games. They never had a conversation or anything in common. They shared a biological mother because it was clear from that one meeting that she doted on that boy in a way she couldn't be bothered to do with her other kids. "That's nice."

"He's going to study international business. I'm sure he would love to talk to you. I know your firm has offices in London."

"I don't know much about the London office. Most of my clients are celebrities."

"Still I'm sure he would like to speak to you. He's approaching manhood."

"His father can talk to him about those things, don't you think?"

"Well, I would like to talk to you, Julian."

"We're talking right now."

"I mean in person. I would like to see you. I

haven't seen you since your sister's wedding. It's been too long."

"It's been a year. We've gone much longer without seeing each other."

"And that was wrong. I don't know you. I would like to get to know you."

"You know me as well as I expect you to know me."

"I hear more about you from your sister than I ever do from you."

"Then you have all the information you need to know."

"I don't. I'm trying, honey. Can't you meet me halfway?"

"I have to go. I'm not alone."

"Are you with Regina?"

"No, we're not together. I'm with Sunny now." He had meant he was with her in that moment, but the way he said it made it sound like they were a couple. And anyone who saw them in bed together would probably think the same thing.

"Sunny?"

"I've got to go. Good night." He disconnected and looked down at Sunny who was staring at him with a raised eyebrow.

"I think I need to get more blankets."

"Why?" He frowned at her.

"It just got very cold in here."

He shook his head and lay back down. "We're not close."

"I can tell. And yet you text your father and your sister all day."

"You're not the only one whose mother abandoned

them. She was supposed to pick me up one day and never showed up. She had disappeared for a year and the next time we saw her she was asking my father for a divorce, so yes I'm much closer to my father and sister than I am to my mother."

"She seems like she wants to change that."

"I don't want to change things. I'm thirty-five years old. I sure as hell don't need a mother now."

She let out a deep sigh, grabbed his iPad and started scrolling through the apps. "I'm going to miss my laptop. How else am I going to binge on *Orange Is the New Black*?"

"If you have something more to say about my mother, then say it. There are few people in my life who are totally honest with me and I need you to be one of them."

"It just makes me sad. You have someone else in your life who is trying hard to love you and you won't let her."

"You do the same thing. Anytime someone tries to take care of you, you shy away from it. You act as if you don't deserve to be loved."

"I was shuffled around to so many foster homes. I lived with people who had taken me in just for the paycheck. I had to learn to take care of myself because I've been disappointed so many times before."

"What about Detective Rodgers? If anyone has shown you that they will always be there for you, I think it was him. It's been over twenty years. He's been by your side longer than your mother."

"I know. I didn't know what it was like to be loved,

but you did. You grew up with it. You know who your family is and where you came from. You know that there will always be people you can go to, who share the same history. And now you have someone who is making the effort to try to connect with you and you won't budge an inch."

"I take her phone calls. I send her a birthday present. I could have completely iced her out."

"And yet you haven't. That tells me something. It might be easier for you both if you did. You're punishing her. You hurt her every time you make her think that there is a crack in the door for her to slide through and then slam it in her face."

"Galen cried for her every night for two months after she left. She was four. She was heartbroken. I'm supposed to forgive that? I'm supposed to pretend that shit didn't affect us."

"No. But Galen seems to be trying. She talks to your mother fairly frequently, it seems."

"Galen is different than me. Galen is hopeful."

"And you always foresee the worst?"

"Maybe I do." He shook his head. "Are you telling me that if your mother reappeared after all this time, you would forgive her?"

"I would love to see her again. There's a hole inside of me that I don't think will ever go away unless I know what happened to her. It only hurts me to be mad at her. Why would I want to hurt anymore?"

He leaned down and kissed her cheek, feeling

something for her in that moment that he couldn't name.

"I'm not suggesting that you spend every holiday together. I'm not telling you that you're not allowed to be mad, but I'm asking to reconsider your relationship with her. You might be happier if it changed."

"I'll think about it."

She lifted her hand to run her fingers through his hair. He wanted to press his mouth to hers but he resisted. He was in a dangerous position in her bed and he knew if he started he wouldn't be able to stop.

"Good night, Sunny."

"Good night, Jules. Thank you for being here."

Chapter 10

Mama was mad at her but for the first time, Sunny didn't care because she was mad at Mama too. Nothing was fun anymore or good or happy. They had been without electricity for so long, and the apartment felt hot like an oven and sometimes it seemed like it was getting smaller in there and it was hard for her to breathe. The blankets covering the windows blocked out the light and the air and the view of the kids across the street who played at the school. Sunny wanted to go back to the days when her mama was happy and used to take her to the beach, when they used to take off their shoes and play in the sand and run in the ocean. There was nothing to look forward to.

Sunny had begun to imagine things during those long, dark, hot hours of the day. She would imagine her and her mama living any place else but this noisy, dirty city, maybe a house in the country somewhere with a garden. In her dream, her mama wouldn't have her crazy eyes, her skin would be golden instead of pasty, and her face would be full instead of deflated. They would laugh and be happy and free instead of scared and miserable. If dreams were wishes. . . . Her mama could take away many things but not her dreams. She was mad at her now, so angry that she wasn't speaking to Sunny. It was the only punishment she could give because Sunny had nothing left to take away. She wasn't talking to Mama either. She was mad too. She didn't feel bad for leaving the apartment after Mama left to go to work.

Her neighbor was an older lady who lived with no one except a cat she called Perrito. She only spoke to Sunny in Spanish and would squeeze her cheeks when she saw her. The lady would always let her in when she knocked. She never asked her about her mama or why she never went to school or why she always smelled of staleness and sweat. She gave her a bath with lots of bubbles and feed her arroz con pollo or empanadas stuffed with delicious meat. They would listen to old music while the lady knitted and hummed along. It was the best part of the day. The lady liked her, and Sunny desperately needed to escape the life Mama had made for them.

But Mama had found out because Sunny got too comfortable one evening in the lady's air-conditioned apartment and fell asleep. She was usually so careful. She would only spend a few hours with the lady and sneak off when the lady fell asleep in her chair. But this time she didn't make it home before her mama, and Mama had been furious.

"You left! You left this place!" her mama screamed and for a second she was shocked because her mama had never raised her voice to her. "I thought they took you. I-I thought they took you away." Her eyes went wilder. "I can't let anything bad happen to you. Safe . . . you have to be safe."

Sunny felt her cheeks burn red, not with embarrassment but with anger.

"I don't want to be safe with you anymore. I want to have lights and food and sunshine. I hate it here. I hate you. I don't want to live with you anymore."

Her mama had recoiled as if she had been kicked in the stomach, and hadn't spoken a word to Sunny since that moment. But Sunny was still mad. Her stomach was still burning.

She got up and began to pull the heavy blankets off the windows and pushed them open so she could breathe in something other than stale air. The sunlight hit her face for the first time in weeks and she almost felt as if something inside her had been set free.

"Sunny, no!" Her mama yelled and scrambled to try and replace the blanket but Sunny held on to it tightly, and her mother gave up and started to weep.

"Sunshine baby, I'm sorry. I'm sorry." She tried to pull Sunny into a hug but she pulled away, unable to stand the smell of her mother's sweat and sickness. *"Don't you love me anymore? Don't you love your mama?"*

She didn't answer her because she couldn't. It was too hard.

"Tell Mama what she needs to do to make you love her again. I'll do anything. Please, baby, tell me."

Sunny backed up and studied her mama and felt sad for her. She wasn't like everyone else. She wanted to tell her mama she wanted to move to the country; that she wanted to go to school every day to hear something besides the sounds of her own thoughts. She didn't know if her mama could manage that, so she asked for the one thing that she knew she could give her.

"I want light."

* * *

Sunny woke up the next morning feeling disoriented. There was a heavy arm wrapped around her and a warm hard body pressed against hers. She felt disoriented but she also felt safe. Completely safe and she couldn't remember the last time she had felt so secure.

"Are you awake?" he asked her.

"Yes."

"Are you okay?" He turned her toward him and looked into her eyes. There was concern in his.

"What were you dreaming about? You were shaking."

"Was I?" She rolled away from him and got out of bed. "I'm going to get dressed and then I'll head down to the bodega and get us some breakfast sandwiches. I think I have the menu in my drawer. I have a coffeemaker here but they make way better coffee than I do. Do you want some?"

"Sunny . . ."

"Think about it. I'll be in the shower."

She showered quickly and got dressed in her bathroom. She needed a moment away from him. She had tried to block those memories. She had felt guilty for saying those words to her mother because soon after that she was gone.

It had been for the best. She had been hurt once before because of her mama. She could have died; as an adult she realized that. Her mother had been dangerous but she had told her that she hated her.

She shouldn't have said it. She would never forget the look on her mother's face when she did.

She left her bathroom to find Julian in her tiny kitchen, washing the glasses in her sink. The coffee-pot had been started and just by the smell she could tell it was better than anything she had ever made.

He was so sexy. She liked having him in her apartment. She had liked his nearness. She didn't want to think about how empty she would feel when he left her today.

"Have you decided what you wanted?"

"I can go with you to get it. I might want to pick up some other things. Is there a supermarket around here?"

"There's one about six blocks away."

"We can take my car. That's too far to carry all that stuff."

"I have a little cart." She raised her eyebrow. "What could you possibly need to get?"

"Your refrigerator is empty."

"You've seen the size of my behind? Do you think I'm in danger of starving?"

"No, but if I'm going to be staying here, we have to have actual food. Do you own a blender?"

"No and you're not staying here."

"I am. Especially after last night. There were two drunk assholes fighting below your window. There were people in the hallway at all hours. This building isn't safe for you to live in alone. So I'm going to stay with you until you move out."

"Julian . . ." She walked over to him and hugged

him. "I appreciate you trying to take care of me, but we both know that you can't stay here for long and as soon as you walk out of here without me, I'm going to lock the door and not let you back in."

"You can try." He smoothed his hands down her back. "I told the locksmith that I was your husband and he gave me the keys. You can't keep me out."

"I'll call the cops and have you arrested."

"You wouldn't."

"You're right. I wouldn't." She was silent for a moment. "But you can't stay here, Jules." She slid her hands beneath his T-shirt to feel his hard back and soft skin. "Because I'll want to do this." She kissed his throat. "And this."

"Don't play dirty. It's not going to work anyway." He closed his eyes and she continued to kiss him. Her nipples tightened, being this close to him, smelling his warm smell, feeling this safe turned her on.

"I'm not playing. I'm not trying to seduce you. I'm doing this because it makes me feel good."

"You shouldn't be doing this."

"No, I shouldn't be doing this." Her hands slid down to his butt. It was like stone, but round enough that made it perfect for touching. "This is a beautiful thing." She said to him. "I love your thighs too. Your arms and chest are perfect as well, but I love your lower body. You must do thousands of squats."

"Damn it, Sunny. Why are you doing this to me? I only have so much self-control."

"You touched me. You stripped me naked and

you touched me all over. It's not fair if I can't do it to you."

"What if I don't want you to do it to me?"

"You don't?"

He wrapped his arms around her a little tighter. "I have to give my consent for this to happen. I still haven't decided yet."

His words made her smile. "Say yes, Julian. I will make you feel very good right here in this kitchen." Her hand traveled to his front and she ran her palm over this thick erection. "Please, say yes."

He groaned deeply and then opened his eyes to look at her. The arousal was undeniable. It made her throb painfully between her legs. "You're going to be the death of me."

"Say yes." She locked eyes with him. "Please say yes."

He was quiet for a moment. "Yes."

Her heart beat faster and she went to her knees before him, but a loud banging on her door startled her.

"Sunny, it's Detective Rodgers."

"And Arden and Danny," she heard another voice say.

"Let us in."

"Seriously?" she asked in a furious whisper. She stood up. "Go get dressed."

"The timing is incredible," he grumbled as he grabbed his clothes and headed to the bathroom.

"I'm coming," she called as soon as the bathroom door closed behind Julian.

She opened the door to see Detective Rodgers

standing directly in front of the door with his arms folded across his chest. "You can't live here. I would never let my kids live here. You're not living here. Your apartment got robbed and destroyed and you didn't even tell me."

"Excuse me? I'm an adult. I can live wherever I want. You can't make me move and how did you find out anyway?"

She heard the bathroom door creak open and Julian stood there looking slightly guilty. "I called him to ask him to talk some sense into you. I didn't tell him to come here."

"Sunny . . ." Arden appeared from behind Detective Rodgers and waddled toward her. "He's right. You can't stay here."

"What are you doing up? You're supposed to be on bedrest! Sit down right now."

Arden's husband shook his head and guided his heavily pregnant wife to the couch. "I told her to call, but she insisted on coming along and threatened to give birth in our living room if I didn't comply with her wishes."

"I'm fine. The doctor told me that I could start to take walks around the neighborhood."

"Yes, you can go to the store to get milk. Not travel twenty damn blocks to confront your friend."

"We drove. Stop being dramatic. I'm going to pop any day anyway and I'm ready to get this kid out of me." She looked at Sunny. "But seriously if you don't move out of this place, I'm going to give birth right here. You'll never get it out of this fabric."

Sunny shook her head in frustration. "I'm fine. I do not want to leave my apartment."

"Why didn't you tell me?"

"I didn't want to worry you." She went over to Arden and rubbed her belly.

"You didn't have to go through this alone."

"I wasn't alone. Julian was with me the entire time." She glanced back at Julian who was now only a few feet away from her.

"Julian doesn't want you to stay here," he said. "Julian doesn't like the thought of you going home alone at night. Julian will be here as long as you are here."

"You're being ridiculous. Where the hell am I supposed to go?"

"You can come stay with us," Detective Rodgers said.

"Or us," Arden spoke up.

"You are both getting ready to move. There is no way that would work."

"There's another option," Julian said softly.

"I can't live with you. That would be absolutely insane." It would be, but that didn't mean a little part of her didn't want to be with him as much as possible. They had been together for three days. She didn't want space from him. She didn't want to be alone, but that was her life.

"Not with me but in my building. My brother-in-law has a place there too. It was his bachelor pad before he married my sister. They haven't been back in almost two years. You could stay as long as you want. You can bring all your stuff."

"Are you sure that would be okay?"

"Yes. I'm sure. They pay someone to go and check on the place. You would be doing them a favor."

She shook her head. "I don't know. I'm not sure I could do that."

"You're doing it again."

"Doing what?"

"Something bad happens and you pull away instead of reaching out for help."

"I don't need help. I can handle it myself."

"Why should you have to handle it alone when I'm here to help you? When we're all here to help you?"

"I've been to ten foster homes and every time I thought maybe it would be the one that would keep me forever, but it never worked out. I always had to move and every time I did, I had to pack up my stuff in a black garbage bag and drag it to the next place. After a while you learn to stop hoping for things and keep your life moving. This is one of those things that happened and I'm just going to have to keep it moving."

Detective Rodgers swore and turned away from her.

Julian stepped closer to her and placed his hand on the back of her neck, forcing her to look him in his eyes. "That's a shitty explanation. I'm here. I'm not going anywhere. You're not going to get me to go anywhere. You're coming home with me tonight."

"You're going home with him tonight," Detective

Rodgers said. "Right now you need a father. And I'm him. I refuse to let you stay here. What's important to you? It's going to get packed right now."

"The trunk." She nodded to the leather trunk that her last foster mother had given to her when she first arrived. It was the first place she had to store her belongings. She knew she wasn't going to win this argument.

"Do you need to put anything in it?"

"No. It's packed."

"Come on, gentlemen. Let's put this in Julian's car."

They left Arden and Sunny alone and as soon as they did, Arden smacked her arm. "What the hell is going on with you and Julian?"

"I don't know. I might fall in love with him." She sat back and sighed.

"You're not in love with him already?"

"We're supposed to be working together, but somehow we became friends and he offered to go with me to Detective Rodgers's retirement party and somehow I ended up in his closet asking him to help me zip up my dress. And somehow he ended up stripping it off of me and giving me the most intense orgasm that I've ever had."

Arden gasped. "Did you have sex with him?"

"No. And it's not because I don't want to. He looks at me and I melt. In fact, you all showed up at the exact wrong moment."

"We interrupted you? Oh no! I'm so sorry. He looks like he would be so good in bed."

"It would be a mistake to sleep with him."

"Why? The way he looks at you . . . It's rare to find a man who'll look at a woman like that."

"We have to work together on a very important case and he has an ex that is still in love with him. They'll probably end up together."

"They won't. Don't think that way. Even if it doesn't last forever or even very long, allow yourself to fall in love, to feel that rush. You always hold yourself back. Why don't you try giving yourself away to it?"

Because she'd had her heart broken before. She didn't know if she could survive a heartbreak with him.

Chapter II

Julian hung up the phone in his office and rubbed his forehead. A very important case had landed on his desk. One of his clients was being charged with assault with a deadly weapon. A reality television star who found her husband in bed with a nanny and then proceeded to chase him down the street in her car. She only bumped him, causing him to fracture his ankle, so it wasn't attempted murder, but, still, his client was facing serious time.

She was expecting him to get her out of jail time. He probably could. He'd had a similar outcome in a case like this before, but this time he didn't feel like doing all the legal maneuvering it would take to convince a judge that she needed counseling over jailtime. She was guilty. Thanks to cell phone video, the whole damn Internet had seen the incident.

He had a lot of long hours ahead of him to win this case, but he was having a hard time concentrating this week. Sunny had moved into his brother-in-law's apartment a week ago. She was just a few floors away from him, but he hadn't seen her once.

He knew she had been just as busy as he was. Another letter had come from Soren's mother. It was more of the same. Promises that they were going to be reunited along with additional cash. The Earls were understandably terrified. Julian hadn't made much progress on the case. He was fairly sure if it came down to a custody battle that the Earls would win. He had been researching family law. Soren's mother had abandoned her. He had no problem destroying her in the courtroom, but he needed more information. More about her past.

But part of him didn't want to drag Soren through that. She was a sweet kid who had been through too much. He thought it might be better to be proactive. To stop her in her tracks before this turned uglier than it had to be.

He had texted with Sunny daily. But he hadn't gotten the chance to speak to her. Work had been busy for her. Arden had her baby. A boy that she and her husband had named Flynn. Sunny had sent him a picture of her holding the baby. She was beaming. He had never seen her so happy. He wished he could see that expression on her face all the time. He pulled out his cellphone and looked at it again. He found himself doing that a lot these past few days. He had wanted to hear her voice and see her face and have her in his presence. But he had stayed away, or maybe she had stayed away from him.

The attraction was there. It was strong and if she

were anyone else he would have taken her to bed a long time ago. But there was something more with her. Something confusing and intense and there was a friendship too. He just didn't want to know her body; he wanted to know her.

He picked up his cell phone and called her, unable to stop himself.

"Mr. King." She picked up on the second ring. "It must be important if you're calling me."

"What if I told you I just wanted to hear your voice?"

She was quiet for a long moment. He hadn't meant to say that, but it was what fell from his lips.

"I would say you're full of crap."

"How are you settling in?"

"It's a gorgeous apartment on Central Park. I could die tomorrow and be fulfilled."

"That's not true. There has to be more you want out of life."

"You're right. I want Indian food for dinner. Will you have it with me?"

"Yes. You want to go out or stay in?"

"In. I have to go make a home visit for a difficult parent. I think I'm going to be too wiped out to deal with a restaurant."

"Okay. Meet me at my place at eight."

"Will you let me buy the food?"

"Don't ask questions you already know the answer to."

"You're such a bully." He could hear the smile in her voice. "I know you didn't call me just to talk. What's wrong, Julian?"

"I was thinking about Soren's mother. Where did this new letter come from?"

"It was postmarked from Maryland. All the letters have come from towns in Maryland or South Carolina."

"I looked up the population of Hope. It's very small. You think someone might know her there?"

"Maybe. But we don't know what name she's going by. We don't know what she looks like. How can we find her?"

"We can go down there and start asking questions. Somebody had to have missed Soren. There has to be a family for her somewhere."

"I always wondered the same thing about myself. How could my mother just disappear without anyone missing her or me?"

"Did you ever find out what happened to your mother?"

"No," she said quietly.

"Don't you want to know?"

"Very badly, but a large part of me is afraid to find out."

Julian's office door opened and his boss, Mr. Bruno, walked in. "I've got to go, Sunny. My boss is here. I'll see you tonight."

"You will. I'm buying dessert and you can't stop me." She disconnected before he could say anything else and again he found himself smiling.

"Hello, sir. How are you?"

"I'm good. But I'm always good. Just wanted to have a little chat with you."

"Of course, sir. Please sit down."

Bruno eased himself into the chair in front of Julian's desk. "You were talking to Sunny? There's still a thing between you two?"

"We're good friends and we're working on this case together. I see her fairly often."

"You can drop this professional bullshit. We both know that if the girl had no tits and a flat ass you wouldn't have looked at her twice."

Julian's fists clenched and unclenched in his lap. This was his boss. He couldn't knock him on his bloated ass.

"I don't feel comfortable speaking about Sunny like this. She's not just a woman off the street. She came to the firm for help with an important case. Mr. Cleese was the one who asked me to help her. The way she looks has nothing to do with anything."

"You're good." He grinned at Julian. "You never drop the act. Not even with me. I don't have a stick up my ass like my partner. You know you can let loose with me."

"It's not an act, sir."

"You know Regina called me. We go back a long way. This firm has been representing her company for years. She has grown a nice little empire."

"Regina's a great businesswoman."

"She asked about you. Wanted to know what was going on."

"There is nothing going on. We are no longer seeing each other."

"I think that's the problem. She played it very cool on the phone because far be it from Regina to show actual emotion, but the fact that she asked about you is very telling. She's got it bad for you."

"I have nothing to say to that. We aren't seeing each other anymore."

"It wouldn't be a good thing if she pulled her business from our firm. Why don't you give her a little attention until she finds someone else to occupy her time? It would bring you one step closer to getting where you want to go in your career."

"Losing her business would be a big loss to the firm but I represent every major athlete in the tristate area as well as some of the biggest music producers in the country. I keep this firm's name in the papers and I win cases. How often do we work for Regina? My clients keep us busy the entire year."

"Are you threatening to leave and take your clients with you?"

"No. I'm just pointing out the things that make me an asset to this firm. Sleeping with the clients is not one of them."

Bruno stood up. The master litigator didn't seem to have an argument for that one. "Just keep your head in the game. You've been a little distracted lately. You're paying clients get first priority. Don't ever forget that."

Julian sat at his desk staring at his computer screen for a long time. He was more distracted now than he had been.

His boss, the man who had a huge say in the next step in his career, said he was distracted. He wanted to say it was unfounded bullshit, but was it? He hadn't seen Sunny in a week. He had barely worked on her case and yet he was distracted by her.

But why? He wasn't sleeping with her. He hadn't kissed her lips yet. And then there was Regina in the background. They had been on and off for years. The had both dated other people in the meanwhile. Maybe she thought that this time wasn't any different than the last time. But there was a difference. They weren't moving forward. He needed to go forward. He had wanted to be partner at the firm, and to have a life partner. But he wasn't so sure about that anymore.

What the hell did he want?

He needed to close things with Regina for good. Nothing else hanging in the air. He wasn't sure what his future was going to look like but he was sure that wasn't going to include her.

He needed to call her, but he didn't pick up his phone. He buried his head in his work instead. The direct line to his office phone rang. Usually, all calls went through his assistant. He answered it to hear an unfamiliar voice.

"Hello, Mr. King?"

"Speaking."

"This is Maxine, Sunny's supervisor. We need you to come down to Manhattan Hospital. Sunny needs—"

He didn't wait for her to finish the sentence. "I'm on my way." He grabbed his keys and his cell phone and ran out of there as fast as humanly possible.

* * *

Sunny kept looking at the deep red smear on the skirt of her dress. It was her white sundress, the one with the pretty little flowers on it. She had loved this dress, but now it was ruined, covered in drying blood that she would never get out. She kept focusing on that spot because she didn't want to think about anything else. Like how the blood had gotten there, or the child who was going to be traumatized for the rest of his life.

"Sunny!" She heard a deep, familiar voice yelling her name and when she looked up, she saw Julian rushing across the ER toward her. There was terror on his face as he approached. She had asked Maxine to call him to ask if he could send someone over with a change of clothes for her. But he came and he looked so scared. Her heart squeezed.

She stood up, realizing that she looked like she had been through a war. "It's not my blood. I didn't mean for you to leave work. I just needed some clothes." She felt herself start to tremble and tried to stop herself but she couldn't. "I'm just here as a precaution. They cleaned the blood off my skin to make sure I didn't have any open cuts." Her voice broke. She stopped speaking. She was dangerously close to crying. She hadn't cried in years. But having him there before her was rocking her foundation.

He took her face in his hands and kissed her forehead. "Let's go home. I'll run you a bath. We'll order dinner early."

"Don't you have to go back to work?"

"No." He shook his head. "I'm where I have to be."

* * *

Sunny went back to Julian's house and just like he said, he ran her a bath filled with warm, soapy water. He didn't seem to care that she got in his beautiful car covered in someone else's blood. He didn't pepper her with questions. He was just there. It was exactly what she needed right then. He was exactly what she needed.

She left his bathroom to find him waiting for her near the door. The worried look never left his face and she felt bad that she had put him through that. "I'm fine, Jules. I promise. You don't have to look at me like that."

He shook his head and grabbed her hips pulling her into his chest. "You're crying."

"No. I'm not."

He took his thumb and swiped it over her cheek. "Yes."

It was then she noticed her cheeks were hot and wet. She was crying. She hadn't cried since her final foster mother's funeral. But she was weeping and she couldn't stop herself.

"Oh, God." She gave a watery laugh. "Tell me to stop."

"Why would I do that? You need to cry." He pulled her head to his chest and smoothed his hand down her back.

"You haven't even asked me what happened."

"You'll tell me when you feel it's right. I just needed to know that you weren't the one who was hurt."

"I went on a surprise home visit to see a parent who has been dodging me for weeks. I've gone to that house a half dozen times and she was never there. But this time when I knocked on the door I saw that it was slightly open and when I walked inside I saw little bloody footprints leading to the bathroom. My client's mother had slit her wrist. There was blood everywhere. He had tried to help her."

"Where was the boy?"

"In the closet. He was hiding, terrified because he didn't know what had happened to his mother. He was covered in her blood and I know the protocol. I know I wasn't supposed to touch him, but he's five and he burst into tears when he saw me and I picked him up and I held him until the police and EMTs came. I stayed with him until they took him to emergency foster care."

"I'm so sorry that happened to you, baby." He kissed the side of her face. "I'm glad you were there for that child. You probably saved him."

"I should have gone yesterday," she whispered. "I could have stopped it."

"Don't. Don't think that way. Don't do that to yourself. I know you tried your best. I know you always go the extra mile for every child. Look at what you're doing for Soren."

His words were meant to comfort her, but they made her feel guilty. Yes, she wanted to make sure Soren stayed with the people who were best suited to raise her, but she was also so invested in Soren's case for herself. Because she needed to follow this crazy thread or it would eat at her. It was selfish.

"Come sit down." He took her hand and led her to the couch. "I ordered almost the entire menu. I have a fully stocked bar. We're going to watch ridiculous movies tonight and laugh and relax."

He wiped the tears that were still rolling down her cheeks. She couldn't stop herself.

"Something came for you today."

"Something came for me?"

"Yes." He walked away from her and into his kitchen where he retrieved a small white box off the counter. "Open it," he said, handing it to her.

She looked up at him suspiciously.

"It won't bite you."

She ripped open the box and her eyes became so full of tears she could no longer see. "How . . ." She took out a barrette. It was very similar to the one that had been destroyed the night of the robbery, but it was gorgeous. Her mother's barrette was simple, cheap, purchased from a flea market for a few dollars. But this one much more than that.

"I have a client who's a jeweler. I sent him the pieces of the barrette and asked him what he could do. There's something else in the box."

She looked again. There was a little jade Buddha.

"I found it when we were moving things out of your place. I had them turn it into a keychain so you can always have it with you."

Her chest heaved painfully. She fell all the way in love with him that moment. She had been fighting it for weeks, but it was no use. He wouldn't let her not love him. He was doing everything possible to make her love him.

She left the couch and threw her arms around him, crying a little harder than before. He hugged her tightly. "You like it? I was nervous about giving it to you."

"Why? It's the most thoughtful thing anyone has ever done for me."

"I didn't want you to think that I was trying to replace your memories of her. I know how upset you were that night. I wanted to make it a little better."

"You're better to me than I think I deserve."

"No, I'm not." He cupped her face in his hands and kissed her. It was the first time their lips had met, which seemed insane. They had shared a bed. He had seen her naked body. He had been with her in her toughest moments yet this was the first time. She shut her eyes. His lips were warm and smooth. The kiss was soft at first, but it was intense. Her heart started to race. Her body went slack, all thoughts in her head stopped. His kiss felt like coming home. His kiss felt like comfort and warmth and safety. His kiss made her want to remove all barriers between them. His kiss was *the* kiss. She didn't think she would ever experience one like it again with anyone else. She would probably never be in love like this again.

"Damn it." He broke this kiss, his eyes still half closed. "You can't kiss me like that."

"*You* kissed *me*."

"I know." He kissed the corner of her lips and

then across her jawline. "But I was hoping your lips
would be dry and nasty and that you would stand
there like a dead fish. You aren't supposed to kiss
me with everything inside of you."

"Why?" She found herself smiling.

"Because my fears have come true. I don't think
I'll ever be able to stop kissing you."

He kissed her again, but there was more heat
behind it this time, more power. His tongue swept
into her mouth, his hands slipped under the T-shirt
he had given her to sleep in.

She had missed him this week. She had pur-
posely stayed away, kept herself busy because she
knew it would be too easy to go upstairs and see
him. Each day she had spent with him she had
fallen more in love. Being in love wasn't good for
her. For her love never lasted forever. People weren't
forever.

She had always thought that. She had held on to
that to prevent anyone from getting too close.

But Arden had been in her life for so long. And
Detective Rodgers. They both loved her. Maybe,
possibly, love wasn't fleeting. Love could stay
around, but she didn't want to get her hopes up.

Her heartbreak would be just as intense as her
love for him.

He wiped the remaining tears from her face
just as there was a knock at the door. "It's probably the doorman with the food. Go make yourself
comfortable."

* * *

Julian walked toward the door still feeling her kiss. He had waited so long for that moment. He had never waited this long to kiss a woman. He had never waited so long to take one to bed, but her kiss was worth it. Her kiss made him feel things that he had never felt before. Her kiss confused the hell out of him. He wanted more of them. More of her.

He couldn't stay away.

He opened the door to see Regina standing on the other side of it. He quickly stepped outside and shut it behind him. "Regina . . . What are you doing here?"

"I stopped by your office and your assistant told me you had an emergency and you left early. You never leave early so I was concerned and thought I would check on you. Is everything okay?"

"It will be. The doorman didn't tell me you were here."

"He just let me up. I have been coming here for years. He told me that there was a woman staying in your brother-in-law's apartment. I thought it was your sister at first. But I should have known better. She's in there, isn't she? The girl? She was your emergency."

He nodded. "I'm not sure this is a good time to talk."

"When is? Every time I see you you're with her."

"I'm not sure what to say to you. There's nothing left for us," he said softly. "I'm sorry. I handled this wrong. This isn't like the other times."

"I just don't understand. You went from wanting to spend the rest of your life with me to being completely done. And I only think it's because you met this girl."

"We're friends."

"Don't tell me you are friends with her. I saw the way you were looking at her that night of the party. There's no way you are just friends. Don't you dare insult my intelligence."

"I didn't say we were just friends. But we are friends. She's my best friend, Regina. It's not about sex or power or trying to climb some stupid ladder. We're there for each other."

"Are you saying I'm not there for you?"

"Yes, and I wasn't there for you, either. We are intimate strangers. You have never let your guard down with me. I haven't even seen you without makeup."

"Are you saying this is my fault?"

"No. I'm not blaming you. But at some point, one of us had to be the one to end this, to realize that this isn't going anywhere. Even if we ignored everything that was wrong with us and got married, do you think we would be happy five years down the road?"

"You can't say that we won't be. We both enjoy the finer things in life. We can debate anything. We can move up together in this world."

"But would you still love me if I went broke? Would you have looked at me twice if I didn't work at that law firm? If I had tried to be with you as a football player, would you have accepted me?"

She opened her mouth to speak but no words came out.

"What if I never even made it to the pro's? What if I was a cop? Or a teacher? Or a limo driver? Would you still want me then?"

"Don't talk about what-ifs. There are no what-ifs. There is only what is."

"The answer is no."

"So, you think that girl would love you with nothing? You're throwing this away for her? Let me be the first to tell you that she would disappear within the blink of an eye if you didn't have all this. The fact that she weaseled her way into your home already should give you a clue. How could you be so stupid? I can build you up. She will only bring you down."

"This isn't about her. This was never about her. This is about you and me." And he knew without a doubt that Sunny would be there for him if he were poor. She would give him her last dollar. She would take care of him. Not just physically, but emotionally. There weren't many things he was sure of, but he was sure of her.

"I don't believe you."

"What if I told you I wanted to move out of the city? That I wanted to give this all up for a simpler life. That I wanted a big family with lots of kids and a big dog? Could you do that for me?"

"Are you insane? I worked too damn hard to get where I am to give it up for some man."

"Some man? I would be the man you married. Your husband. Your life partner. And I'm not asking you to give up anything. You would still have your company. I would be asking you to build a different kind of life. But in the end, I know you wouldn't be happy so I wouldn't ask that of you. But if we can't weather small changes, I can't see how we could get through major ones."

"I don't believe that you want to give all of this up."

"I'm not sure what I want." He was quiet for a moment. He was on track to become partner. That meant more power. More prestige. That would mean he finally made it and no one could doubt his skills or call him a token ever again. "But I do want a family someday. I want to be closer to my family. And I want a wife who wants to give me children. Those things are very important to me."

The door creaked open and Sunny appeared wrapped in the bathrobe that he kept in the guest bathroom. "I'm so sorry to interrupt," she said quietly. "The doorman called up. The food is here. I'm going to go down and get it and then I'm going to stay downstairs. You shouldn't have this conversation in the hallway. Regina deserves more than that."

"No. Absolutely not. I don't want you to be alone tonight."

"I'm fine. You've done enough for me today." She touched his cheek and then seemed to have thought better of it. "Thank you for everything."

He watched her get on the elevator and everything inside of him screamed not to let her go.

"She's been crying," Regina said.

"Yes. One of her clients killed herself. Sunny was the one to find her body and her son. I had to pick her up from the hospital today. She was covered in blood."

"That's terrible."

"She has a very tough job. She tries to save everyone and never thinks about taking care of herself."

"She's one of those altruistic do-gooders. Your sister told me that you once were thinking of becoming a civil rights attorney. Fighting for the little guy instead of getting people with too much money on their hands out of scrapes. She said you'd almost forgotten what it was like to be with normal people and she wasn't sure you were better for it. She was taking a dig at me. But there was truth in what you said. Maybe you don't have it in you to build an empire. Not because you're not capable, but because you're not hungry enough for it."

But he was hungry for it. Or he had been. Just a little while ago. He was so damn confused. "Is that why you said no to me the first time I asked you?"

She shook her head. "I'm not exactly sure why I said no. I wanted you to love me. I wanted it to be different, but maybe I wanted something I knew that you could never give me." She started walking away and he saw the hurt in her eyes; even though it was hidden well, the hurt was there and he didn't like that he was the one who caused it.

"I'm sorry, Regina."

"I am too." The elevator came and she got on it and as soon as the doors closed Julian ran down the four flights of stairs to Sunny's apartment. She was standing in the kitchen in front of the large bag of food she had just brought up.

"What are you doing here? I thought you were talking to her."

"We're done. There's nothing left to say."

"You didn't have to come down. I would have been fine."

"I'm here. I'm not going away."

She nodded and he could feel that whatever they had upstairs before Regina came was gone.

Julian kept his word and stayed with her that evening. She hadn't wanted him to stay. She felt like he was doing it out of obligation, because she had cried and showed him her most vulnerable side. He had felt sorry for her and that was the last thing she wanted from him.

She had just started to feel . . . feel . . . she couldn't describe the way she was feeling about them. She loved him. Her body wanted to be near him. Her heart couldn't help but to feel connected to him. Then Regina showed up and it felt like someone had thrown cold water in her face. She hadn't heard much of their conversation. Only muffled voices through the door and when the doorman called, she had stood rooted to her spot for a few minutes, afraid to get any closer, afraid that she would be infringing on their privacy. But she knew she shouldn't be there while he was speaking to the woman he had been planning to marry. She knew she was in the way; that he wouldn't be able to fully engage with Regina if any part of him was focused on her on the other side of the door.

So she left, but he followed her not ten minutes after and they ate dinner together and they watched funny movies and they chatted about the most inane things but nothing lifted her spirits.

She had pretended for him because she didn't want him to feel obligated to her anymore. She had sent him upstairs around eleven, claiming exhaustion, but she couldn't sleep that night. Because every time she closed her eyes she saw that bloody, terrified little boy and his lifeless mother, naked and half submerged in a tub of water. And when she wasn't thinking about them, she was looking at the pained looks on Julian's and Regina's faces when she walked in on their conversation.

He had said he didn't love her, but there must have been some love there. No one stayed with a person they didn't love for so long.

Sunny got out of bed at five-thirty when she couldn't stand the barrage of thoughts any longer. There was a message from Maxine on her phone ordering her not to come in that day. She almost ignored the directive because the thought of staying alone in an apartment that didn't even really belong to her sounded worse than going in and trying to help someone else.

That was how she coped with things. When she was a kid she threw herself into her studies and as an adult she buried herself in her work. But today she was too tired, too shell shocked. If she couldn't give all of herself to her clients she shouldn't even bother going in.

There was a knock on the door just as she was

starting the coffeepot. She jumped, but went to it anyway looking through the peephole to see Julian standing on the other side. She let him in. He looked exhausted too.

"I knew you'd be up."

"You're not planning to invite me on your early morning workout, are you? Because if you are I'm about to tell you where to take your invitation and shove it."

He grinned at her. "No. How are you feeling today?"

"Raw," she said. There was no other word for it. She was feeling like a scrape that wouldn't heal. She hated that feeling. It seemed so much of her childhood was spent feeling that way.

The remainder of the grin melted off his face. "I'm here because I know you didn't sleep last night."

"How do you know?"

"I know you. I know when you're lying to me. I couldn't sleep either."

"Were you thinking about your conversation with Regina?"

"No." He took a step forward and grabbed her by her hips. "I was thinking about you." He wrapped his arms around her. "All night. I'm sorry about Regina."

"Why should you be sorry? You don't owe me anything. You needed to have that conversation."

"Yes. I did, but I wish it hadn't happened last night." She hated herself for loving the way his arms felt around her, how little tingles broke out all over her skin. She was so close to him, but she wanted to get closer. She slipped her hands up the back of his shirt, running her hands across his muscled back.

"Everything is resolved now?"

"Yes. She thinks you're the reason we aren't getting back together."

"Oh? You told her that wasn't true, right?"

"I did, but I was lying."

She swallowed hard and looked up at him.

"You confuse the hell out of me and make me question everything I have worked for these past ten years and then there's the fact that I want you so much it hurts."

"Julian . . . What the hell are you saying to me?"

"I don't know." He shook his head. "My life is very different since you walked into it and I'm not sure if I like it."

"Then why are you here?"

"I took the day off. I want to spend it with you."

He said he was confused, but he was confusing her. Was she just a distraction for him? A rebound? A place holder until he found what he was looking for?

He cupped her face, tipped her head back, and kissed her. His mouth was warm and searching. It was easy to get lost in his kiss and she almost did, but she pulled away from him and looked into his very beautiful green eyes. "You're not allowed to hurt me or toy with me or use me. I'm not interchangeable just because you got bored with someone else."

He seemed surprised by her comment. "I would never toy with you and of course you're not interchangeable or somebody I'm just passing the time with. You're my friend, Sunny, and I don't ever want to hurt you. But I'm very attracted to you and no matter what I do it doesn't seem to change."

"So what happens now?"

"You take me into your bedroom and . . ." Her breath caught and her heart started pounding. She wanted to feel him on top of her, inside of her. His lips. His hands. His breath. It all turned her on. It all made her throb between her legs. "Go back to sleep."

"Sleep?"

"You need to rest."

"I won't be able to." She stepped back slightly and placed her hand between them, running her hand over his erection. It was hot beneath the fabric and long, traveling down his thigh. He was a very large, very successful, very gorgeous man and he must have been with dozens of women. She wasn't sure she would live up to them.

"I can barely concentrate with this thing touching me. How do you suggest I sleep with it pressed into my back?"

"I was hoping you wouldn't notice. I wasn't going to try anything with you."

"But who said I wasn't going to try anything with you?" She slipped her hand inside of the workout shorts he was wearing and pulled him out. She swallowed hard, intimidated by the weight, length, and sheer beauty of him.

"What are you thinking?" His voice was strained. She heard how heavy his breathing had become. "You looked scared."

"I'm thinking a lot of things." She stroked him with both of her hands. "Does it hurt to be this hard?"

"Yes, but I've become accustomed to it since knowing you."

"You don't have to feel discomfort. You could find any woman you want and get them to come home with you."

"I don't do that." He placed his hand over hers and guided her on how to stroke him.

She lifted her lips and set a gentle kiss on his lips. "You make me feel . . . So damn good."

"What else were you thinking?"

"That I wasn't sure if I could satisfy you and that no wonder Regina wanted you back. If you turned her on half as much as you turn me on, the poor woman is going to need an intervention."

She went down on her knees before him and ran her tongue up his shaft. The heat of him was warming her face. "Only you can satisfy me because you are the only one that I want."

She wrapped her lips around him and took him into her mouth. He buried his fingers in her curls and let out a guttural moan. She felt power in this. Power to make him feel good. Power to make his control slip. Her sexual experiences were incredibly limited. In college, she had been touched by boys. In adulthood, she had been kissed by men but that was it. She didn't feel comfortable enough, safe enough to let her guard down. She wasn't naïve. She knew about sex, about pleasure. She wanted to give it. She wanted to receive it. But she had been violated before. She wanted to choose who she shared this with.

Julian grabbed her hand and pulled her up. "But wait. I wasn't done."

"But I will be far too soon, if you keep doing that."

"That's the whole point, Julian. I want to make you feel good. I want to do this just for you."

"Don't do this for any man who won't do it for you."

He pulled her underwear down, pushed her against the nearest wall and went down on his knees. He tossed her leg over his shoulder, opening her to him. He looked up at her for a moment before he put his mouth between her legs. He licked the length of her and if his hands weren't on her hips she would have slipped down the wall and dissolved in a puddle of mush. "You taste good." He licked again, deeper this time. It couldn't be possible for any woman to be this aroused. "Tell me what you like," he said, kissing her there. "I want to do all those things to you."

She could barely speak. Barely make sense of things in her mind. "I like you, Julian. I like everything that you do."

He rose and crushed his mouth to hers. The kiss was so intense, so passionate that she needed it to go on forever. He made her feel so good all the time. She just wanted to return the favor, but he had bested her again. She reached for his erection and began to stroke him. No slow, exploring strokes, but ones that matched the intensity of their kiss.

But Julian King wasn't satisfied with that. He was the type of man who went pleasure for pleasure. He lifted her up and took her to the couch, laying them both down so that they were on their sides, their bodies touching. He wrapped her leg around his hip and slipped two fingers inside of her while his thumb caressed her nub.

"Julian," she moaned.

"Keep kissing me." She did what he asked, giving him the deepest kisses she could manage all while sliding her hand up and down his powerful erection. She had never been this intimate with anyone. She wished she could have felt this sooner, had met him sooner. But if she had, she might not have been ready for it, ready for him.

She was trying to hold off her orgasm to make the feeling last longer, but she couldn't hold it off anymore. He was too much. His taste, his scent, his touch were too much for her senses and she couldn't keep control. She broke the kiss and cried out and he shuddered against her, a warm wetness seeping into her hand.

He gathered her closer and kissed her forehead and her cheeks and then her lips and she wanted to cry again. She was still feeling too raw, but it was a beautiful moment and she wouldn't forget it. It was a beautiful moment that she wanted to repeat over and over again.

"Alex had a Jacuzzi room built here in his single days. Have you been in it yet?"

"No."

"Good. I think it's something we should try together."

Chapter 12

Julian woke up next to Sunny a few hours later. She was cuddled into him, buried beneath the blankets in the guest bedroom. His sister and brother-in-law hadn't been to this apartment in years. They had given their permission for her to use it as if it were her own, but she chose to stay in the smaller guest room. She didn't want to be in the way even when there was no possible way she could.

She should have her own home. A real home. Not some small rented place. But he knew it would be nearly impossible to do on her own. It would be so easy for him to give her that. Whatever she wanted. She didn't seem to want much of anything. But she needed more. She needed to be loved. She needed to be taken care of. Not with money or things. Her soul needed it. That he wasn't so sure he could do. He could have married Regina because she could take care of herself. She never displayed her feelings. She never revealed herself to him. But with Sunny . . . She was strong and fragile. She was caring and sweet and loving and the thought of having all of her or being responsible for her happiness was overwhelming. His life was not for her. The hours. The intensity of his job. His drive for something greater. She deserved a nice husband with a quiet life and a handful of kids. He could see her being a mother. There was so much love inside of her.

He didn't want to hurt her. She warned him not to hurt her. But what if he did? What if in a few years he decided that he didn't want that kind of life? What if he got bored? What if he wanted something different?

The pressure of being with her was too much. He wanted to make love to her and in a way, he did that morning, but he couldn't join his body with hers in that ultimate way. Sex had never had that much meaning for him, but with her it would. With her it would mean something. And once he crossed that line with her, he was committing himself to being with her.

"I know I should get up," she said softly. "But I don't think my bones are functioning."

"It was the Jacuzzi. I've never seen anyone so delighted to be in one."

"I've never been in one."

"No?"

"I don't often get to live in the third homes of professional football players."

"You've never been to a resort with a Jacuzzi?"

"No. I've only been on little trips. Weekend girls'

getaways. I've always wanted to go to an island though. Or maybe just back to the ocean. I have a very clear memory of my mother and I going to a quiet beach when I was little. We used to spend hours there and I would lay next to her with my eyes closed and the sun beating down on my face. I've been to the beaches here, but it just hasn't been the same. The water is different. The sand is different. It's just different. I felt so happy then."

"How old were you?"

"Maybe four. It's before Mama got sick."

"You remember when she got sick?"

"Yes. Clearly. It was like a before and after picture. We had a house and a routine and security and then we were driving cross country and living out of a car. And then moving from motels and shitty apartments every other month. It was like paradise and hell. There was no in between."

"And yet you tell me she loved you and that you still love her."

"She did love me, Jules. And I loved her so much because I can't forget how happy things used to be. She was paranoid. But everything she did was to protect me. I just didn't need that kind of protection."

"I'll take you to the beach."

"When?" she asked with a delicious smile.

"Today. Any one you would like? I can get a helicopter."

"Forget about the helicopter. Let's get a private jet and go to Bora Bora."

She was joking, but he was serious. He could fly them to the Hamptons for the day. He had so many football playing friends with second or third homes out there. It would be easy for him. "Bora Bora is a long flight. We could go to Puerto Rico. They have beautiful beaches. We could eat really good food. Have drinks right in the pool. I'm serious. We could go."

"Julian King." She kissed his cheek. "I don't want you to take me to Puerto Rico. I would be happy to go to Coney Island though. Maybe eat a couple of hot dogs. In fact, I would be happy just to eat anything right now."

His cell phone began to ring from his shorts that had been tossed on the chair when they came in the room.

"I'll get it for you." Sunny popped out of bed wearing a tiny nightie that she had put on after they had gotten out of the bath. It was short and white and so well-worn that it was nearly see-through. He grew hard again. He willed his body to behave because he had just talked himself out of taking that step with her, and yet in the next moment, he was planning to sweep her away.

She handed him his phone and he saw that it was his baby sister calling.

"Hey, snot face sister."

"How are you, my stupid smelly brother? I called your office line first."

"I'm taking a day off."

Sunny kissed the side of his neck. "I'm going to give you some privacy," she whispered.

He wrapped his free arm around her. "You don't have to go. I'm in your bed."

"I'll make coffee. Talk to your sister. Family is important."

She walked out and Julian watched her, having a hard time taking his eyes off of her.

"Where are you? Could have sworn you just told a woman that you were in her bed."

"I'm in your husband's former bachelor pad."

"With the friend you asked if we minded stayed there for a while?"

"Yes. I told you about Sunny."

"I had originally thought Sunny was a boy Sonny until we got a handwritten note, a dozen brownies, and a rent check with sunflowers on it."

"She paid you rent? I told her she didn't have to. Everything she owned worth anything was destroyed and now she is paying rent to the two of you."

"I'm sure she doesn't want us to think she's a mooch. Who is she, Julian? Mom told me you were with her when she called a couple of weeks ago. She asked me about her and for once I couldn't rat you out."

How could he describe who Sunny was to him? She wasn't his girlfriend, or a fling, or a lover. But she wasn't just a friend either. She was important to him. He cared about her. "It's none of Mom's business who she is."

"She wants to know about your life, Jules. She wants you to be happy. And she's trying. How long are you going to punish her?"

"Sunny said the same thing. I'm not punishing her. I just can't forgive her and I don't know how you can."

"She's my mother and sometimes I think the best thing she could have done for us was leave. Remember how Dad used to work all the time before she left? He cut back his hours and stopped working weekends. He ate dinner with us every night. He took us on long vacations. He was at every single game, recital, and parent-teacher conference. We may not have had a mother who could take care of us but we had a father who did, and we had a better childhood than most people in this world."

"I guess you got me there. She made Dad a better father by being a terrible mother."

Galen made a soft noise. "What else did Sunny say about Mom?"

"Sunny has no family so she thinks that I should make the effort to fix things with Mom."

"She has no family?"

"She grew up in foster care and then became one of those bleeding heart social workers, so of course she would suggest fixing things with Mom."

"She sounds smart, Jules."

"She is."

"Who is she to you?" Galen wouldn't let it go. She needed a definition. He wasn't sure he could give her one.

"She's my friend. She's my good friend and I care about her very much."

"And what about Regina? I'm sure she wouldn't be happy about you being friends with another woman."

"We're done. For good."

"Good. I hate her."

"I know."

"I really hate her. Like so damn much."

"I know."

"She is the worst person for you. She makes you pompous and uptight. She would skin puppies for their coats and the fact that you spent so long with her makes me like you a little less."

"Galen, did you call just to insult me?"

"Yes." He could imagine the mischievous smile on his sister's face. He missed her. She was the closest person to him when they were growing up and now that she was married, he rarely got to see her. "What other reason would I have for speaking to you? I want to see you. It's been too long. I miss my stupid big brother."

"I want to see you but I've got cases piling up."

"You always have cases piling up. You can't take a long weekend to see your sister? Daddy will be coming down to Fripp Island this summer. He has a lady friend he's been seeing. He told me he wants me to meet her. I think it's very serious. They are looking at houses."

"What? Dad is seriously dating someone? Why didn't he tell me?" He was sure his father had seen women over the years, but he had never shared that part of his life with them. Julian was positive his father would never risk love again. Never remarry. But apparently it was a possibility.

"When is the last time you spoke to him for more than five minutes? He didn't want to share something like that with you in one of your famous rushed conversations. The only reason I get to speak

to you for this long is because you took off work. I
think I have Sunny to thank for that."

And apparently he was too busy to know what
was going on in the lives of the people he cared the
most about. He didn't feel good about that. In fact,
he felt like the world's biggest asshole.

"Alex and I are going to be at the house on the
island until he gets cleared to go back and play. You
have the rest of the summer to come see us. I'm not
asking you to make any promises, but I'm asking
you to try. Alex and I have some things we want to
talk to you about."

"What kind of things?"

"Just things. Try to come down."

"Okay. I will." He would. He would have to make
some time. He had told Regina that his family was
important to him and he had seen less of them because of her. Maybe because he knew they would
never accept her. Maybe because being around
them reminded him of who he once was and made
him forget who he wanted to be.

"And bring Sunny too."

"Galen . . . It's not like that."

"Oh, but I think it is."

Sunny walked back into the room with two mugs
of coffee in her hands. Julian looked so damn
beautiful sitting up in bed shirtless and completely
relaxed. He was going to break her heart. She knew
it just by looking at him. He wasn't for her. Not in
the long run. They both knew it. After this case was

over they were going to be done. It was for the best.
But for now she was going to enjoy him. Enjoy this
beautiful rare day she had off.

He put his phone on the nightstand. "You didn't
have to bring this to me. I would have come out."

"I wanted to do something nice for you for a
change."

He took the mugs from her and put them down
on the nightstand as well and then he reached for
her, pulling her on top of him. "You do nice things
for me."

"Like what?" She wrapped her arms around him
and rested her head on his strong chest.

"You like me."

"Lots of people like you. You're a good man."

"That's not true. My colleagues hate me. They
think I don't deserve to work at my firm. The only
value my boss sees in me is my former career. But
you just like me. If I had none of this, you would
still like me."

"You're unhappy." She looked up at him, realizing
it for the first time. "Your job makes you unhappy. If
you don't feel like you're being valued then find
someplace that will give you more satisfaction."

"I'm not unhappy. I just want more. I want to
prove to them that I'm good enough and by making
partner, no one can doubt that. I'll have everything that I have been working so hard toward for
the past twelve years."

"Are you sure you'll be happy after you get there
or will it just be more of the same?"

"I don't know, Sunny. But I've come this far. I

can't give it up right now. How many people who look like me and came from where I did get to be a partner at one of the top firms in the country?"

If that's what he wanted, then that's what she wanted for him. To be happy. To be fulfilled. To feel like he left an indelible mark on the world. "I know you'll make partner soon. But if you decide that it's not for you there's no shame in leaving. You don't have to prove anything to anyone."

He cupped her face in his large hands and kissed her so incredibly deep. It was painful to love him so much. "We need to get dressed now because if we don't get out of this bed soon I'm going to want to stay all day."

"What if that's what I want, Julian?"

He looked at her for a long moment. She could see the arousal in his eyes, feel it pressed against her. "We rarely get the day off. Let's see more than these four walls."

He took her on a lunch cruise up the Hudson River. Sunny had never been on a boat before. She couldn't take her eyes off the water or the scenery of the city as they passed through it. He was giving her another experience. She could find no words to thank him. There was nothing in return she could give a man who had experienced so much. All she could do was love him. She sensed he needed that. Sunny was sure that Regina had loved Julian in her own way and that his mother did too, but they couldn't love him the way he needed. He needed to feel like he mattered. That's why he drove himself so hard. He was a huge man who seemed to have everything anyone could ever want, but there was a hurt boy inside of him. Sunny had overheard a tiny bit of his conversation with his sister. He was still holding on to his anger over his mother's abandonment. That would hold him back. That would keep him seeking the approval of those who wouldn't matter in the long run.

She turned to him just after they stepped off the boat and onto dry land, and she hugged him tightly. "Thank you, Julian. That was so beautiful."

"You don't have to thank me again. I've never seen anyone so happy on a boat."

"I've never been on a boat before."

"No? Not even a rowboat? My dad used to take us fishing all the time."

"Really? Did you catch anything?"

"No. Galen refused to touch the bait or take the fish off the hook. So basically we just sat in a boat all day and ate junk food."

She grinned. "Sounds like my kind of day. Did you have fun?"

"Yeah. It was some of the best memories I had with my dad. No phones, no work. He was just with us."

"When is the last time you went fishing with your dad?"

"Right before I went into law school. I had gone wild after my football career ended. I'm a big man, but my father literally hauled me off my ass and dragged me fishing. I was hungover, booze coming through my pores. The last thing I wanted to do was go fishing, but he made me sit on a boat and just think. I needed that. It changed my life."

"You should go fishing again."

"You think I need a life change?"

"No, I think you need to spend time with your dad and your sister with no phones and no disruptions. It sounds like the most delicious thing on earth."

A pang of longing hit Sunny. It was times like these she wanted to find her mother more than anything else. Just to ask her questions. Who was her father? Did he know about her? Did he love her? Who was her family? She needed to know where she came from.

"What's wrong?" He touched her cheek.

"Nothing."

"Don't lie to me. I know you too well."

He did know her. He could read her emotions. "I was thinking about Soren and this case and how we don't seem much closer to finding out who her mother is."

"Let's go visit her."

"Right now?"

"Yeah. I'll win in court if it comes to that. I'll destroy the birth mother. You don't have to worry about the adoption not going through. But I would like to get more information upfront about her."

"I don't want her destroyed, Julian. I just want her to realize what is best for her child. And that is not traumatizing her again with a custody battle."

"You came to me because I have a reputation for causing witnesses to break on cross. That's how I win my cases."

"No. I came to you because I thought you were a good man. And because I thought you were sexy."

He grinned at her. "It doesn't matter why you came. We still should talk to Soren."

"But it's your day off."

"I took the day off to spend it with you. I'm with you so I'm good. Call Soren's parents. Ask them if we can come by."

An hour later they were at the Earls' home. They lived in a two-bedroom apartment in a quiet neighborhood in Midtown. Even though the apartment was much smaller than his, Julian felt that this place was much homier than his own. The first thing he noticed was that there were pictures of Soren everywhere, as well as her framed artwork and soccer cleats and dance shoes. It looked like the apartment of a family that was involved with their kid. It was how every kid should grow up.

"How are you enjoying your summer?" Sunny asked Soren as she hugged her close.

"It's been good. We are going to Lake George tomorrow. Mom showed me pictures of the house we're staying in. It's right on the lake. We are going to rent a boat and there's an amusement park up there."

"That sounds amazing!" Sunny said, giving the girl a squeeze. "I'm so happy you're going."

"Soren, why don't you go see if you can pull the pictures up on your computer so we can show Sunny. Print them out. She might be interested in renting it too."

Soren looked puzzled for a moment but did as her foster mother asked.

"I'm so glad you called today," Mrs. Earl said in a quiet tone. "I was going to wait until we got back to show this to you, but I'm happy to see you because I don't think I'll be able to enjoy my vacation without sharing this with you." She opened up the wall safe and pulled out a large envelope. "Another envelope came today. There was five hundred dollars in there and a letter saying the usual, but this time there is a return address on it."

Julian took the envelope from her. There was an address on it. No name, but sure enough there was an address from Maryland. "She's usually more careful than this."

"Maybe she wants to be found," Sunny said. "Maybe we can reach her."

"I thought about it," Mrs. Earl said. "I thought about driving down there and asking her what the hell is wrong with her. I had a shell of a kid. One who was too terrified to ask me for a glass of water. She hoarded her food for the first six months, afraid we were going to stop feeding her. This woman can say that she loves her all she wants, but she abused her. The only good thing she did for that child was leaving her at your agency."

"You aren't going to lose Soren, Mrs. Earl. You have my word. There's no way."

"I just want the letters to stop. I want to go to sleep at night and not be afraid that my kid is going to get snatched off the street."

"Jeannie . . ." Sunny's voice was choked. "I'm so

sorry you're going through this. I wish I could do more."

"Do more?" Jeannie laughed. "You've done more for us than anyone else ever has. You convinced me to become a foster mother after my daughter passed away. You're the reason we have gotten this much happiness these past few years. I didn't think I would be able to feel anything but numb. You've given me a gift by making me a mother again."

Tears began to roll down Sunny's cheeks and Julian wrapped his arm around her and kissed her forehead.

"I don't mean to cry. I'm so emotional these past couple of days. I'm sorry."

"Don't apologize! We're going to miss you once the adoption is finalized."

"I won't get to see Sunny anymore once the adoption is done?" Soren came out of the back, holding papers in her hand.

"You will if your mom and dad let me. I'm not supposed to have favorites, but you're mine."

Soren grinned at her but only briefly. "Why are you crying?"

"Your mom was saying nice things to me. Plus, Mr. King promised me dessert and I got so excited I started to cry." Sunny stepped away from Julian and took Soren's free hand. "We need to ask you questions about your mama, Soren. I know it's hard to talk about her but there are some things we need to know."

"She's trying to get me back."

Jeannie looked horrified. "How do you know?"

"I figured it out. You and Papa are worried. You hide the mail from me. Mr. King is here. I just know."

"And what do you think about it?" Jeannie asked her.

"I'm not going back." Soren balled her fists. "I don't care what anybody says. I will run away."

"You aren't leaving us. I would never let it happen."

"Neither would I," Sunny said. "That's why Mr. King is here. We want to talk to you about your mama so maybe we can find her and talk to her."

"You can tell her that I want to stay with my parents. They are going to buy a house in the country. We looked at some last weekend. And there's going to be a yard and Mom said I could have a dog and maybe a cat. You tell her that I love them. Tell her I won't go back."

"What's her name?" Julian asked.

"Her name is Gracie."

Sunny jumped slightly as if the name startled her.

"What about her last name?" Julian asked, crouching before her.

"It changed a lot. She told different people different names. She used Smith the most."

"Do you remember any of the other ones?" Sunny asked her.

"Sometimes it was Johnson. That was my daddy's last name."

"Is there anything else you know about your father? Something you haven't told me before?"

"I don't think so." She shook her head. "Mama was sad that he couldn't be with us so she took me to New York and then she got sicker and then things got really bad." Soren's eyes filled with tears.

Sunny went to Soren and hugged her tightly, smoothing her hands down the girl's back. "I know how hard it was for you and I promise you it won't happen again. We need to ask you a few more questions and then we'll stop. I promise."

"It's okay."

"Where were you right before your mama took you to New York?"

"We lived in South Carolina. But Mama had family in Maryland."

"Have you met them? Did they ever try to find you after she brought you here?"

"She had an aunt. But she was old and she died and that's when Mama went out of her mind."

"Just one more question," Julian said, stepping forward and placing his hand on Sunny's back. He felt the need to touch her then. He wasn't sure why but she looked as if she was in just as much pain as Soren. But it made sense. Her life had been just as hard as Soren's except no family had come to love her. "What was your father's first name?"

"His name was Richard and he lived in Meriden, South Carolina."

They had gotten all the answers they came for, but Sunny's head was spinning because a thousand more questions popped into her mind. Was it possible that she and Soren had the same father as well? There were too many commonalities at this point, but it was too crazy to be true. Sunny's mother was mentally ill. She heard voices. She saw things that weren't there. How could she have gotten her act together to orchestrate this? How could she take care of another child for as long as Soren was with her mother? How could she have found the agency where Sunny worked? And find out where the Earls lived? And if she had known Sunny was there, why write to Soren and not to her? It didn't make sense. None of it made sense. But they had more information. A path they could try to follow.

Julian had taken them to a bakery so they could lighten the mood. Sunny could barely concentrate, but it was nice to see Soren so relaxed and bubbly with her foster mother. They were very connected and anyone who had eyes could see that they belonged together. Blood might be thicker than water, but water kept you alive. And Soren needed the life that this family could bring to her.

Julian took her hand in his and squeezed her fingers, causing her to look up at him. "I'm going to buy a dozen of those cupcakes for later. Which ones should I get?"

"Whatever you want, Julian."

"But what do you want?"

"You know what I like. Just make sure there's a chocolate one in there."

He gave her a soft smile and then spoke into her ear. "Everything will be okay, Sunshine. I promise." He looked up at Soren. "You want to help me pick out some cupcakes? Maybe your mom will let you take a couple home."

Soren nodded and left the table with him, leaving Sunny and Jeannie alone. "What is going on with you and the lawyer? And please do not tell me nothing. The day Soren met him she came home and told me he was beautiful. I thought it was just a childish infatuation, but she was right. He's incredibly beautiful and my husband told me he used to play pro football. Karl told me that it took everything inside of him not to scream like a teenage girl at a boy band concert when he met him."

Sunny smiled. "He is beautiful. He's an excellent lawyer and I have no doubt in my mind that if it comes to a custody case, Julian King will win. He's invested. He's good man."

"I'm happy to hear that, Sunny. But you didn't answer my question. He can't stop touching you. He's not just someone you're working with."

"No." She shook her head. "We're very good friends."

"Good friends? The way he treats you. . . . There's more there. There has to be more."

It wasn't just her then if other people could see it. She felt like she was special to him. She felt like he might share the same feelings she had . . . like love. "Our first priority is to your family."

"My family would like it if you were happy. Don't hold back on him because of us."

"Mom?" Soren came running over to the table followed by Julian. She was holding a large pink box. "Mr. King bought a bunch of pastries. He said they were for Papa because he didn't get to come with us today. Can we bring them home?"

"Of course. We've got to get going. Please thank Sunny and Mr. King for taking us out."

"Thank you, Mr. King." She hugged Julian, which was rare for Soren. She had never showed this kind of affection before. She had come so far from the half-starved, mute kid who was scared of everything and everyone.

The rest of them said their good-byes and they went their separate ways. Julian took her back to their building and walked her to her apartment. She opened the door to let them in, but he stopped her. "I need to say good-bye right here."

"Right here?" She turned to face him and wrapped her arms around him and kissed his chin. "You're sick of me already?"

"No. I want to come inside, but I looked at my phone and I have seven missed calls from my office. I have a very angry client. She is facing jail time and is mad that I disappeared for a day and a half or so says my assistant who sent me a very lengthy text."

"I feel terrible. You took off for me."

"No, I didn't. I took off because I wanted to be with you. I wouldn't change that for anything. Today was a good day. But now I have to go into the office."

"You can't even take an entire day off? I know this is what you want. But I hope down the road when you are partner and you have a family of your own that you'll be able to take some real time off to enjoy them."

Julian made a soft noise and then cupped her chin in his hand and kissed her sweetly. It took her breath away. "I have to go," he said when he lifted his lips from hers. "I'm going to be busy for the next couple of weeks, but I will be working on Soren's case."

She nodded, feeling saddened. She had known that they couldn't happen and he was backing away. His career would ultimately come first.

Chapter 13

Julian rubbed the back of his neck trying to work the stiffness out. He felt as if he was chained to his desk. He rarely saw daylight these past few days. He woke up, worked out, came to the office, and stayed at his desk until nine, sometimes ten o'clock at night. He was working in overdrive trying to get ahead on his cases. He was making headway. He'd settled a few cases. He was progressing in avoiding jail time for his angriest client, but he felt like shit. His head hurt. His muscles were stiff and tight. He was pissed off all the time for no reason.

"Mr. King," his assistant called him from the doorway. "I'm heading out for the night. Do you need anything before I go?"

"No." He shook his head. "I thought you had left hours ago."

"No. I was trying to get all of the little stuff out of the way so you could stop working fourteen-hour days."

"I appreciate it. I'll make sure your paycheck reflects."

"You always do. You're a good boss, Mr. King. All the legal secretaries want to work for you. You say please and thank you and you don't try to stick your hands up our skirts. If you ever leave this place, I'm coming with you."

He smiled. "Thank you. I don't think I'm going anywhere until I make partner so you might have to wait awhile."

"You'll make it and soon. Have a good night. Make sure you get some rest."

"I will. Good night."

He was alone for about twenty minutes when he heard a knock at his door. It opened slowly and Sunny stepped inside his office holding a small box in her hands. He hadn't seen her in ten days. He had counted them. He had spoken to her a few times. He texted her every single day, but he hadn't seen her face and he missed the hell out of her. Every time he stepped away from her this feeling got worse. It felt like he was missing a part of himself. That was crazy. He had known her a few months. His career had to come first. But missing her was starting to wear on him.

"I was in the neighborhood and I thought I would drop off some soup."

He had told her that he wasn't feeling well and here she was with soup. She was so sweet and his chest loosened as soon as he saw her. "You were in the neighborhood?"

"Yes, I had a meeting with Mr. Cleese."

He frowned at her. "Why? I saw you speaking to him at the party. What's going on?"

"We speak at least once a week. I've been to his house once. He's an incredible man. You should get to know him outside of this."

"You've been to his house?"

"He lives in a brownstone on the upper west side. It's beautiful. It's a lot less pretentious than I thought it would be."

"Why have you been to his house? Are you sleeping with my boss?" he asked, half joking. He believed her when she said she was meeting with Cleese. There was no reason for her to lie. But he couldn't think of a reason why she would meet him.

She walked over to him, placed the box of food on his desk, and then sat on his lap wrapping her arm around him. "There's only one lawyer I want to sleep with." She kissed the side of his face. "How are you feeling? I bought you chicken and rice soup and tomato soup and a turkey sandwich and some hot tea. I wasn't sure what you wanted."

"Whatever you bring me is what I want." She wore a blue skirt with white flowers on it. It had ridden up when she sat down, revealing her creamy thigh to him. He set his hand there and stroked her soft skin. "Why have you been meeting with my boss?"

"It's his news to share. I'm sure you'll find out soon enough."

"Sunny . . ."

"You know I can't reveal private information. Just like you can't. What do you want to eat? You probably can't remember the last time you got up from this desk." She tried to get up but he wouldn't let her go. He had missed her closeness. He didn't want to give it up now.

"I will eat whatever you give me." It almost hurt to look at her. She was so beautiful. And thoughtful and sensitive. "Why did you come here tonight?"

"Because you said you weren't feeling well. You seemed off for the past few days."

"Bullshit."

"I missed you," she admitted. "I don't want to miss you. I don't mean to miss you, but I do and today, as much as I wanted to, I couldn't stay away."

Julian crushed his mouth to hers, kissing her with everything pent up inside him. He felt the same way she did. It was hard to stay away. There was something intense between them, something strong that he really didn't want to think much about because it shook him.

Heat shot right through him as the kiss continued and he grew hard instantly. She turned him on like no one else could. And all she had to do was be in the same room with him. He was unable to go more than a few minutes without touching her. That wasn't him. No PDA. No taking time off work to be with a woman. No wanting to be with a woman more than he wanted air to fill his lungs. He was losing himself in her.

Sunny noticed his arousal. She reacted by moving her bottom against him. Her hands came up to his throat to loosen his tie and then his top buttons.

"Lock the door. I need you, Julian. I can't wait anymore."

He broke the kiss and looked at her. He was tempted to do what she asked. "We can't have sex here." Not for their first time. If it were anyone else he might have risked it, but he wanted more for her. For them.

"Then come home with me." She gave him a kiss that was slow and deep and sexy. No woman had ever kissed him like that. No woman ever made him unsure he was going to be able to recover after going to bed with her.

She was dangerous to him.

"I have so much work to do here." It was true. The more time he spent with her, the less he cared about his work. He had to care about his work. He needed to make partner.

"You want me. I can feel it. Why do you keep pushing me away?"

"I'm not pushing you away. I'm just trying to keep my head above water. But it's too hard to stop this."

She ran her hand over his erection. "Yes, it's much too hard."

Her dirty joke surprised him, made him laugh aloud. This was one of the thousand reasons he wanted her. "Sunny, I can't promise you a serious relationship right now. I can't promise you much time at all. I don't want to hurt you."

"Okay. I won't get hurt. I'm not asking you for a relationship. Just come home with me."

He couldn't say no. He had no more fight left in him. He had to have her. He wouldn't feel at peace until he did. "Give me an hour and then meet me at my place. I have to finish up a couple of things."

"An hour." She kissed him again. "Don't keep me waiting."

"Don't expect to get any sleep tonight."

Sunny walked out of Julian's office feeling as if the ground was moving beneath her. She couldn't catch her breath. She was going to make love to the man she loved tonight. She couldn't wait to feel his weight on top of her. His hands all over her. Him inside of her. She wanted to get closer to him. He was the only man she had ever wanted.

"Um, Sunny, is it?" She paused for a moment, looking over her shoulder to see Julian's other boss, Mr. Bruno, coming out of his corner office. She was surprised to see him here so late. He didn't seem like the type of man who actually still worked. He looked perfectly groomed, unlike Mr. Cleese who had his sleeves rolled up and a tiredness in his eyes when she walked in. She wanted to tell Julian why she was meeting with him. Why she had gone on a home visit. Why she was so happy to have met him because he was about to change someone else's life. There was goodness in Mr. Cleese.

Mr. Bruno, however, was another story. She turned around to face him, holding her head up. She didn't like him, but she didn't want him to know how uncomfortable he made her.

"Yes?"

He looked her up and down taking in every inch

of her. She kept her hands at her side but it was a struggle. She immediately felt like she needed to smooth her skirt. Fix her hair. Anything so the intensity of his stare would lose some of its potency.

"You're here late on business."

"I have a heavy caseload. I have to do some things after hours."

"Yes." He took a step closer, but she didn't back away. "To get what you want you have to do certain things after hours and behind closed doors."

"Excuse me?"

"First you were holed up in Cleese's office for an hour and then you go in to see King. Davis is too much of a stuffy bastard to ever consider cheating on his wife, but it makes me wonder why he's been spending so much time with you. I walked into his office and he was on the phone with you. He hung up quickly, which means it must be personal."

"You should ask your partner. It's not my place to divulge."

"Discrete, are you?"

"I shouldn't have to say this because it's none of your business, but there is nothing unprofessional going on between Mr. Cleese and myself." She turned around to leave, but she felt a hand wrap around her shoulder.

"Of course not. I'm sorry for suggesting it. He wouldn't know what to do with a girl like you. Your body alone probably has him confounded."

"This conversation is done."

"Nothing is done until I say it's done." His grip on

her shoulder increased. For one horrible moment she felt trapped. She had been placed in this situation before. Some man tried to use his power over her, tried to put his hands on her. Try to take something she didn't want to give. "You can't tell me that nothing is going on with King. He broke up with his girlfriend. He's taking off from work. He defended you to me like you mattered to him. You must be giving it to him real good. You should see your lips. Puffy and kiss swollen or were you doing something else with them?"

Sunny's hand flew out and cracked Bruno across the face. "You're disgusting."

"You must like it rough." He used his bulk to push her body against a wall. His hand sliding beneath her skirt to cup her behind. He had an erection and he was pressing it into her, making sure she knew what he was after. "Whatever King is doing for you, I can do more. Why would you want to be with him when you could have the top of the food chain? I can set you up. You would never have to work again."

"No!" She lashed out at him, everything going black. Her hands connected with his face. Her knees came up, anything she could do to keep him away. But then a flash of man came at them and Julian was there shoving his boss into the wall so hard that the plaster crumbled.

"What the fuck do you think you're doing to my girl?" Julian's hand went around Bruno's neck, lifting him slightly off the floor. "You think you can touch her? You think I won't kill you?"

Sunny had never heard Julian's voice sound so deadly. She believed him in that moment. Bruno's face had gone purple. "Julian." She grabbed his arm. "Let him go. I'm okay now."

"He had his hands on you. You were struggling beneath him. I should snap his neck."

"And then I would lose you to prison. I don't want to lose you."

He let Bruno go and Bruno slid down the wall gasping for air. "You tried to kill me. You're fired. Get your shit and get out."

"Fine. I don't want to work for a scummy piece of shit like you anyway."

"Not so fast, King." Mr. Cleese had appeared from his office. He was furious. "You are not fired. My partner has spoken far too quickly."

"What the hell are you talking about, Davis? He tried to crush my windpipe. I'm one of the most powerful attorneys in the country. His career is done."

"Your career is the one that should be done. You committed sexual assault on Ms. Gibson when you put your hands on her. I heard her scream. I walked out and saw you touching her. Julian made it across the room far faster than I did, but you weren't going to get away with it. Not this time. You have taken far too many liberties with women in your time here. I have turned my back because they seemed to have wanted your attention, but this woman didn't and you crossed the line. If she goes to the police, which she's within her rights to do, I will back her."

"I've known you since law school," he sputtered. "I helped make you relevant in this industry."

"And I kept this place from imploding more times than I can count due to your bad behavior. You've slept with clients and judges and opposing counsel. You've had shady dealings with mobsters and CEOs who have done despicable things in the name of profit, and I stood by you as your partner because we needed each other, but we don't need each other anymore. You are far too risky to the firm."

"You think I can't leave this place and take all the clients with me? You don't think I'll ruin King in the process? If he was stupid enough to let some pussy get in the way of his career, then he deserves to go down."

"What did you just say?" He lunged forward but Sunny stepped in front of him and Cleese grabbed his arm. Sunny wasn't sure even the two of them could stop him.

"You think your attempted rape trial won't be all over the media? You may have friends in high places, but so do I. Especially in the DA's office. I'm sure they are looking for a reason to watch you burn."

"I won't press charges if you make Julian partner," Sunny blurted. He had worked so hard for it. It was all he had ever wanted and he was going to lose it all for her. All because she couldn't get away from Bruno fast enough.

"Are you crazy?" Julian turned to her. "If you

want to press charges, I will go down to the police station with you. He can't get away with this."

Sunny stood firm. "Julian makes partner right now or I'll press charges. It will affect the integrity of the entire firm."

"No. I refuse to let you do this. I don't want it this way."

"He deserves it. You see how hard he works. You know his record. He's the best lawyer here."

"Come in tomorrow morning at seven and we'll discuss it," Mr. Cleese said. "Bruno, you and I are going to discuss your retirement and how you are going to completely turn over the day to day operations to me."

"But I . . ." Bruno sputtered, red faced.

"That's it. Ms. Gibson. I'm sorry. The situation will be remedied immediately. Mr. King, please escort her home."

They left Julian's office that night but they barely spoke another word and when they got to their building, Julian went to his apartment and Sunny returned to hers, thinking that what happened was a sign. They were never going to be together.

Julian didn't sleep at all last night. He didn't feel good about what Sunny had done for him. Bruno needed to rot in hell, but he had almost killed him. He saw his eyes bulge out of his head. He saw him gasping for breath. Julian had never been that angry before, yet he could have killed last night, without a thought to anything else he had worked for. He would have killed for her and she had made a crazy side deal for him—what the hell did that say about them? Who else in his life would make that kind of sacrifice for him? He didn't want to think about it. The possibility of what it meant was overwhelming.

He had to think about the next step for his career because he sure as hell couldn't take a partnership this way. His coworkers already doubted that he belonged there. They might never find out about what took place that night but he would know. Walking in the office every day and knowing how he had achieved it would make him feel dirty.

He dressed in a suit and headed straight for Mr. Cleese's office, prepared to listen to whatever unearned offer he was about to receive.

"Can I get you something, King? Some coffee. You look like you haven't slept in a year."

"Something like that, sir."

"What has Sunny told you about our meetings?"

Julian was surprised that he had brought it up. "Not much. She said you are a good man and that she had been to your house, but that was it. She told me it was a private matter."

He nodded. "She kept her word. I've known a lot of people in my time on this earth and Sunny is probably the most generous and kind person I've ever met. It's not hard to see why you're taken with her."

"Taken with her isn't how I would describe it. It's like I was hit by a freight train. But we're not together. I've been trying to keep a professional distance but it's impossible when she's all I think about." He didn't know why he was admitting that to his boss. It may have been exhaustion or insanity, but he couldn't stop himself.

"I've been thinking a lot about her lately as well, but maybe not in the same way you have. That night at the party I had shared with her that my wife and I never had any children but we always wanted some. We had tried to go through the adoption process but at the last moment it had fallen through when the birth mother wanted to keep the baby. We were devastated and so we haven't tried again. I don't share that story with many people, but somehow I found myself telling her about it. We parted ways that night and I was surprised when she called me the next day if I would still like the chance to impact a child's life." Cleese smiled, which Julian wasn't sure he had ever seen before. "She told me she had a pair of siblings on her caseload, a little boy and a little girl who needed a good home. The boy had been in foster care for nearly his entire life and at ten his chances of getting adopted were getting slimmer by the moment. But there were a few families that said they would only take the girl. Sunny asked me if we would just meet them. So we met them, not sure what to expect. We knew the kind of lives lifelong foster kids had, the kind of baggage they carried."

"Sunny was a foster kid. No one ever adopted her."

"I know. She told us. She had everything stacked against her, yet she made it to where she is. She's remarkable and so were the kids we met that day. The boy is so smart. I felt like I was speaking to someone much older than ten. The little girl is sensitive and shy and sweet and she clings to her brother. She told us that she refused to go any- where without him and I told them that we would take them both. I surprised everyone in the room. Most of all myself. But my wife was feeling the same way. We've had quite a few visits with them and they are coming to live with us next week. We are going to adopt them. Sunny has been incredible through- out the process. She has answered every question we've had. She's checked in with us daily. She's re- assured us when we were afraid but ultimately, she's made our dream come true. She's going to give us the opportunity to have a family. I'm fifty-five years old. I'm going to be a new father and I couldn't be more excited."

"That's incredible, sir. I'm very happy for you."

"Thank you. I know the path my life is about to take. The question is what path is yours going to take? The partnership is yours. But not because of what happened last night. It was always yours. We were going to announce at the end of the quarter. But I'm not sure that's what you want. You work incredibly hard and your work is impeccable, but I'm not sure that what we do here fills you up. You're the type of man who won't be happy unless he finds value in what he does. I know you don't love defending reality stars and athletes when they throw fits."

"No," he admitted. "I thought maybe if I made partner that I would be able to do more important work."

"You can, but I want you to think about it. I want you to really think about your career. You have ten weeks of personal time. I'm making you take some of it. At least a month. You are not to come back until you are sure about the path you're going to take."

Sunny heard a knock at her door around six-thirty that night. She hadn't lingered at work that day. She was exhausted, bone tired from not having gotten any sleep the night before. She had been worried about Julian, about his career, about how it was so close to ending last night. She knew that Bruno trying to force himself on her wasn't her fault. Just like the last time someone trying to force themselves it wasn't her fault, but there was still that guilt. Because each time a man tried to take something from her that she had never wanted to give, her life changed drastically. The last time it had caused her to lose her mother for good.

She opened the door to find Julian there looking just as exhausted as she felt. "You're home early."

"I've been banned from work." He walked inside and dropped into a chair at the kitchen table. "Please tell me there is some sort of alcohol in here."

She nodded and rushed to the fully stocked bar his brother-in-law kept. "Is bourbon okay?"

"Paint thinner would be fine with me at the moment." Her hands shook as she poured his drink. She wanted to question him, to blurt out an apology, to say something, but she kept her mouth shut because it seemed like the most sensible thing to do.

She dropped a couple of ice cubes in his drink and sat down across from him. "What did Mr. Cleese say?"

"That you're the reason he's going to be a father and he couldn't be more grateful to you."

"I'm grateful to him and his wife. I knew Jack and Brenna needed someone special and the Cleeses are kind and patient and giving. They could give them the kind of experiences most people will never have. Now what did he say about you?"

"That the partnership is mine if I want it. That it was going to be mine at the end of the quarter regardless of what happened."

"That's incredible, but why are you banned from work? Did they suspend you for what happened last night? It's not fair if they did. You could fight it."

"I'm not suspended. Mr. Cleese ordered me to take some vacation time. I'm not to come back until I know what I want to do with my life. He thinks that the partnership might not be what I really want."

"Oh." Sunny had thought the same thing. She didn't think it would make him happy in the long run, but she couldn't convey that to him. "What are you going to do?"

"It depends. How much unused vacation time do you have?"

"A lot."

"You want to follow the trail of the letters and go to the beach?"

Her breath caught. "Yes. There isn't anything I would like more."

Chapter 14

Julian looked over at Sunny as they drove down the long, quiet road that would lead them to the small town in Maryland from where Soren's mother sent her letters. She hadn't said much to him on the trip down. He could tell she was nervous and excited and maybe a little bit sad. But he still found her so pretty. She wore the barrette he had given her on the side of her head and let the rest of her ringlets flow free. She looked like a throwback to another era, and he was having a hard time keeping his eyes on the road.

"Stop looking at me, Jules."

"I'm admiring your hair."

"I wanted to wear it today." She touched the barrette. "For years I kept it locked away. I was going to keep this one locked up too. I was even going to put it in a safe-deposit box, but I decided that that would be pointless. I want to wear this. I want people to see it. It's important to me and I want to keep it close."

He took one hand off the wheel and took her hand in his. She liked his gift. She appreciated everything he had given her, no matter how big or small. Regina didn't seem to care about anything he had given her, but maybe that wasn't a fair assessment, because he had never gone out of his way to give her something he knew would mean a lot to her. He hadn't cared enough and it still puzzled him why he would choose her to be his wife. He was lucky she said no. "Are you hungry? We've been on the road since five this morning and you barely ate any of your muffin."

"We can stop if you're really hungry, but I don't think I'll be able to eat until we go to the address the last letter came from."

"I don't have to eat right now. You packed a lot of snacks for us. When you handed me that lunch box I felt like a well-loved kindergartner headed for his first day of school."

She smiled softly. "I'm afraid if I have children they are all going to be terribly chubby. I need to feed people."

"To show them you care?"

"I guess so. Food represents security for me. I remember being hungry. I remember not knowing when or if I was going to eat again. I would never want someone in my care to feel that way. I might overdo it."

Shit. The life she led. He couldn't wrap his head around it. He had never known what it was like to not have those essential things. He had never been grateful just to eat. "You can feed them as much as you want. I'll make sure they exercise."

She glanced over at him and when she did, he realized what he had said. The implications of it. He hadn't meant that. That they were going to have children together and. . . . And. . . . But what had he meant?

She didn't say anything to him. She just looked at the navigation system and then back out of the window. "We're almost there. This is a sweet little town, isn't it?"

"Yes. It is. What did your boss say when you told her you were taking a month off work?"

"She said hallelujah and told me she hoped that I would be spending some time with the nice young lawyer she spoke to that day."

"I don't know any nice lawyers. I'm not sure they make them."

She grinned at him and he knew in his gut that he was going to be making love to her before the end of this trip. Not a hookup. Not simply sex. He was going to make love to her. But he didn't want to think about what would happen afterward. How things would change between them. He was just going to live moment by moment.

The GPS alerted them to their destination. They pulled up in front of a small white house with a set of flower boxes in the window and a small porch with a rocking chair on it. The windows were open and there were sheer gauzy curtains blowing in the breeze.

"It's lovely." Sunny opened the door and got out.

He followed behind her. "It reminds me of the house I had when I was little. Before Mama took me to New York." She made a soft noise. "I loved that little house."

Julian squeezed her shoulder. This was hard for her. It was bringing up a lot of memories of her childhood. He couldn't have done this job if he were her. It would have been too hard for him. He hated looking back.

"Are you ready?"

"No. But let's do this."

She took the lead and walked up the porch. He watched her take a deep breath before knocking on the door. They waited but there was no answer. Julian knocked this time. His knock much louder than hers.

An older woman came out of the little cottage next door. "Can I help you?"

"Hi." Sunny stepped forward. "We're looking for Grace. Do you know if she's here?"

"Grace? Oh no. She hasn't been here for at least a week. Is there anything I can help you with?"

"We need to speak with her. Do you have a number for her or know where we can find her?"

"Grace is really private. She seems nice but doesn't talk much to the neighbors."

"What about her husband?" Julian asked. "She comes here with him, doesn't she?"

That wasn't a fact they were sure of, but Julian had a hunch.

"Yeah. He's really friendly. He works a lot though. He's the district manager for some company that's based a couple of towns over. They spend half the month here and I think he said they live somewhere in South Carolina. Hope is the name of the town, I think. I couldn't tell you the address though."

"Is there anyone else in town who might know them a little better? Like how to reach them?"

"You can try to find out at his company."

"Do you know the exact name of it?"

"No. I just knew it had to do with shipping, or trucking." The woman shook her head. "Something like that. I can't even tell you his full name. Grace just calls him Heff."

"Thank you, Ms. . . . ." Sunny said.

"Just call me Dottie. Everyone does. Should I tell them you were looking for them when they come up?"

"That's okay. I'm planning on seeing Grace soon. I was just hoping to catch her before they left town."

"You actually can tell her we were looking for her," Julian took his card out of his pocket and handed it to Dottie.

"You're a lawyer? This is a big important firm in New York City." Dottie looked up at him. "I've seen you before. You represented my favorite soap opera actress when she pitched a fit in that boutique."

"That was me." He nodded.

"I was watching stories of that like a hawk. There was all sorts of chatter at the senior center about what they would do with her storyline if she got locked up. That show revolves around her."

"I know and she really is a good person, so we did our best to get her back to work as soon as possible. Please let me know if Grace shows up. I'm sure I can arrange a few autographed pictures of your favorite actress to be sent to your front door."

"I will let you know! This is exciting." She turned to go back into her house. "Wait until I tell the girls."

"Was that the smartest thing you just did, Julian? What if she does tell her? Should we have given her a warning?"

"I don't see why not. All along Grace has had the upper hand. She's known where Soren is. She's threatened to take her away from the family who loves and cares for her. I want her to know that we're on her ass and that the most powerful law firm in the country is onto her. She should be afraid that we are going to press charges or sue her for emotional distress on top of my legal fees."

"But you're doing this for free."

"She doesn't know that. She should be afraid. She should be just as afraid as Soren was when she thought she might go back."

"Julian, she might not be as evil as you paint her. Her side of the story might be different."

"There is no her side. There is only one side. You've got to stop doing this. You've got to stop chickening out when it's time to come down hard on her. You came to me for a reason. This is how I win. This is how we are going to keep that family together."

"I'm not a lawyer. I'm a social worker and you may be perfectly content in breaking down people but my job is to help them put themselves back together. I came to you because I needed help, but that doesn't ever mean I'm going to celebrate someone else's downfall." She stepped into his SUV. "Can we eat and go check into our hotel rooms? I need a break."

The view from their hotel room was almost too beautiful for words. Julian had booked a room on the Inner Harbor in Baltimore. She had been expecting to stay in some national chain hotel, but Julian had surprised her again. He had rented a two-bedroom suite on one of the top floors. It had huge windows and from them she could see the gentle waves of the water below her and the way the sun was causing it to shimmer. She was a ball full of nervous energy, but being near the water soothed her. It made her almost feel like that was where she should be. Not the hot, dirty city. She had been anxious the entire ride down. Anxious about Soren. About possibly meeting her mother, about possibly meeting their mother. She had asked herself what she was going to do if it had been her. Would she feel the need to embrace her, or would she feel angry like she had many times during her childhood?

How could you leave me locked in that closet?
How could you leave me?

In her mind she knew it was for the best. She knew she wouldn't have survived living with her mother for much longer. And rationally she knew her mother was mentally ill, but it didn't mean that she wasn't still angry, that she wasn't still hurt, that she didn't blame her for Sunny never feeling safe until now. Until Julian. And she knew he wasn't permanent. Just a little taste of what it was like to feel this way. He had to take a month off of work, a month from the life he claimed to love, to reevaluate. The partnership was going to be handed to him. It was what he wanted. It was what he had worked so hard for all these years. To prove he was more than just a token, that his hard work meant something.

She wouldn't blame him if he took the job and relished his life as a high-powered attorney, but she didn't think he would be happy. Not all the way happy.

He certainly wasn't going to be happy with her when he found out what she had done.

"This is a bit of the way to go for ice cream," he said to her as they left downtown Baltimore and ventured out into the suburbs.

"I know. I saw the place on some television show and I thought we could try it. I heard it was one of the best custard places in the country."

"I did ask you what you wanted to do tonight. I should have known you wouldn't have said catch a play or ask me to take you to a symphony."

"Would you prefer me to be more cultured?" she asked seriously.

"I prefer you as you are."

"I'm sure my novelty will wear off soon." She smiled but she meant it. It was another reason she knew they couldn't be together long term. She wasn't enough for him. She wasn't sophisticated enough, or rich enough, or quiet enough to fit into his world. "You don't have to rent fancy hotel rooms for my benefit. I could sleep in a motel just fine. It will be like old times for me."

"Your mother . . ." he said, knowing what she was thinking.

"I guess you could say that was the fun part of her mental illness. She made it a game. Every day she would tell me we were going on a new adventure. I thought it was so much fun to sleep in a different bed every night and she would feed me fast food and chips and I got to have so much soda. I had no idea." She shook her head. "I'm sorry. I'll stop talking about my past."

"Why? You don't have to with me."

"I don't usually talk about her with anyone."

"Not even Arden?"

"No, I never wanted to let anyone know how truly screwed up I am."

"You're not."

She grinned at him. "We both know I am."

"I like when you talk about her to me. It makes me feel special."

"You've seen more of me than anyone else, Jules. You've seen me at my worse. You're more than just special to me." She stopped herself from telling him that she loved him. She would keep that to herself. He already made her feel too raw. "I was serious about spending so much money on this trip. I don't need anything but you."

He touched her knee. "I like to see your face when

you experience something for the first time. It's selfish. I don't do anything for you. I do it all for me."

"I wanted to do something for you, but I'm sure you're not going to like it," she said to him as they pulled onto the road that led to the park where the ice cream stand was.

The park was empty, most people must have been home for dinner by now, but there was a car in the parking lot. A white Mercedes and Sunny knew who it was even before seeing the driver's face.

"What are you talking about? You know I like everything you do for me."

"Your mother is in that white car."

He tensed. "Excuse me?"

"Remember yesterday when you were getting in the shower and you asked me to pick up your phone because your sister was supposed to call?"

"Yeah." He pulled the car to a stop and looked at her. She could feel how angry he was.

"Your mother called and I picked up just to tell her you were in the shower and that you would call her back, but we started talking and she asked me how you were, how you really were because you never tell her anything. I didn't know what to tell her, so I told her that we were on our way south to see your sister. Her voice got so sad and she told me she hadn't seen you since your sister's wedding and before that it was your law school graduation. I could hear the tears in her throat as she told me that she had only seen you twice in ten years. I told her we would meet her here. I know I shouldn't have done it, but the words popped out of my mouth and I didn't take them back. I couldn't take them back. She just wants to see your face."

"You should have minded your own damn business."

He got out of the car, slamming the door behind him. She followed him and walked just behind him as he approached his mother who was standing behind her car.

"Hello, Elaine!" Sunny walked ahead of Julian and shook Julian's mother's hand. She wasn't sure what she had expected the woman to look like. She was hoping she would be ugly, or there would be some kind of nastiness pouring from her soul. Julian was so angry with her, so hurt by her. But she looked like a typical upper-middle-class suburban mother. She was petite with straight, blond hair and delicate features. She could see Julian in her. His eyes. His cheekbones, the shape of his chin. Despite their different sizes and skin colors, it was hard to hide the fact that they were mother and son, and unlike most mothers and sons, no one seemed happy to be there. Sunny didn't have to look at Julian to know how angry he was. It was radiating off him.

Elaine looked nervous, almost afraid. And as much as Sunny was aware she was risking Julian's wrath, she knew she wouldn't regret what she'd done. How could he move on with his life with this hanging over him? He knew where his mother was; he could do what she so desperately wished she could. He could ask her why she left.

"Hello. You must be Sunny. I'm so happy to meet you."

"I'm happy to meet you, too. Julian didn't know I arranged this meeting. I surprised him."

"Oh. He's going to be very upset with you."

"I know. But I think things happen for a reason and there was no need to waste this opportunity. I'm going to walk down the road to give you two some privacy."

Julian watched Sunny walk away. He was furious with her. She had no right to arrange this meeting. He would see his mother on his time, on his terms. Just because her job was to put families together didn't mean she had the right to meddle in his. He wasn't one of her clients.

"Don't be too mad at her, Julian. She's a sweet girl. She only meant well."

"I know she meant well, but that doesn't change the fact that I didn't want to see you."

The hurt flashed in her eyes and Julian was surprised that he didn't like to see her pain. He shouldn't give a damn about her feelings. She didn't want to see them. She stood in open court and told a judge she didn't want custody. She didn't ask for visitation rights. She made it clear she wanted nothing to do with them.

"Well, at least you finally admit it. You have used every excuse in the book. The words sting, but at least they are the truth."

"Don't try to guilt me. You don't get to act like the victim. You're the one who disappeared on us. I waited for you at school for over an hour. I sat outside by myself and watched every parent come to pick up their kid. You never came and I wondered if you were hurt or dead. I had to pick up Galen and look into her worried face and tell her everything was going to be okay. But you weren't hurt or dead. You were just gone. It would have been easier if you had died, because then it would have been over. Instead of reappearing every few years pretending as if you give a shit about your kids."

"Julian, that is the furthest thing from the truth. I did care. I loved you. I had to leave."

"You had to leave?" He shook his head in disbelief. "You could have at least said good-bye. You could have at least tried to make us understand. Galen cried every night for weeks. Every time she heard there was a car accident she checked to see if it was you. Dad had to hire a private investigator to track you down and even when he found you, he wouldn't tell us where you were. He told us you didn't want to be found."

"There's more to that story. If you would just listen, you would know why I did what I had to do."

"I don't want to hear your excuses. There is nothing you can say that is going to make me think that what you did was just. You got married again. You had another kid. You live this perfect little life in the suburbs with your socially acceptable husband and the only time you think about those other undesirable kids you have is when the guilt is too much for you. Are you surprised at how well we turned out? Have you told your family how successful your little disgraces are?"

"Now you wait a minute! My leaving had nothing to do with you or your father or the color of your skin, so you stop that right now."

"You don't get to tell me what to do. Only a mother does and my mother died the moment she told a judge that she didn't want us. This conversation is over. I have nothing left to say to you."

He walked away from her and down the road toward Sunny who hadn't gotten very far at all. She was sitting on a bench, probably just out of ear shot of the conversation. He was so damn mad at her. He had pushed all that anger down below the surface. Now he felt like he was a kid again. Like he was thirteen years old and pissed off all the time. His father had taught him self-control. Discipline. He told him he would never go anywhere in this world if he didn't have any. And he had taken those lessons and made himself into something. But right now he didn't give a shit about any of it. He wanted to break something. He wanted to scream and rage, anything to distract him from feeling the way he was feeling.

Sunny looked up at him. There was a sad expression on her face and for a split second he wanted to not be mad at her.

"You butted in."

"I know."

"You went behind my back."

"I did."

"My family is none of your goddamn business! You had no right. You overstepped big time."

"Maybe I did. But there has to be a reason you're so mad at your mother. If everything was fine you'd be okay with spending five minutes with her."

"I told you what she did to us."

"She left you. I get it. I've been left too."

"Don't compare your mother to mine. Your mother was crazy. Mine just didn't want to be bothered with us."

"She was sick. Not crazy. Don't call her that. And I don't know why my mother left me, but you can find out why your mother left you. All you have to do is talk to her. I would give anything to talk to my mother again."

"I don't want to hear your sad orphan bullshit right now. I'm not in the mood for it."

Sunny flinched as he said the words and Julian knew that he had gone too far, but he was too damn mad to take it back.

"I'm not your mother or opposing counsel. I don't care how mad you are, you don't get to be an asshole to me."

She walked away from him and back to the car. He followed her silently and didn't say another thing to her for the rest of the night.

Chapter 15

"Sunny? Do you want some ice cream?" Harvey asked as he walked into the kitchen.

"No, thank you," she said quietly as she watched him pull off his wrinkled work shirt and take the iron out of the cabinet.

Mama had told her to call him Daddy, but Sunny knew that she never would. She didn't know who her daddy was, but this man wasn't him.

Mama had met him a few weeks ago while they were living in the motel downtown. He worked in the office building next door and had been watching them. Every time they went in or out he seemed to be there. Just staring. . . . Mama hadn't noticed at first, but Sunny had. She had felt his eyes on her and then one day he walked up and he took the bag of groceries from Mama's arms, telling her that women as beautiful as her shouldn't carry their own bags. Mama had smiled at him and then started to talk in that fast way she did when she was excited.

Soon he was there all the time. Giving Mama presents. He bought her a bracelet and a pair of earrings. He had food delivered to their room and then he had given Mama a lot of money so they could get an apartment. Mama had been so happy. She said that he must love them because he was taking care of them so well and that he never wanted anything from her. He gave Sunny presents. A doll. A yo-yo. But Sunny didn't feel like Harvey loved them.

She didn't like being near him because he always stared at her. His eyes followed her wherever she went and for the first time since Mama had taken her away from their home, Sunny felt like everything wouldn't be okay.

Mama had left her alone with him tonight. She had a cleaning job and Harvey had volunteered to watch Sunny.

It was the first time she had been alone with him and she was mad at Mama for leaving her with him. She didn't like Harvey. She didn't like the way he looked or smelled or acted.

"Why don't you come into the kitchen, Sunny. I could use some company while I iron my shirt."

Sunny walked over slowly but stayed on the far side of the kitchen table, too far away for him to touch her. He tried to touch her a lot. He rubbed her back and kissed her cheeks. Mama had told her to never let anyone touch her. She told her never to take candy from strangers and never let anyone inside of their apartment, but she was doing all the things that she told Sunny never to do.

"What are you doing all the way over there? Come closer."

"I can see you from here," she said quietly. He always seemed so nice to her, but she had seen Harvey angry. She had seen him kick the stray dog that lived in the alley beside the building. The dog just came up to him. The dog didn't do anything, just walked up to him looking *for food. Mama hadn't noticed, but Sunny had and since then she really didn't want to be near him.*

"Oh, come on, sweetheart. I just want to see your pretty face."

She inched closer not wanting to make him angry. He nodded his approval and turned around to iron his shirt.

"You like living in this apartment instead of that motel, right?"

She had at first. Switching motels every week was starting to get old. But she didn't realize how much Harvey would be there. He didn't live there. He went home every night but he was there a lot during the day. He came over in the morning before he went to work. He stopped by on his lunch hour. He had dinner with them every night and was there all day on Saturdays. It was getting harder and harder for Sunny to stay away from him.

"It makes Mama happy."

"You like it when your mama is happy, don't you?"

She nodded.

"You love her." He turned around to face her. "I could make your mama very happy. I could bring you to live with me in my house. I have a little yard. We would put a swing set in there for you. There's a nice school in my neighborhood that you can go to."

Sunny didn't say anything. A house with a yard sounded nice. And school . . . She had missed school so much. She had missed friends and books and being in a happy place.

"Come here." He held out his hand to her. She didn't attempt to take his hand but she moved closer. He sat in a chair and patted his lap. "Sit with your new daddy."

Sunny shook her head. She wouldn't sit in his lap. She always listened when her mama told her what to do,

*but she couldn't call him daddy and she wouldn't sit on
his lap.*

*He grabbed her wrist and something inside of Sunny
screamed no. She didn't know what he would do but she
wouldn't let him grab her. She bit his hand as hard as she
could.*

*"You little bitch," he swore. His eyes changed. He looked
like when he kicked the dog.*

*Sunny knew she had to get away. She tried to run, but
he grabbed her again, and took the hot iron off the table.
She fought him. She kicked and scratched at his hand, but
she couldn't stop him from pressing the iron into her skin.
He held it there, pressing it down with all his weight.*

*She screamed out in agony. She could smell the scent of
burning skin, but she couldn't see anything because everything had gone black.*

*The door burst open and she could hear heavy pounding
footsteps. Her eyes focused and she could see her next-door
neighbor with a baseball bat in his hand. He looked at her
curled up on the floor and then at Harvey before he swung
the bat wildly and smashed Harvey in the head.*

*Harvey went down. His body hitting the floor with a
thud she would never be able to get out of her head. There
was blood everywhere, pooling around his head in a messy
circle. Sunny would never forget that smell too, the lifeless
look on Harvey's face.*

*Her neighbor walked over to her and crouched down
beside her. She tried to scramble away, too scared to be near
him. "I'm not going to hurt you." He put both his hands up.
"I just need to see what he did to you."*

*Sunny moved her hand to reveal her wound. All of her
brown skin was gone, just red and pink and white were*

left behind. Looking at it made her stomach churn and she gagged at the sight and the smell of her own skin.

Her neighbor cursed. "I'm going to call my mother to come help. Can you tell me what happened?"

"He tried to make me sit on his lap and I didn't want to so I bit him. He took the iron and burned me. He keeps trying to touch me."

"He's a fucking pervert. He won't bother you anymore."

The man walked out and a few minutes later returned with an elderly woman and two other men. They questioned her about Harvey, about where he was from and how Mama had met him. The old woman was taking care of her shoulder, pouring water on it over and over again when Mama walked in.

"Sunny! What happened?" Mama looked scared. She had that crazy look in her eyes that she got when everything became too much and she didn't know what to do.

Her neighbor turned to Mama and backed her against the wall. "You stupid bitch. You don't just leave your baby with the first fucking guy you meet. He's a pervert. If you had any sense you would have been able to see that. He tried to touch her. He burned her and all because you're too damn stupid to know that you shouldn't trust anyone you meet on the street."

"Harvey?" She looked over to him as he lay still on the floor where he fell. "Is he . . ."

"Whatever he is is your fault!"

Sunny felt hands touch her face and she lashed out, clawing and kicking until she felt heavy arms restrain her. "It's me, Sunshine. I'm not going to hurt you."

She shook off her terror and sat up. Her night clothes were sticking to her body. "Julian?"

He switched on the light beside her bed and she saw the damage she had done. His cheek was red and raised from where she had scratched him. "I'm so sorry. I was dreaming. I thought you were . . ." She shook her head. "I'm sorry."

"I heard you cry out. I got scared."

"I'm fine now." She lied. She hadn't dreamed about that night in many years. It was another one of those huge moments in her life, one that changed everything. One that had made her mother slip further and further into her mental illness.

"Why are you clutching your shoulder?" The concern never left his face as he pushed her hand away. Her burn was there, bright red and raised from her skin. There were times she wished she could cut it off, kill any reminders that it was ever there, kill any reminders of that night.

"What the hell happened to you?"

"I need to take a shower." She got out of bed and rushed into the bathroom closing the door behind her. She glanced at herself in the mirror. Her curls were plastered to her head, her eyes were huge and still filled with fear as if she was five again. She got in the shower and let the hot water run over her head, trying to wash away the memories of that night, but she couldn't. They were a part of her. They always would be. She was never going to escape what happened that night. It made her who she was.

She got out after the water had turned cold, ran

a comb through her curls, slathered lotion on her skin, anything she could do to prolong opening the bathroom door. She knew she wouldn't be able to go back to sleep. She never could sleep after that dream.

But she couldn't stay in the bathroom all night and when she opened the door Julian was still there. Her soaked sheets were in a pile on the floor and fresh ones were on the bed in their place.

"Thank you. You didn't have to do that."

"I know I didn't . . ." His voice broke. The emotion was so strong in it that it brought tears to Sunny's eyes. "I don't have the right to ask what happened to you, but I need to know, Sunny. I have to know who hurt you."

She climbed back in the bed and looked up at him. "Will you hold me?"

"Of course." He crossed the room and pulled her into his arms.

She just absorbed his warmth for a few moments. The safe feeling returned again. She only felt this way with him. She hated that no matter what she did, she couldn't create her own safe space. She didn't want to need anyone, but right now she needed this comfort. She needed him.

"There was a man who used to hang outside of the motel where we were staying. He befriended my mother by buying her gifts and giving her money until she fell in love with him. It only took a few weeks. He had gotten us an apartment and he had convinced my mother that he would watch me while she worked overnight. I was so young but I knew what he was up to and I avoided being alone with him, until one day I couldn't avoid it any longer. He tried to force me to sit on his lap and I bit him. That made him angry and he took a hot iron and burned me."

"Shit," Julian swore. "He's a fucking monster. Please tell me that your mother pressed charges and that he went to prison and that's the end of the story."

"No, it's not. My-my mother never got to press charges." She debated how much she should tell him. No one knew about this. It was her darkest secret. The things she was most ashamed of even though she knew it wasn't her fault. "My neighbor heard me scream and burst through the door with a metal baseball bat. He bashed Harvey in the head and two guys picked him up and took him somewhere. I think . . . I think they killed him."

Sunny felt Julian's body grow rigid. "He was a monster. He hurt you. He was trying to do unspeakable things to you. If your neighbor hadn't come . . . Damn it, Sunny. I don't want to think about it."

"I've never told anyone that. I try to pretend that I'm okay, but I'm not. I'm not sure I'll ever be." She felt herself trembling. She hated that she couldn't stop herself. She hated that she was still so affected by it twenty-five years later. "Sometimes I feel broken."

"You're not broken," he said firmly. "I don't think I know anyone who is as strong as you are."

He kissed her cheek. She turned her face toward his and pressed her body against his, wanting more of his closeness. She kissed his lips lightly. She was looking for more comfort, but that spark of heat was there and she kissed his lips again. It was a deeper, slower kiss this time and it immediately made her want more.

But she felt so emotional and her eyes filled with tears. "Touch me," she whispered.

He untied her bathrobe and slid his hand down her naked body. His hand was heavy and steady and warm and it had set every nerve in her skin on fire. He kept kissing her and kissing her, his tongue sweeping into her mouth softly and deeply. She felt like she were melting into him, like she could be one with him.

He ran his fingertips across her nipples, which aroused her even more than she thought was possible.

"You're so sweet," he said, kissing her cheeks. "I want to be with you all the time. So much that I can barely think."

"Be with me tonight." She wrapped her leg around his hip, opening herself to him. She took his fingers and brushed them over her wetness. "I want you. I need you."

"I need you too, but I don't have a condom."

"I've been on birth control since I was sixteen and I know you were tested after you broke up with Regina."

"Yes." He kissed the side of her throat as his fingers delved farther into her wetness. "I've never made love to a woman without protection before."

"I've never made love to a man before, period. It will be a night of firsts for us both."

He froze and looked into her eyes, some of the

heavy lust gone, now replaced by shock. "You're a virgin?"

"Yes. I thought you knew."

"You can't be. The way you move when I touch you. The way you kiss. The way you moan. You are sexual."

"I am a grown woman who has lived nearly thirty years." She slowly ran her palm down his erection. "I explore my body, the way I want to explore yours. I think about what feels good. I think about you and I touch myself and I say your name and I see your face and I imagine how good you would feel inside of me."

"But why haven't you been with anyone, Sunny?"

"I was waiting for you," she said honestly. "I was waiting for someone I could trust with my body."

He looked at her for a moment before he crushed his mouth to hers and then he rolled on top of her and his heavy body felt right to her. She felt safe beneath him. She felt blissful.

He pushed himself inside of her, but she couldn't describe the feeling. There was no pain. There was only the most intense pleasure. And rightness. This felt right.

He was being so gentle with her, deep kisses and long, slow strokes. He was controlling himself. He was such a powerful man. He could do whatever he wanted to her and she would gladly let him, but he was making love to her. He was whispering her name between kisses, he was looking her in the eyes and there was something there she couldn't name.

She was so painfully in love with him and she knew

nothing would ever change that. No matter where their lives took them, she would never forget him or this night or how he made her feel.

She wrapped her legs tightly around him, urging him to go deeper, to move a little faster.

"Stop it," he whispered. "You feel too good."

"I can't stop. I'm barely holding on."

"Don't," he said through gritted teeth. "I want this to be everything you want it to be."

"I just want to be with you."

He stared into her eyes and gave her a kiss so deep that it felt like he was trying to kiss the soul out of her. She kept her eyes open. They wanted to drift closed but she forced them to stay open so she could see him, the strain in his face, the sweat on his brow, the look in his eyes. She didn't want to forget a moment of this. Her body moved against him, not knowing what she was doing, but it felt natural, it felt good. He pumped deeper inside of her and faster and she dug her nails into his shoulders, pressed her mouth into his neck to muffle her cries.

He pushed hard inside and it caused her to break and her toes curled and the waves of intense pleasure took her breath away. He let go with her and she felt his warmth spill into her and she liked the feeling. She felt closer to him than anyone ever before in her life.

His body was hot and heavy on top of hers and she loved the sensation. She felt so safe and warm and happy. She wrapped her arms around him and kissed the side of his face.

He pulled himself off her. "I'm crushing you."

She missed his weight, his smell, his warmth, the way he filled her up. "I didn't mind."

He looked down into her eyes with concern in his. "Are you okay?" He cupped her cheek. "I didn't hurt you?"

"No. It was perfect. Thank you."

He gathered her into his arms and rested his lips on her forehead. He was very quiet and she could feel that there was something churning inside of him. He was thinking hard about something and Sunny felt her insecurities rise even though she knew they shouldn't. She had wanted nothing more from him than this.

"What's the matter, Julian?"

"I'm feeling a lot right now."

"Is one of those things regret?"

"I regret not making love to you months ago. I knew we would end up here. The pull was too strong. You're my best friend, Sunny, and I feel like knowing you has changed me. I'm not sure I recognize myself anymore."

"All that from having sex with me once. Damn, I must be good in bed."

He laughed out loud and pulled her on top of him. "You are," he said, still smiling at her. "I imagined being with you a thousand times. All the things I would do to your body." He ran his hands down her back, arousing her again.

"It wasn't like you expected?"

"No." He sought her lips and gave her a slow but incredibly sexual kiss. It wasn't sweet like the kisses he gave her before. "You gave me your virginity and now I'm selfish. I don't want you to ever have sex with another man as long as you live, no matter what happens."

"Oh . . ." She rubbed her body against his. "There's only one way for me to even consider that."

"What's that?" He grinned.

"You're going to have to make sure all my needs are satisfied."

"I think I can do that."

"Are you sure, Mr. King? I have so many of them."

He rolled her back over and pushed inside of her. "Be careful what you ask for, Gibson. I might never leave you alone."

Julian sat on the edge of Sunny's bed while he waited for her to get ready. He was in a weird place. His body felt calm, satisfied in a way he didn't think was possible, but his mind was a jumble. He couldn't shake what Sunny had told him last night. She had witnessed a man being killed right in front of her eyes, but it was the man who was trying to groom her, the man who was brutal enough to burn a small child with an iron when she fought to stay away from him. And her mother. . . . Too stupid, or selfish, or sick to know that she should never let a strange man watch your child.

How the hell did Sunny stay so strong? How the hell did she survive it? He wasn't that strong. His life hadn't been that hard. He had a family and a support system. He had opportunities. She had to fight for everything she had and she still didn't have a lot.

And he had made love to her. Finally. He had waited so long. He had been afraid to before because he knew what it would mean. He would want more of her. Crave more of her. She was a drug to him. There were a thousand things going on in his mind. His career. His future. His family, but the only clear thoughts he had seemed to revolve around her. He hated it. It wasn't him. His career had always come first and now the only thing he was driven to do was be with her. Protect her. Save her even though she didn't need him to do any of that.

She walked out of the bathroom wearing a little sundress that hugged her curvy body just right. Her feet were bare. Her curls were short and springy. She was adorable and sexy and just looking at her made him hard.

"I got coffee while you were getting ready. I wasn't sure if you wanted to eat breakfast here or stop somewhere else."

She placed a few items in her bag and then walked over to him and wrapped her arms around him. Hugging was new to him. It sounded odd, but it was. He never shared this kind of closeness with Regina. They never touched just to touch. She never just pressed her body to his without seduction in mind. And he had never attempted it with her or any other woman, for that matter. He wasn't affectionate. At least he didn't used to be, but he savored Sunny's every touch. He leaned into it. It made him feel like he had never felt before.

"I don't care where we eat, just as long as there is a lot of it and it's bad for me." She kissed his forehead and because he wasn't satisfied with that, he lifted his chin and pressed his lips to hers.

She let out a little moan as if his kisses were delicious and he found it arousing. He knew he should let her go. They had to get on the road. They needed to eat, but he was more hungry for her than any food. He kissed her again and skimmed his fingers up the backs of her thighs.

"You're not wearing any underwear," he said when his fingers found her bottom to be bare, round, and smooth.

"You weren't supposed to put your hands that far up my dress." She gave him a sexy grin and turned away from him.

"I think you planned that. You didn't put any on because you wanted to turn me on so much that it's hard for me to think."

"I just forgot to take them in the bathroom with me."

He followed her around the room, grabbed her arm, spun her toward him, and kissed her.

"I want you again. This is why I waited so long, because I knew once I had you, I would never be able to have enough of you. You're going to have to start carrying a hose with you."

"No." She closed her eyes and leaned into him. "It feels good to be wanted."

"How are you feeling?" He slipped his fingers between her legs to find her wet already. "Are you sore from last night? We don't have to have sex. Tell me what you want."

"I've always dreamed about you taking me against a wall in a hotel room." That mischievous grin crossed her face again and it turned him on so much his hands trembled as he pulled her dress up and pushed against the nearest wall.

She tore at the fly on his shorts and he was inside of her in moments. She was so tight and wet and he could barely control himself. Her legs were wrapped tightly around him, her fingers dug into his back and she cried out his name over and over. And then she climaxed. He felt her clench around him and it drove him over the edge. He let out a string of incoherent words and then carried her to the bed, laying her down gently.

"That was . . . I liked that," she said with a smile.

"You let me know if there is anything else I can do for you. I'm happy to be of service."

"Anything?"

"Anything. I would do anything for you."

She ran her fingers through his hair. "Call your mother. Please. For me. It feels wrong to leave it like that."

"You're thinking about my mother after sex like that? I feel inadequate."

"I'm still seeing stars. There's nothing inadequate about you, but please call her. I won't ask you for anything else."

She didn't ask him for anything. Only to take this case and his life ended up being better for it. "Okay," he sighed. "I'll do this for you."

* * *

He was surprised when his mother picked up his call on the first ring. He wasn't sure he would have if the tables had been turned. She agreed to meet them in the same park they had met in the day before, but this time Julian knew what was coming.

He got out of his car to see his mother already waiting beside hers. Sunny grabbed his hand as they walked toward her. His heart was pounding a little harder than usual. He wasn't sure why. If he had to put a name to it, he would say he was slightly nervous. But for the life of him, he didn't know why.

"Hello," Sunny greeted his mother with a bright smile. "Thank you for coming back. I hope we get the chance to talk one day."

"Hello, Sunny. Thank you for convincing him to return. I know my son wouldn't be here without you."

"I'm pretty sure that a big part of Julian wants to be here. Or else I would have never gotten him to come back." She looked at Julian and kissed the side of his face. "Just listen," she whispered. "I'll be near the pond. Come find me."

She let go of his hand and walked away. He hadn't wanted to let her go, but he did because he knew that this conversation was one that he needed to have alone.

"I know my opinion doesn't mean much to you, but I really like Sunny. The only thing I have ever wanted for you was to be happy and with her I don't have to worry that you will be."

Happy . . . Is that what he was with Sunny? He wasn't sure he would describe it that way. He didn't know how to describe the way he felt when he was with her. He had never felt this feeling before. There was a heady rush whenever she was near him and he missed her when she was gone. Then there was uncertainty because she wasn't what he wanted for his life. But she was presented to him, like some sort of gift he never knew he wanted.

"She's a thoroughly good person. She's strong and she's kind and she always puts everyone else first. I can't say that about many people but I can say that about her. And sometimes I feel like I don't deserve to know her."

"What a beautiful thing to say." She smiled. "I hope you tell her that."

He should have told her that, but wasn't sure he was able to. "I'm supposed to listen, but I have one question. Why the hell did you leave us the way you did?"

"I know you think I left you because I was unhappy with my life and that I regretted marrying your father, but that wasn't it. Your father is a very good man and he was very good to me. My family wasn't happy when I brought him home at first, but I didn't give a damn about that. What you don't know is that I had been pregnant again after Galen. From the start of the pregnancy I knew something wasn't right, so your father and I agreed not to tell you until we were sure the baby was going to be okay. When I was around seven months pregnant, the baby died inside of me and I had to give birth to him. Do you remember when I was in the hospital when you were a kid? We told you it was my appendix."

He nodded. He did remember. He had remembered her gaining weight and always being in pain, but he had never thought she was pregnant. They had been so happy when she was pregnant with Galen. That time, he could only remember his parents being worried all the time.

"The loss of that baby hit me incredibly hard. I developed a deep depression that I never sought help for. I thought it would go away on its own, but it didn't. It only got worse. A lot worse. I started having vivid visions of hurting myself and hurting both of you. It's why I used to lock myself in my room whenever you two were around. I was afraid of hurting you. Your father confronted me, telling me that if I didn't get help he was going to have me committed. He was right. I needed to be committed, but I was so angry with him for telling me I was unfit, so I left. I drove across country alone and was found by the police when I tried to break in to someone's home. I was committed to a hospital for five months."

"Did Dad know you were in the hospital?"

"Yes, but I asked him not to tell you. I was ashamed. Ashamed of being sick. Ashamed for having those thoughts of hurting you. It took me a long time to be okay. It was a lot of therapy. A lot of medication changes. I was so afraid that those feelings would come back that I was too afraid to see you or your sister, to be alone with you. I was afraid to face you. You were better off with your father. It took me a long time to feel like myself again. Years and years and by the time I felt safe again, it was too late. You both hated me and I hated myself for not getting treated earlier."

It was too much information to process at once. He turned away from his mother. He couldn't look at her any longer. He couldn't stand to see the pain on her face, or the tears in her eyes.

She was sick. She had been a danger to them. She had been ashamed.

"I wish you would have told us." His voice came out choked. His throat burned. He didn't sound like himself. "I spent so long being angry at you. Why the hell couldn't you just tell us?"

"I didn't know how. I didn't think you would understand. But I love you. I have always loved you and the biggest regret of my life is that I didn't see you grow up. That I can take no credit for the incredible man you have become."

He turned back to her and wrapped her up in a quick tight hug. "I'm sorry," he managed to get out. He kissed her forehead and then walked away from her, blindly walking down the path toward Sunny. He found her and she looked toward him without him even calling her name. She ran to him and wrapped her arms around him. His face was wet and hot. His chest burned and it took him a while to process what was happening to him.

Sunny never asked him what happened, she just ran her hands down his back and whispered soothing things in his ear.

It struck him in that moment that he wasn't alone,

that he didn't feel alone for the first time. He had never realized that he felt that way before, and it shook him. He pulled away from her and stared at her for a long moment.

"I think we need to eat. I feel like French toast or maybe a western omelet or maybe both," she told him.

It was the perfect thing for her to say to him in that moment. He took her hand and as he walked he began to think that it would be impossible to go back to a life without her.

Chapter 16

Sunny had never asked Julian what his mother said to him. They had gone to breakfast and drove nearly seven hours to get to South Carolina, but he remained silent on the matter until they stopped at a hotel that night. They were only about an hour away from his sister's home, but she could tell he was exhausted. He showered and climbed into bed with her and started to tell her the story, not just what his mother had told him, but his memories of his childhood and how he had felt then and how he felt now. He had been in so much pain and she had hurt for him. She understood him better now. She felt closer to him.

He had made love to her afterward. Long, slow, intensely passionate, and intensely sweet. And in the morning, they got up and drove the rest of the way to the little island off the coast of South Carolina and Sunny felt like Julian had taken her to paradise. He had had his contact at his law firm put out a search for Grace's husband, hoping they could track them down at the South Carolina home. In the meanwhile, they would relax. Have a real vacation. It was the first one Sunny had ever had.

The house was lovely, which was an odd word for a home of its size. It was more like an estate that overlooked the ocean. But it was homey and it felt like a place like she could stay forever.

"Alex used to come here as a kid with his parents and he had seen this house every year and promised himself he would own it one day. It was only supposed to be a summer home, but he fell in love with my sister here and this is where they stay most of the year."

"I don't blame them. It must be hard to leave here."

"Let me take you inside to meet them."

Sunny was nervous entering the house. She had met Julian's mother yesterday, but she didn't think much about it because of the nature of her relationship with Julian. But she was about to meet the rest of his family. The people he loved the most, the people who were the closest to him. She had always felt awkward around families. She had never really belonged to one. She didn't know how to interact with them. She'd had her last foster mother who had taken care of her better than anyone else, but she hadn't had her for very long, a little over a year. It was just the two of them and it was a quiet life until she had gotten sick and the cancer had quickly taken her away.

"They'll like you," he said softly just as they were entering. "I promise."

Sunny heard a loud scream and then saw a flash of pink launch toward Julian.

"My big dumb brother is here!"

"Hey, little stupid sister." He spun her around, hugging her tightly.

"I missed you," she told him as he set her down. "You can't wait so long to visit."

"I have some time off now. I'm not rushing to get back to New York. You'll be sick of me before I leave." He looked over to the large man with wavy brown hair who was standing just behind Galen. "Hey, Alex." He gave his brother-in-law a brief hug.

"Good to see you, man. We're glad you're here."

"Is that my boy?" Another large man, this one older, came from down the hall. He rushed and swept his son up in a huge hug. Julian did resemble his mother, but he was his father's son.

Sunny felt emotional standing there watching the family reunion. It was sweet, but it made her feel empty. It made her hate herself a little for feeling jealous that she would never get this greeting, that there was never a home for her to return to.

"Guys," Julian said when he let go of his father. "I want you to meet Sunny. Sunny, this is my father Peter, my sister Galen, and my brother-in-law Alex."

"It's nice to meet you. Julian only has wonderful things to say about all of you. Thank you, Galen and Alex, for letting me stay in your apartment. I really appreciate it."

"You sent baked goods to us," Alex said. "Those were the best brownies I have ever had. I have to hug you."

He hugged her and then Galen hugged her and then Peter hugged her. They were warm and friendly and she liked them immediately.

"Galen, can you put Sunny in the seashell room? I think she'll like the view from there."

Galen frowned at him. "Of course. If you're sure that's what you want. And you would like to stay . . . ?"

"In the same place I stayed in last time."

"Okay . . . Let me show you to your room, Sunny." She looked at her husband. "Can you start the grill? Julian, grab the bags and meet us upstairs."

Sunny followed Galen upstairs and listened while she gave a brief tour of the house.

"It's all so incredibly beautiful," Sunny said to her. "Thank you for allowing me to tag along with Julian and thank you again for the use of your apartment."

"You don't have to thank me." She smiled. "My brother told me your apartment was broken into. He was concerned. Extremely concerned. In fact, I've never known my brother to be that concerned about anyone before."

"He's sweet. He can be a macho ass sometimes, but he's a good man and it's rare that I encounter anyone who cares as deeply as he does."

Galen gave her a soft smile, took her hand, and led her to the sitting area in front of the bay window that looked out on to the beach. "I worry about my brother. Do you think he's happy?"

"Maybe that is a question you should ask him."

"He won't tell me. Everything is always fine with Jules, but I wonder if he is really as happy with his life as he thinks. There's no one else for me to ask."

"I tricked him into meeting your mother so that he could really talk to her."

Galen's eyes went wide. "He probably hit the roof."

"He was furious with me and told me to mind my business at first. But he feels better. He's going through a lot right now, Galen. He had been planning to marry Regina and working furiously to become partner of his firm when I had first met him. I want him to be happy. God knows that's the only thing I want for him, but I can't answer that question for him."

Galen nodded. "I'm glad he's not going to marry Regina. I hated her."

"She's cold, but I do think she loved him in her own way."

"You've met her?"

"A few times. She hates me. She looked at me like I was a bag of rotting garbage. I know she blames me for their breakup, but we met afterward and we truly were just friends."

"She looks at everyone she doesn't think is on her level like that. Meaning anyone who makes less than six figures a year. I saw her reduce a waiter to tears once when he accidentally gave her fried instead of grilled chicken. We were at a soul food restaurant."

"She wanted grilled chicken over fried? Now I know she's evil."

They both laughed as Julian walked back into the room. "What's so funny?"

"Your face," Galen said as she got up and crossed the room. "I'm going to check on Alex and Dad.

Every time I ask them to start the grill, it takes them a good thirty minutes. They argue over the charcoal placement and I'm usually left starving." She squeezed his arm and gave him a little nod before she walked out.

"My sister likes you," Julian told her as he placed her bag on the bed.

"I like her too. She's beautiful. I thought you were gorgeous, but you in female form is damn near breathtaking. I'm a fairly confident person but I feel inadequate here. Your brother-in-law is hot too."

"You're the sexiest woman I have ever known." He walked toward her with that look in his eyes and a little smile on his lips. He hugged her and she closed her eyes and rested her head on his chest.

"I'm going to miss you tonight."

"No, you won't. I asked for you to be put in this room because it is close to mine and far away from Galen's room. My father's room is downstairs so it will be very easy to sneak out of my bed and climb into yours."

"That's naughty."

"I know, but I can't go back to sleeping without you."

"Are you saying sex with me is addicting?"

"Yes, but I like going to sleep with you. I like turning over and feeling you next to me."

She hugged him a little more tightly. She didn't say anything because if she did she would have told him that she loved him. She wasn't ready to tell him that and she was sure he wasn't ready to hear it from her, but he had to know. He had to feel her love. She couldn't hide it.

"Will you take me down to the beach sometime?"

"Yes. We can go wherever you want."

She stood on her tiptoes and reached up to kiss him. She meant for it to be a light kiss, but Julian deepened it and she felt the warmth spread through her and her body get liquid.

"Stop," she whispered as she pulled away. "Don't start something that you can't finish," she said with a smile.

"I can't help myself. I can't believe I made it this long without you."

"You could have been with whoever you wanted. You weren't lacking for sex."

"It wasn't the sex. It was you. I was missing you."

When he said things like that, he sounded like he loved her. Like this wasn't a fling, or friendship, or something that was just temporary, but she couldn't let her mind take her there. She couldn't count on forever, because forever never lasted for her.

Julian felt more at peace than he had in years. This wasn't the place he had grown up, but he felt at home here. Maybe it was because he was with his family. He hadn't realized how much he missed being around them until he was with them again. They had stayed up very late last night, just talking and laughing. Sunny had sat beside him on the couch, close to him, but not touching. She had been quiet, taking them all in, but seeming to enjoy herself. He knew that this was awkward for her. There was no one person she had spent her entire life with, no one person that she had a shared history with. No one who she looked like, who shared the same traits, no one who could tell stories of her as a little carefree girl.

He wanted this trip to be carefree for her. He wanted this trip to be one of those happy memories she could keep. They were all down at the beach. Their chairs pushed all the way up to the shore, their toes being gently lapped by the water.

He looked over at Sunny. Her eyes were closed. Her face was turned up to the sun. There was a slight smile on her lips. He had a hard time pulling his eyes from her. She looked like she belonged here, wearing a bathing suit, her curls bigger and wilder, her skin browner and sun-kissed. She looked like a goddess.

"Hey, guys," Alex said to them. "I'm going to head inside and make us some sandwiches. We can eat out here on the beach."

"That sounds nice, baby," his wife replied. "We're not having dinner till late tonight. We can have a nice big spread."

"I'll help you." Sunny popped out of her chair. "You want spicy mustard instead of mayo, Julian?" she asked as she ran her fingers through his hair. She then seemed to think better of it and removed her hand. "And turkey rather than ham?"

"Yes, to both." He grabbed her fingers and squeezed. "You remembered."

"Of course."

"Hey, Alex," Galen said. "How come you aren't asking what I want?"

"You'll eat what I bring you, woman, and you'll like it." He winked at her, gave her a grin, and then tugged Sunny's hand away from Julian and led her into the house.

"Thank you for being so kind to Sunny," Julian said to Galen when they were alone.

"Why wouldn't I be kind to her? She's very sweet."

"You've hated every woman I have introduced you to."

"Not all of them. Some of them were just using you. I could see dollar bill signs in their eyes whenever they looked at you. And then there was Regina. You two didn't even seem to even like each other. There was no easiness there. You two were using each other."

"You really think so?"

"Yes. She got a young hot shot boyfriend. And you got an older woman who gave you some respectability. It's different with Sunny."

"She's my best friend."

"Yeah, and what's with the friends act?" She frowned at him.

"What do you mean?"

"You two aren't sharing a bedroom. She definitely tries not to touch you when we're around. I saw you grab her, push her against the wall, and kiss her like you two were long lost lovers when you thought no one was around. You don't have to sneak around."

"What about the no unmarried couples sharing a room rule?"

"That rule doesn't exist here."

"You told me the last time I visited that I shouldn't bring Regina because it would make Dad uncomfortable."

"That wasn't because you two weren't married. It's because Dad hated her too."

"I get it, Galen. You hated her. You hated every woman I have ever dated."

"I don't hate Sunny. That should tell you something. How could I hate anyone who looks at you the way she does?"

"Does she look at me a certain way?"

"Yes. There's love in her eyes, Julian. You have to see that and even if you can't, you have to feel it."

He was quiet for a moment as he thought about Sunny. She looked at him in a way that no one else ever had and she did things for him, for his well-being, for his soul that no one else would ever do for him. "She is love. She would give you her last dime if she thought you needed it."

"And she's deeply in love with you. I'm surprised she hasn't told you."

"She hasn't."

Galen frowned at him again. "You act as if that is something you might not want to hear."

"Any man would be lucky to be loved by her. I feel like she would say it if she felt it."

"Maybe she thinks you aren't ready to hear it. Maybe she thinks you don't love her back. Maybe she thinks you are afraid of commitment and have had such disastrous relationships with women who are clearly wrong for you because you have unresolved issues with your mother and she doesn't want to get her heart broken. But she does love you. I don't know everything. But I know that."

He couldn't describe the feeling that welled up in his chest. He was having a hard time envisioning his life without her. His life before her seemed quieter, emptier, simpler. He couldn't say he was happy then. Was he happy now? He didn't know. His career had come first. He was supposed to be taking his time off and thinking about what he wanted. But he couldn't think about it, didn't want to think about it, because every thought in his head revolved around her.

That's not what this time was for. He was wasting it. But how he could be wasting it when being with her made him feel so good? No one had ever made her feel this good. "Damn, Galen."

"Damn is right."

"Let's change the subject. When were you going to tell me you were pregnant?"

Shock crossed her face. "Did Alex tell you?"

"Not exactly. I saw him rub your belly last night. That's not something he would normally do. I'm happy for you. You'll be an incredible mother."

"He's so excited." Her eyes filled with tears. "I'm so happy. We were going to tell everyone at dinner tonight. I wanted my family around me when we announced. That's why I wanted you to come down. I want to see you more. I want you to feel the same kind of happiness that I have."

He grabbed her hand. "That would be nice, Galen. That would be incredibly nice."

Chapter 17

"Damn it!" Galen smacked her patio table as Sunny grinned at her. They were sitting in the back of her house, overlooking the ocean, a deck of cards between them.

"I forgot how fun this game is."

"It's only fun for you because you've won five games in a row."

"I heard when you're pregnant your brain slows down a bit. I'm sure you'll beat me after you have the baby."

"Okay, we'll have rematch here in exactly a year. But I think you're some type of ringer. Some sort of Spit champion who has won competitions with huge cash prizes in Vegas or somewhere."

"Nope. I was a foster kid. I once had a foster mom who would force us to play each other every night. Only the winner got to eat. I learned to get fast out of necessity."

Everyone got incredibly quiet around them. Julian's father and his new girlfriend stared at her.

Alex shook his head. Julian and Galen gave her matching sad looks.

"That was a joke! I was never forced to play Spit for food."

"I've heard some of your stories, Sunny," Julian said. "At this point, I would believe anything you told me."

"That didn't happen. I had some challenging times, but my childhood wasn't all bad. I do think being in foster care helped with my card playing skills. I've been placed in homes with lots of other kids and often the thing that connected us was playing games. I got good at a lot of them. I'm really good at chess. I used to hustle old men in the park after school for money. They never thought I could beat them. It's how I saved up enough money to buy my first CD player."

"I love chess," Julian's father said. "I would love to take you on. I'm pretty good myself and I'm not going to be fooled by your cuteness."

Sunny smiled at him. "I'm thirty. My cuteness has long worn off. But challenge accepted. After dinner."

"I think you're still cute," Julian said, giving her a little wink.

"I think you're cute too. You want to play me in chess?"

"No way in hell." He laughed.

Sunny had noticed the change in him since they had been there the past week. He was quieter, calmer, but he smiled so much more than he had in the past. He was happier and she knew it had everything to do with his family.

They were such good people. She had been nervous to be around them, but her fears were for nothing. They had welcomed her just like she was a part of their family. Especially Galen with whom she had spent the most time. They had stayed up all night a few days ago just talking and laughing. If that was what it was like to have a sister, Sunny would adore it. They had completely lost track of time that night until Julian came to get her around four A.M. to bring her to bed. The same bed they had been sharing since their second night there.

He had told her that he had a hard time sleeping without her. And now that she had slept in his arms every night, she was starting to think she would never get to sleep without him again. Every day her love grew deeper, more solid. But there was still that fear inside her. She couldn't let herself get too comfortable with him. Nothing lasted forever with her. But if something could, she wanted him to be the one who would always be there. It was too much to hope for. There was too much up in the air. Being in the warmth of his family had made her forget why they had come to South Carolina in the first place.

They—no, she was on a journey that had started over twenty years ago when her mother left her. A huge part of her never wanted to leave this place, but that was her fear talking.

Nerves were bubbling up inside her often, pulling her from sleep at night, pulling her from the peaceful feelings that surrounded her on this island. She felt like she belonged here, more than anywhere else in her life. She was surrounded by the ocean and the sun and kind people and it brought her back to when she was four, before Mama had pulled her out of school and away from safety. Before she knew that there could be such enormous fear and that people could hurt her.

But her mind could just be playing tricks on her, lulling her into a false sense of security. She owed this to Soren to go on. To the Earls. She needed to take herself out of the equation even though she felt like she was a huge part of it. Even if they did share a mother, Soren didn't belong with her. She belonged with people who were safe, who could love her as she needed to be loved. She deserved the life that Sunny never had.

And that's why she didn't tell Julian about her possible connection to Soren. Sometimes she wanted to. Sometimes the words bubbled up inside of her and threatened to overflow.

It didn't feel good anymore to keep it from him. He knew everything about her. But this. She needed to keep some part of herself to herself. Even if it was just this. It was for protection.

"You okay, Sunny?" He touched her shoulder.

"What?" She rubbed her temple.

"You spaced out there for a moment."

"I've got a bit of a headache. It must be too much sun and not enough water."

"I'll get you some." Julian's father stood up. "And maybe a little snack."

"You don't have to." She shook her head. "I'm fine."

"You should go lay down for a little while," Galen said, looking concerned. "I'll bring you some aspirin."

"No one has to bring me anything. I'm fine. Thank you for being so kind. I can take care of myself."

"But that's the thing about having a family, Sunny," Peter said. "You don't have to take care of yourself. We're here to take care of you."

Her eyes filled with tears. It was the most beautiful thing to say.

Chapter 18

The next day Julian found himself alone on the patio staring out at the ocean. He had always known that his sister and brother-in-law's home was in a beautiful part of the country. He had even been to this house before on a few occasions, but this was the first time he really noticed how truly beautiful it was here. He hadn't thought he was a beach person, but he could get used to this life, this pace. Get used to being this close to his family. But he knew it couldn't last forever. There was a big job waiting for him when he got back home. Cleese had wanted him to take time to think about what he wanted, yet as hard as Julian tried, he couldn't force himself to think about work.

It was a no brainer. He had to take the job he had always strived for. But now that he was away from it, he didn't miss it. He figured that the time would come when he did miss it, and probably soon. This vacation would just be a nice memory for him. One he would hope to repeat more often.

Sunny came out of the house carrying a large glass of lemonade in her hand. She was smiling. He had seen her smile more this week than he ever had. He had seen her lose some of her edge. He had seen her relax. He had seen her let her guard down. It made her even more beautiful to him.

"Hey." She handed him the glass. "I thought you might be thirsty."

He took the glass from her, set it on the table, and then pulled her into his lap. "Thank you. How are you today?" he asked in her ear.

"I'm happy," she whispered. "I feel weird saying it, but I am. This place makes my soul happy. Thank you for bringing me here."

"Don't thank me, Sunny."

"Why not? I'm thankful."

"Sunny?" Galen called. "Alex and I are going to get ice cream now. I know I said after lunch, but I'm pregnant and I can change my mind if I want to." She grinned. "Would you like to come with us? Dad's girlfriend is coming too."

"Of course, I want to come. After I heard about the cupcake sundae I won't be able to think about much else until I have one." She looked back at Julian. "Do you want to come with us?"

"I'll stay here. I've been eating way too much on this trip. I'm going to get a big gut and not be able to fit into any of my suits."

Sunny slipped her hand up his shirt and touched his still hard stomach. "I wouldn't care if your belly gets big. I would still think you're sexy." She kissed him and gave him a sassy grin. "Plus if you get chubby it will make me feel better about myself."

He touched his lips to her ear. "There's nothing about you that I would change," he whispered. "Not a damn thing."

"Are you guys looking for Angie?" Peter asked, referring to his girlfriend as he came onto the patio. "She went walking on the beach."

"I'll go get her," Sunny volunteered and hopped off Julian's lap.

Julian watched her as she bounced away from them and onto the sand. She really was happy here. Her happiness affected him deeply.

"I want to give you something, son." Peter reached into his pocket and pulled out a small box. Julian frowned in confusion at his father. "Go on. Open it."

Julian did as his father asked and saw that it was his grandmother's diamond ring. "When my parents first got married they could barely afford the simple bands they wore, but my father worked and saved for twenty years to be able to afford a ring like that for my mother. I remember the day he gave it to her. She was so shocked. My father was a frugal man. If it wasn't on sale, we didn't own it, but on this he spent. And when my mother was convinced that it was really for her, she cried. She cherished this ring and right before she died she gave it to me to pass on to you for when you found the right girl."

"What?" Julian blinked at his father and back at the ring.

"I know it's old-fashioned and simple and that you were probably considering something more modern, but I think Sunny would like it. We're so glad you brought her home to us, Julian. I knew you were thinking about marrying Regina and I couldn't picture giving up my mother's ring to that woman. But I am happily giving it to you for Sunny."

"But Dad . . ." He didn't know what to say. "It's only been a few months."

"You're in love with her. I can see it in your eyes when you look at her. You smile more. You're happy. You're better because of her."

He must have been in love with her. What else could this feeling be? He had never felt it before. Never felt it with this intensity. He thought it was obsession. He thought he was losing his mind. But he was in love with her. Incredibly in love with her.

And he didn't want to be.

It made everything more complicated.

"Julian," Galen said softly, "you can't see a future with her?"

"I can," he said truthfully.

But he wasn't sure if it was the future he wanted.

Sunny walked into the bedroom she shared with Julian to find him sitting in front of the window that overlooked the ocean. It was clear he was deep in thought and she was about to walk away so she wouldn't disturb him, but he must have heard her footsteps because he turned around and looked at her.

"I didn't mean to bother you. I just came to get

my sweatshirt. I was going to go for a walk on the beach."

"Alone?"

"Yeah." She felt awkward. "I know we're leaving soon. I want to spend as much time near the water as I can. I don't care how gray it is outside." For the past couple of days she had felt that way. He had gone incredibly quiet on her.

She felt like he might be getting tired of her. They had been together every single day. With his family. There was no work. No real space between them.

She was giving him his space. She had too much self-respect to force him to be around her when he'd rather not be.

"Can I go with you?"

"If you're asking because you think I shouldn't go alone, you don't have to worry. This is not New York City. I'm not going to get snatched."

"I want to go with you because I want to be with you."

"Oh." His statement knocked her off guard. "Of course, you can come."

He nodded and got out of his chair, grabbing both of their sweatshirts before they headed out to the beach. It was cool outside, damp and cloudy. The wind was blowing just a little too hard to make it comfortable, but they were alone. Everyone else was inside, cuddled up with books or in front of the television.

They were quiet for a long time as they walked

down the empty beach, watching the waves churn in the ocean. Sunny knew that there were other people on this island but it didn't feel that way. She never thought she would like the feeling. She had grown up in New York. She had been in foster homes with many children. She didn't know what it was like to sleep truly by herself until she had gotten her first apartment. She never thought she would be comfortable without the hustle of the city outside of the window. Never thought she would feel calm without knowing that all she had to do was step outside to see, to speak to another human being.

But here it was different. It made her feel calm. Even though emotion was roiling inside of her, she felt more at peace than she had in years. The water was a powerful thing. She wasn't sure how she was going to go back to life without it.

"It's going to storm again tonight," he said, breaking the silence.

"It feels like it. I love it though. I love the feeling in the air. I love the sound of the thunder. I like how the entire beach lights up when lightning strikes. It's exciting."

"This is why they love you," he said to her. "Rain-storms excite you. Simple things make you happy."

"Your family is incredible. I'm so glad to have been able to spend this time with them."

"They wish I would have brought you home sooner," he said softly, "I never get to spend this much time with them. It is good to see everyone so relaxed."

"But it's weird having me around, isn't it? I can go stay at a motel for a few days so you can have some time alone with them."

"No." He frowned at her and shook his head. "I want you with me." She didn't know why she was surprised by his reaction, but she was. He was too polite to tell her he wanted her away, but she thought he would take her up on the opportunity to be here without her. "You have to stay."

"I know your family thinks that I'm your girlfriend and that we're serious. It has to be weird for you. I can tell them it's not like that. That we're . . ." she trailed off. She didn't know what they were, only that she loved him and that she should have protected her heart a little better.

She would be so sad when this came to an end. But she couldn't say she wasn't prepared. She expected that this happiness was only here for a little while. An experience for her to learn from.

"But it *is* like that. You're more than my girl-friend." He paused and looked away from her for a moment. He looked tortured for a moment. "You're my best friend and my life has changed since you came into it." He grabbed her hand and pulled her close to him, wrapping his heavy arms around her. Immediately she felt warm. "This snuck up on me," he whispered. "I was planning on spending my life with someone else and then you came along. This wasn't supposed to happen."

She didn't know what to say to him. He was right. Neither one of them had planned on this. But it had happened and it wasn't one sided. It was intense. And when they were together it felt right.

But maybe not for him. He was unsure. She could tell. She could feel it, but she wouldn't waste her time trying to convince him. If he had to think so hard about them, then that was a sign.

She wanted to spend the rest of her life with him. It wasn't something she had to think about. It was something that she just knew. It was also something she knew that would probably never be possible. This trip was ending. Soren's case was ending. They were going back to New York next week.

"Say something," he said.

"I think it's starting to rain."

"Sunny . . ."

She looked up at him. "I think I want fried shrimp for dinner. And strawberry milkshakes for dessert. I want to bring back souvenirs for my friends before we leave, and I want to take a thousand more pictures before we go so I don't forget this place."

He cupped her face in his hands and tilted it up toward his own and kissed her. "I've missed you these past couple of days. Why have you been keeping yourself away from me?"

"You seem like you needed the space."

"I didn't. I would tell you if I wanted space from you. I want to be with you every moment of the day."

She believed him. That was the crazy thing. He had barely said anything to her in the past couple of days but at night he reached for her and made slow, sweet love to her and then he held her while they slept.

It confused the hell out of her.

"I'm crazy about you, Mr. King. You know that, don't you?"

"No. I don't. Tell me more."

Thunder cracked above them and then the rain started to fall. They weren't close to the house, about a half mile down the deserted beach.

He grabbed her hand and tugged her in the opposite direction of the house. The rain started to come down hard and Sunny could barely see, but she trusted Julian to lead her in the right direction. They came to a little shed with kayaks around it.

Julian said something to her but she couldn't hear him over the storm. He flung open the door and pulled her inside. There were more boats and a couple of jet skis and stacks of towels.

"Alex and Galen own this too, but they are not much for water sports since Alex's injury."

"I'm glad you brought me here. We would have been drenched by the time we got back to the house."

"We're drenched now." He unzipped her hooded sweatshirt and peeled it off her body. He grabbed a towel off a shelf and ran it gently across her face before he kissed her. "I don't think I'll be able to concentrate with these clothes sticking to your body."

"You wanted to come for a walk with me." She pressed her lips to his. "Are you mad that I'm all wet?"

"Mad? No." He hooked his thumbs into her shorts

and pulled them down, taking her underwear with them. "I'm a lot of things right now. I'm cold. I'm happy. I'm turned on as hell, but I'm definitely not mad."

"Get naked, Mr. King."

He pulled his sweatshirt off over his head, revealing his smooth, slightly damp chest. He never failed to arouse her. He didn't have to do much; he just had to be.

She stepped forward and unbuttoned his shorts, looking into his eyes as she slid them down his powerful legs.

"Go sit on that bench," she ordered as she kicked off her flip flops and removed her clothes completely.

His eyes were full of arousal and she felt powerful as he did what she asked. She straddled him, keeping her eyes locked with his as she slid down on his erection.

He groaned. She loved the feeling of him inside of her and she almost didn't want to move. But he wouldn't allow her to stay still. He slipped his hand beneath her shirt and squeezed her breasts. She couldn't help herself, her hips rolled and feeling him go deeper inside felt too incredible to describe.

"You're so sexy," he whispered as he took her hips and moved her hips while she rode him.

She had never felt sexy before but he made her feel that way now. It was why she could never get enough of him. "I love you." The words slipped out, but she wasn't embarrassed. It was the truth. She wouldn't take it back. She loved him. It was that simple.

But she wasn't even sure it registered. They both said things when they made love. Sometimes she was so far gone she couldn't make sense of what she said.

She could tell he was on the edge. He was thrusting into her as she moved on top of him. His fingers were digging into her skin. He deeply moaned her name and that turned her on even more. She felt her orgasm building and she wanted to slow it down. She wanted this time, like every time with him, to last longer.

But the pull was too strong and her feelings were too intense. She broke and he took her mouth at the same moment, kissing her roughly and deeply as he came inside her.

And he kept kissing her, but his kisses got softer and sweeter and his hands came up to cup her cheeks and she felt . . . intoxicated. Heady. Delicious. Satisfied.

"Shit," Julian cursed as he briefly lifted his lips from hers. "Damn." He pressed his lips to her shoulder. "How do you do that to me?"

"Do what?"

"Make me wish that we were the only two people in the world so that I could always have you all to myself."

She smiled, but she felt like crying. His words were too beautiful. "It's still storming." She got off of him and faced the small window so she wouldn't have to look at him. She would crumble if she did.

"Looks like we're stuck in here for a while." He got off the bench and started to clear a spot on the floor of the shed, taking towels off the shelf and placing them on the concrete. "There's a blanket here. Come lay with me and keep me warm."

He held out his hand to her and she took it, snuggling into him, feeling that immediate sense of safety whenever his arms were around her. "That was the first time I've had sex outside of a bedroom."

He kissed her throat. "It won't be your last."

"I hope not." They were quiet for a moment and Sunny could feel herself starting to drift off to sleep but she forced her eyes open. Their time here was too short to spend it sleeping. "I got a call from Mrs. Earl earlier today. They've closed on their house. They'll be moving in late August. They've also gotten a court date for the adoption. It's soon. In a month. They are excited and terrified at the same time."

"Things will work out for them."

"You sound so sure."

"I am sure. My contact from the firm called. I think we found Gracie. This will all be over soon. Things will work out because they have to. I won't have it any other way."

"Do you really feel that certain?"

"Yes. This case changed everything for me."

He had almost lost his job, assaulted his boss, upset his clients, spent hours with his attention elsewhere because of her. And now he was here, not even knowing the entire reason they had come. She had wanted him. It was hard not to feel guilty, but she didn't regret anything because her life changed so much as well.

"I don't want to talk about any of that," he said quietly. "We're on vacation. Let's talk about vacation stuff."

"Like what?"

He was silent for a long moment. "Dream houses. What did you imagine your dream house to be when you were a kid?"

"I had lots of dream houses. But I really just wanted my own room. With a big bed and lots of books."

"That's it? Come on, Sunny. You had to have dreamed of more. My dream house changed a lot. When I was a kid, I thought it would be really cool to have a houseboat."

"Seriously?"

"Yeah. My dad's friend had one and I thought it was the best thing ever. And then when I was in college, I wanted the ultimate bachelor pad with flat screen TVs on every wall and video game systems and big leather recliners. And a full-sized bar."

"And you made that dream come true."

"Yeah. My first place," he smiled. "I had so many parties."

"And so many women," she said, laughing.

"No, not then," he said seriously. "After I had gotten hurt and the doctor told me that I couldn't play anymore, I went through a phase where I overindulged. Too many women. Too much booze. Too much excess. I became someone I didn't recognize. I became someone that I hated."

"And what changed?"

"I cursed at my father. I had never done that before and he grabbed me by the collar and shoved me into a wall so hard the plaster crumbled. I was drunk and numb and in a fog until then. I saw how angry I had made him, but more than that I saw how disappointed in me he was and that broke me. I decided to go to law school then."

"Which led you to your current dream home."

"Sort of. My place matches the image I wanted the world to see."

"You dream of more?"

"I dream of different. But I asked you first. Tell me about your dream house."

"It's not a mansion or anything. But something spacious, with a lot of windows. Something that feels homey with huge soft couches and a kitchen with one of those islands in the middle. And since I'm dreaming, I would like it to be near the water, just so I could open the windows and feel the breeze. I would like space for a garden. It's one of the things I remember from when I was very little. My mama had a small garden where she would grow tomatoes. I would like a yard too, with a swing set and a wraparound porch so I could sit outside and just watch the evening pass by. I wouldn't want it to be empty, either. I want lots of people and food and noise. That's my dream." She felt a little embarrassed, revealing her deepest desires to him. "I know that must sound so simple compared to what you and your sister have."

"No." He kissed her forehead. "I think it sounds beautiful."

Chapter 19

Three days later they had left that beautiful island and were back on the road headed toward what could have been Sunny's past. She should have been more nervous. Her stomach was churning, had been for the past couple of days. But she couldn't totally blame it on the upcoming confrontation. She had been so sad to leave the island. She couldn't hold back the tears as she said her good-byes.

Galen cried too, and assured her that they would all be together again. That they would make plans for Thanksgiving. Sunny nodded through her tears but she wasn't sure of that. Julian had all but disappeared in the days before they left. She had thought after they had spent the time in the shed that things would continue on, at least for a little while longer. But he had gotten even quieter than before and then he was gone. Literally gone for hours each day following up to their leaving. He wouldn't tell her where he was. He wouldn't talk to her at all. She felt completely shut out, but she wouldn't show him that it was bothering her. She spent time with his family. She had laughed. She had taken pictures. She had shown him how strong she was. They had to finish this journey.

She needed him to finish this case. And then they could go their separate ways.

He had reached for her hand a few times as they drove to Hope. Briefly locking his fingers with hers at traffic lights. She let him hold it. She didn't squeeze back. She didn't look at him. She just let the silence envelope them as they drove along.

"Are you hungry? We can stop before we check out this address that the investigator found."

"No. I would like to get this over with so we can get back to our lives. I know this was a lot to ask of you."

"You didn't ask this of me. It was my idea."

"Right," she said and turned back to the window and looked at the sweet little town that they were entering.

It looked familiar. Sunny sat straight up. It could be her mind playing tricks on her, but the place looked eerily familiar. In a word, it was charming. There were gorgeous historical buildings lining the streets and a beautiful town green that led right up to city hall. She looked out of the driver's side window to see a little park. She remembered playing there as a child.

She knew this place. This is where she had come from. This was what she thought of when she remembered home. It had been twenty-five years but she could feel it in her blood that this was her home. This was the last place she had been happy.

Well . . . This was the last place she had been happy before these past couple of weeks.

"You're excited," Julian commented.

"This reminds me of the town I used to live in before my mama moved us away."

"It's beautiful here. You must have been sad to leave it."

"You have no idea."

He turned down a street that had large stately homes. The wealthy lived here. It made sense. All the money that was being sent to Soren had to come from somewhere.

He stopped at the very end of the block at perhaps the sweetest looking house.

There was a porch with four white rocking chairs lined up in a row.

Sunny sat there paralyzed just looking out the window at the house they had tracked Grace to.

"Are you ready?"

"No." She took a deep breath and opened the door. "I don't think I'll ever be."

She got out of the car and began walking up to the front door, Julian was behind her but she could barely focus on him because her heart was pounding too fast.

She didn't give herself a moment to think as she reached the door. She rang the bell before her feet turned her body around and took her away from there.

There was a muffled voice coming from inside

and then a woman appeared. Pretty. Not much older than Sunny. She was African American with short, curly black hair and large round eyes. Sunny swallowed hard, finding her voice.

"Hi, I'm Sunny Gibson. This is Julian King. We're looking for Grace."

A worried look crossed the woman's face and she took a step back. "I'm Grace."

"You're Grace?" Sunny asked. Her voice barely audible.

Julian stepped forward. "You're Soren's biological mother?"

"I am." She nodded.

The words hit Sunny like a physical blow. She didn't find her mother. It had been a crazy thought. A crazy obsession for the past few months. She felt so stupid. She had taken a coincidence and let it run her life. She had made Soren's case all about herself and in the process she had lost her objectivity.

Out of all the questions she had asked Soren, the one she never asked, was what does your mother look like. She would have learned that this Grace's skin was brown not white, that her hair was black not blond. That she was far too young to be Sunny's mother.

Sunny stood there. Her mind spinning. Her chest hurting. She wasn't going to find her mother. She needed to stop. To forget about that kind of closure. She needed to think of her as dead and move on with her life.

It was the logical thing to do, but the devastation that ran through her was powerful. She was finding it hard to breathe, to not weep with sadness. But this trip was not about her. It was about Soren.

Soren who could get closure.

Soren who could have a lovely home and a happy family.

Soren who had all the chances Sunny couldn't have.

Sunny forgot about herself and focused on Julian. His face was twisted with anger. His body was tight. He was in high-powered attorney mode. He was terrifying to regular folks.

"Did you or did you not realize the psychological harm you put the child through when you kept contacting her? Are you unaware of the impact of your abandonment? That she didn't speak for an entire year? That she suffers from trauma? That she doesn't trust easily? And you want to take her from her parents? From the only stability that she has ever known? It won't happen. I work for the most powerful law firm in New York. I have every resource available to me for this family. You'll never win in court. You're unfit but just in case you want to try me, I'll keep you so twisted up in legal briefs that you'll be bankrupt by next year. As it stands right now, I should have you charged with stalking."

Grace looked terrified, but she held her head high. "I will not be threatened in my own home."

Sunny stepped in front of Julian. They had come too far to let this all fail now.

"I'm Soren's social worker. I was there from the very beginning. I have been with her through multiple foster homes and therapists. I found her this family. And Grace, they love her. She has thrived with them. I've seen her blossom into this bright, loving child. I know you never meant to hurt her, Grace, but you did. And if you try to force this relationship, she's going to resent you. It's not going to be the happy reunion you had in your mind."

"But I can take care of her now," she said with tears in her eyes.

"She needed you to take care of her then. You broke her trust. That's something that you have to regain."

"How?"

"Slowly and over time. And the worst thing you can do is threaten her security with her new family. She'll never forgive you for that. You have to meet her on her terms."

"What if she never wants to see me again?" Grace asked and Sunny could feel her heartbreak. She felt sorry for the woman, but not sorry enough to allow her to continue down this road.

"She still loves you. Eventually she will."

"I was a drug addict. I am an addict, and I hit a really hard patch when Soren's father died. But I'm clean and I've been clean for well over a year."

"How are we supposed to know that you'll stay clean? Last time you had her, you abandoned her. This time she might end up dead," Julian spat out. "What happened to your other daughter? I've read your letters. I know you did something to her."

Grace recoiled as Julian's words punched her. "She drowned. I turned my back for a second and she drowned in a pool. I didn't mean for it to happen."

"Were you too high to pay attention?"

"Julian, stop it right now," Sunny warned. She turned back to Grace and grabbed her hands before the woman got hysterical. "I think I'll be able to eventually get you some contact with your daughter, but not if you go about it this way. The family needs to be in agreement. Mr. King may be rude, but he is correct. You won't win this court case. Your rights were correctly and legally terminated," she said gently. "There are other ways to try to regain a relationship. But the first thing you have to do is let Soren make the decision. And you're going to have to respect whatever she decides."

"I'll think about it."

"Please do." Sunny pulled her card out of her pocket and handed it to her. "If you need anything, please call me. I'm not your enemy. I'm here to help."

Sunny turned and walked away. There was nothing else to say. Grace needed to process this and hopefully make the right decision because if she didn't, she would have a huge fight on her hands. Julian would destroy her.

They got back in the car and Sunny sat there silently. She felt like all the air had been let out of her. Like a little bit of her life had been drained.

"That woman is full of shit. She acts like she's so innocent. She had to know she was terrifying that whole family."

"You didn't have to go so hard. This isn't court. We were there to have a conversation. To hear her side of things. You could have made her more persistent in getting Soren back."

"I had to say something. You just stood there frozen. You knew what we were coming here to do. Why the hell did you look so shocked?"

She sat there for a moment, debating whether she should tell him or not. It wasn't something she was going to shake immediately. It wasn't one of those disappointments she was going to bounce back from.

And she had wanted to tell him. For months she wanted to tell someone, tell anyone about everything that was churning in her head. "I had thought that Soren's mother could be my mother too," she said in a voice that was barely above a whisper.

"What?"

She pulled the letters out of her pocket. Her letters. The ones that were so dear to her. She had placed them there this morning before they left. She had taken them when she left New York, feeling like this trip would finally give her the answers she needed. "Her mother's letters were so similar to mine. I used to live in this town. I remember it. I have a younger sister somewhere. I needed to know if Soren was it."

He went deadly silent and she felt him grow tight beside her. "You have been lying to me the entire time we have known each other."

"I haven't."

"A lie of omission is still a lie. Did you even want to help Soren or was this all about you?"

"You know I wanted to help her! I would have done the same thing for her even if I didn't have the suspicion. The Earls are who she should be with and I will do everything in my power to ensure that she will stay with that family. You know me better than that."

"I feel like I don't know you at all. You could have told me. There were a million times you could have told me."

"I didn't tell you because I thought it was too crazy to be true. And it was. I was wrong."

"What else haven't you told me? God damn it, Sunny! I changed my entire life because of you. My career. My goals. My future. And you can't even tell me the truth? What does that say about us? I feel like everything was a lie."

"You've been trying to push me away for this past week. You're looking for a reason to end this. Just end it now. Don't wait till we get back to New York. Don't try to let me down easy. Just do it. You're not going to break me."

Confusion poked through his anger. "What the hell are you talking about?"

"Just face it, Julian. I'm not who or what you want. I'm not polished and sophisticated. I'm not enough for you. And instead of telling me that like a man, you have been pushing me away. Going silent on me. Making me feel like shit."

"Don't change the subject. This is about you lying to me. This is about our whole relationship being based on a lie. I can't even look at you right now."

"What was the lie? I didn't tell you that I was curious to find my mother? It sounded too crazy. It was too crazy. I didn't trick you into any of this. I still needed help for Soren. You can turn away from me, but if you have any kind of decency, you'll still help that family. I may have been wrong for keeping that part of the story away from you, but there was never anything that I have done that was malicious or dishonest. I fell in love with you. I gave you my body. I let you into my heart. But it's clear you don't feel the same way. You've been looking for your escape path." She opened the door and stepped out. "I'm not going to wait for you to let me down. This is over."

She slammed the door and started walking down the street. Her eyes were so filled with tears she couldn't see. But somehow she knew where she was going. The town still smelled the same. It sounded the same. The breeze felt the same on her skin. This was her home. This was the place where she once felt the safest in the world. This is where her mother had been.

There was a little cottage not far from the other Grace's home. It was adorable, white, with blue shutters and a pretty garden on the side of the house. There was also a sign that said vacancy. This is where her mother had worked. It was coming back to her now. It was a bed and breakfast. The owners had let her and Mama live upstairs for free in return for Mama's work as the cook and caretaker there. It was all coming back to her.

She knew her mama wasn't there, that she wasn't in this town anymore, that she had been gone for years. But she needed to be here right now. She needed to be where she last remembered her mama well. Sunny needed to be where she was last truly innocent and happy.

She knocked on the door and a few moments later an older woman answered.

"I saw the vacancy sign," she said, her voice broken with tears. "I was hoping I would be able to stay here for a little while."

The woman's eyes passed over her, seeing that she had no luggage, that she was completely alone, just nodded, reached for her hand, and pulled her inside. There were no words exchanged and no questions asked. It was exactly what she needed in that moment.

Julian shut his eyes after Sunny slammed the door. He knew he should have gone after her immediately. But he was too mad. He had always been so good with words. He was good in the courtroom. He never lost a case; he was that convincing, but he couldn't talk to Sunny then. He couldn't express himself. He couldn't explain to her why he was so angry.

She knew everything about him. All of his pain. His fears. His history. She had seen a side of him no one had and she had kept this part of herself from him.

He would have helped her find her mother. He would have gone to the ends of the earth to make sure Sunny was completely happy. But she held that back from him and it made him doubt her. Made him doubt her trust of him.

She showed him how much she loved him in a thousand ways every day. And he had heard her say it that day in the shed. He believed her. He felt her love. But he didn't say it back. He didn't say anything because he had never told a woman that he loved her before. He didn't know how to express the scope of his feelings in words. So he figured he would say nothing and try to show her instead. But instead of making her feel like he wanted her, he made her feel the exact opposite. He had to let her know that he was in love with her. That he wasn't trying to push her away. That he wanted, no needed, her by his side because life wasn't full without her.

He got out of the car and walked down the street. She couldn't have gotten far. Not even five minutes had passed. But he didn't see her in either direction. And when he got in his car and drove around the sweet small town, he couldn't spot her either. So he called her, and called her and called her until her voicemail was full. But she never picked up. He got a single text, though.

> I'm safe. You don't have to worry about me anymore.
>
> Anymore.

There was finality in that word.

It hit him square in the chest. He had taken hard hits before, but this one was the worse. He had let her go. Sunny was somewhere out there in the world thinking she was unloved.

He had to do everything in his power to change that.

It had been nearly a month since Sunny had seen Julian. She knew the split would be hard for her, but she didn't anticipate the low level of misery that never lifted. She had gone back to work, tried her best to be present. In fact, she threw herself into her job, but the fulfillment wasn't there. She found no joy in it anymore. She missed Julian too much and the warm, humid air of South Carolina and the sand between her toes.

She had been disappointed before. She had been hurt before, but she had learned to shield herself, to bounce back. But this time she couldn't, and she was angry at herself for not being able to pull herself out of her misery. She had been alone before. She had felt deep loneliness before but this time it was too deep to describe.

But today was a happy day. It was adoption day for Soren. Grace had agreed to back off. Sunny was able to set up a phone call between Grace and Soren with Soren's permission. It had broken Sunny's heart. She watched Soren cry silently while she listened to her mother's voice for the first time since the day she left her. This child had been so hurt, so traumatized, but she had made her wishes very clear. She wasn't ready to see her biological mother and she never wanted to go back.

Grace had to accept that. It would take time for Soren to forgive. To finish healing and maybe one day there would be enough space in her heart to welcome Grace back in.

Sunny had met the Earls at their home. They were all packed up and ready for their move upstate. Soren greeted her at the front door wearing a simple pink dress, her hair blown out straight for the special occasion. She looked like a little adult. She had come so far from the filthy, bruised, half-starved child she had been when Sunny found her.

Tears sprung from her eyes and continued to roll down her face the entire time she was in their apartment. It was the end of a chapter for this family. They were starting a new life in a new place. Happiness for them peeked through the mess Sunny was feeling along with a little pride. She had helped these people. She had made a difference in their lives. It was why she became a social worker.

They had gone to the courthouse. There was no Grace in sight. No last minute attempts to stop the adoption. Sunny let out a slow breath of relief, but her breath immediately caught again when she saw Julian walk into the courtroom. He introduced himself to the judge as the Earls' lawyer who raised her eyebrows at his presence. She obviously recognized his name. He was one of the most powerful lawyers in the city. He didn't make appearances in family court.

But Sunny had forced him into doing things he didn't normally do. Things he didn't want to do. He had felt used by her. Maybe she did use him. Maybe she should have told him. But she couldn't feel guilty because she had loved him. She did love him and she wouldn't take any of it back.

Some of her greatest joy came from being in love with him.

The court proceedings went very smoothly with the judge talking to Soren first and then the Earls about their life together and their future plans. And then it was done. The papers were signed and Soren's last name officially changed and Sunny cried again. And so did the Earls. All of them hugged Sunny, thanking her for what must have been the hundredth time that day. They gave her a gift. A locket with a picture of Soren and her together at Soren's last birthday.

Sunny put it on immediately. It was one of those things she would keep beside her heart forever. Soon it was over. The Earls were off to celebrate with a lavish lunch at Soren's favorite restaurant. She watched them walk away as a family. She kept her eyes on them until they disappeared from sight, just to avoid looking at Julian who was standing behind her.

"Sunny . . ." he finally said.

She turned to look at him. He was so handsome in his suit. He was once again the image of the powerful attorney she had met when she begged him to take her case. He was partner now. His dreams had come true. He finally was who he had always wanted to be.

"Thank you for coming today," she said to him. "It meant a lot to the Earls. And thank you for all that you have done for them. It made a huge impact on their lives." She turned away from him, ready to leave for good, but he grabbed her wrist.

"I need to talk to you."

The tears that were so close to the surface all day came again. She had never cried. For years she hadn't. She had forced herself to turn off that part of herself, but with him she became raw and open. Her wounds were sore and not ready to be picked at.

"We don't have to do this. I think we should both move on with our lives."

"I can't," he said, and his voice sounded choked. "I can't because there's something I have to tell you."

"I'm not sure I can hear it. Being near you hurts too much."

"I'm miserable without you, Sunshine. I haven't been able to function. I'm in love with you and I have been for a long time."

She turned to face him. "Excuse me?"

"I love you. I love you. I love you. I've never said it before. I didn't know how to tell you. I wasn't pushing you away. I was making plans for us." He pulled out his phone. "I went looking for houses in those days before we left. I found this one. It's not far from my sister's place."

He started swiping through pictures on his phone. It was a large three-story home with a huge wrap-around porch that overlooked the ocean.

"There's a porch swing," he told her. "And rocking chairs and my favorite part is the hammock that can fit two people. There are six bedrooms and on the side of the house there is already a little swing set.

And there's the kitchen. It's got an island just like you wanted and a double oven. This is the kind of room the family gathers in."

"Why are you showing me this?"

"I bought it."

"You what?" The shock of his statement made her take a step back.

"It's not as luxurious as Galen and Alex's place, but I thought it would be good for us."

She shook her head, trying to make some sense of his words.

"I was going to bring you there after we left Hope." He pulled a small box out of his pocket and got down on one knee. "I was going to propose to you with my grandmother's ring on the porch." He opened the box and revealed a simple but lovely diamond ring. "I was going to tell you that I needed to grow old with you and make babies with you and love you for the rest of my life. But I didn't want to blow the surprise. So I didn't say anything."

"I thought you didn't want me. That you didn't want that kind of life."

"I'm resigning from my firm. I want more than a career. I want you and whatever is going to make you happy. Marry me, Sunny. I can't go through this life without you."

She nodded and wrapped herself around him. "I love you. I'm so sorry. I've been so miserable without you."

He stood up, his arms still around her. "I would have helped you find your mother. I'll still help you.

I would give you the entire world if I could, just don't hold any part of yourself away from me."

"I thought you would think I was crazy."

"I do think you're crazy, but I love you because of it and I want to be crazy with you."

"Say you love me again. I need to hear it."

"I love you. I'm in love with you. Please be my wife."

"Of course, I will." He spun her around, put the ring on her finger and then they left the court house, ready to start their lives together.

Epilogue

"You're going to keep me?" the little boy asked Sunny as she tucked him into bed.

"Yes, Tyler." She kissed his forehead and then his cheeks. "Your social worker said we could. We are going to go to the courthouse to see the judge and then we'll sign papers that say you will be ours."

"Forever?" he looked up at Sunny, the skepticism in his face clear.

"Forever," Sunny said. "You are our boy. Our son. No more foster care."

Julian watched Sunny scoop Tyler into her arms in a ritual that was becoming a nightly thing since they decided to adopt him. It was very important to Sunny that they foster a child. They had two of their own, a little girl that was just over eighteen months and another girl that was six months old. Julian was holding their youngest now, feeding her the last bottle of the night. They had been married for five years. And happy. Julian hadn't thought this kind of happiness was possible.

After he resigned from his job, they had married a month later in a small ceremony on the beach in South Carolina and then he took her on a three-month honeymoon around the world. He had thought that that would be the happiest time of his life, but he had been wrong. Watching her love their children made him even happier. She had so much love to give. And when she told him that she wanted to foster almost a year ago, he agreed, but he knew it wasn't going to work because Sunny was never going to be able to give a child back once she loved them. And she fell hard for little Tyler, who was abused by his birth mother and tossed around three foster homes in his short life.

"And I can call you mommy?"

"If you want to."

He looked so unsure. He didn't trust easily. It had taken so long for him to be this comfortable with them. To let Sunny hold him. "I will if you want me to."

"I would love it if you called me mommy, but it has to be your choice. You can call me Sunny if you want to."

"I will call you mommy." He looked at Julian. "Can I call him daddy?"

"Yes," Julian answered for her. "I would be very proud to have you call me daddy."

"We love you." She placed him back beneath the covers. "We won't stop."

"Even when I misbehave?"

"Especially then. We will always love you. We will

never give you back. Even if we get mad. Even if you misbehave, you will always have a home here."

He nodded. "I love it here."

"I'm glad." She kissed him again. "Good night, Tyler. We'll see you in the morning."

Julian put their daughter, Juliana, in her crib and followed Sunny out of the room.

He grabbed her hand and slipped his fingers through hers as they walked down the hallway. "It was a very brilliant idea to put Ana's crib in the room with him. He hasn't been scared, which means we haven't had a four-year-old sleeping between us."

"He's never had his own room before. It's a big change for him."

As soon they crossed the threshold of their bedroom he shut the door and pushed her against it, kissing her deeply. She wrapped her arms around him and melted into his kiss.

Her reaction to him never changed. Five years and three kids later and she still smiled when he walked into a room. His heart still raced when she touched him. He missed her whenever he was away from her for more than a few hours.

"Don't kiss me like that, Mr. King."

"Don't be so damn cute, Mrs. King."

"I missed you today." She rested her head against his chest.

He had opened up his own law practice that he ran out of the house, but his business had grown faster than he expected and he had to hire more lawyers to help with the work, which meant he had to move his practice to a small office downtown. He couldn't pop upstairs to kiss his wife when he had a free moment, but working outside of the house might have been a better move. He stopped working every day at four-thirty to make sure he was home by five. He left work at work. His weekends were free. He took long vacations. He had more of a life now than he had ever had.

"I missed you too." He kissed her cheeks and then down to her neck.

"Stop kissing me," she moaned. "I want to talk to you."

"I've already sent out the invites for Tyler's party. The whole family will be there for his adoption day."

"Thank you, but that's not what I want to talk to you about."

He stood up straight and looked down into her eyes, which held a little fear. She had gone to the doctor today. She told him she had been feeling a little run down lately and thought she was getting a cold.

"Please don't tell me you're sick. I can handle anything but that."

"Okay, I'm having a torrid affair with the young hot lifeguard on the beach. He satisfies me in ways you never could."

"You're hilarious. Now tell me what's wrong."

"I'm pregnant," she whispered. "Again. I'm three months along."

"You are?" He grinned at her. "That's amazing."

"You're happy?" She looked up at him unsure.

"Of course, I am."

"But you said I can't foster any more kids after Tyler. I thought you didn't want more children."

"I don't want you to foster because foster care is temporary and you have a very hard time giving them back. When our first foster went back to her mother, you cried for three days. And before Tyler's birth parents' rights were terminated you were a nervous wreck. I can't bear to see you like that. We can adopt from the system, but let's only take them if we know we can keep them. I want as many children as you'll give me." He rubbed her belly. "I'm very happy about it."

"This is why I love you."

"I love you too. And I have some news for you."

He had hired a private detective to track down her mother. There had been so little to go on. Grace Gibson had left almost no trace. "We found your sister. She's twenty-seven years old and lives in DC."

Sunny gasped. "Are you sure?"

"Yes. She's the daughter of Warren Bates."

Sunny frowned. "Why do I know that name?"

"He's the millionaire tech mogul who ran for Congress a few years ago. There's talk he might run for president."

Sunny was having a hard time processing that. Her sister didn't live in foster care. She lived a life of privilege. She had lived without their mother. She wondered if she had known her like Sunny had.

"Does she know about me?"

"I don't know. We can do whatever you want, Sunny. Just tell me and I'll get it done."

She thought about it for a moment. Her sister probably led her own quiet life. She wasn't sure if she wanted more family. But Sunny had searched so long. "I want to meet her." Even if she didn't want a relationship, Sunny wanted to meet the person she shared the same blood with. She wanted to know what she looked like. Wanted to see if they had even the smallest things in common.

"Okay. We'll do it. Just let me know when you're ready."

She nodded, feeling completely heady. She was one step closer to closure.

Don't miss Jamie Pope's next book

ONE WARM WINTER,

Where we meet Sunny's sister.

It's coming to you in April 2019
Available at your favorite bookstore or e-retailer.

Connect with

Visit us online at
KensingtonBooks.com
to read more from your favorite authors, see books
by series, view reading group guides, and more.

for sneak peeks, chances to win books and prize packs,
and to share your thoughts with other readers.

facebook.com/kensingtonpublishing
twitter.com/kensingtonbooks

Tell us what you think!

To share your thoughts, submit a review,
or sign up for our eNewsletters, please visit:
KensingtonBooks.com/TellUs.